T0265735

MURDER OF A HERMIT

Also by Carol Miller

Moonshine mysteries

MURDER AND MOONSHINE
A NIP OF MURDER
AN OLD-FASHIONED MURDER

The Fortune Telling mysteries

THE FOOL DIES LAST *
DEATH RIDES A PONY *

* *available from Severn House*

MURDER OF A HERMIT

Carol Miller

SEVERN
HOUSE

First world edition published in Great Britain and the USA in 2024
by Severn House, an imprint of Canongate Books Ltd,
14 High Street, Edinburgh EH1 1TE.

severnhouse.com

British Library Cataloguing-in-Publication Data
A CIP catalogue record for this title is available from the British Library.

ISBN-13: 978-1-4483-1057-9 (cased)
ISBN-13: 978-1-4483-1058-6 (e-book)

All Severn House titles are printed on acid-free paper.

MIX
Paper from
responsible sources
FSC   FSC® C013056
www.fsc.org

Typeset by Palimpsest Book Production Ltd., Falkirk,
Stirlingshire, Scotland.
Printed and bound in Great Britain by TJ Books,
Padstow, Cornwall.

Praise for the Fortune Telling mystery novels

"Fans of paranormal cozies will have fun!"
Publishers Weekly on *Death Rides a Pony*

"An entertaining plot, colorful characters, light romance, and a satisfying ending make this a pleasant and engaging read"
Booklist on *Death Rides a Pony*

"Fans of Steven Hockensmith's Tarot mystery series may want to check out this cozy"
Publishers Weekly on *The Fool Dies Last*

"Ghosts in the attic, smokescreens, wacky characters, and a vengeful killer add up to good fun for cozy fans"
Booklist on *The Fool Dies Last*

"Pleasing characters spark the first entry in an often amusing mystery/romance series"
Kirkus Reviews on *The Fool Dies Last*

"Fans of humorous cozies with a little mysticism will want to try this one"
Library Journal on *The Fool Dies Last*

About the author

Carol Miller is the author of three Moonshine Mystery novels, including *Murder and Moonshine*, which was named an Amazon Best Book of the Month and a *Library Journal* Starred Debut of the Month upon release. *The Fool Dies Last* was Carol's first novel with Severn House and the first entry in The Fortune Telling Mysteries series. Carol is an attorney and lives in Virginia.

www.carolmillerauthor.com

For my parents

Acknowledgments

I am grateful to my marvelous editor Victoria Britton at Severn House, along with Joanne Grant, Martin Brown, Penelope Isaac, Mary Karayel, Rachel Slatter, and Piers Tilbury.

I am also grateful to my wonderful agent Kari Stuart at CAA, along with Phoebe Rhinehart and Jennifer Simpson.

And as always, I am grateful to my dearest family and friends. Thank you.

ONE

'He's back,' Megan Steele announced.

'Again?' Hope Bailey said in surprise.

'Yup. That's the third time I've seen him at the window in the last hour, and each time he's made it one step closer to the door before retreating.'

Megan was sitting at the aged, coffee-brown pine table that Hope used for her palm and Tarot readings. Set in the front corner of Bailey's Boutique – the little mystic shop owned by Hope and her sister, Summer, in the historic district of downtown Asheville, North Carolina – the table bordered the large row of windows that faced the street, providing Megan with an unobstructed view of the sidewalk and all passers-by.

'Are you sure that he's coming to the boutique?' Summer asked.

'Yup,' Megan answered again. 'At least, that's how it appears to me. He isn't circling the block or approaching any of the other shops. He just lingers at the corner of the brownstone as though he's trying to muster up his courage to enter. He makes it a few paces toward the door, then he suddenly turns around and hurries back to the corner.'

'How odd of him,' Hope mused, taking a rusty tin with an illegible label that Summer handed her. She and her sister were at the back wall of the boutique, with Summer standing on the rickety herb-and-tea counter, sorting through the containers of infrequently used dried flora and infusions on the upper shelves.

'Maybe he's shy,' Summer suggested. 'If he hasn't been here before, he could be nervous about what to expect. People get all sorts of peculiar misconceptions about the shop into their head. He might be waiting for another customer to come inside, so he can follow on their heels and feel more comfortable.'

'If that's the case, then he'll end up waiting a long time,' Hope replied, 'because Tuesday mornings are almost always slow for us.'

Her sister nodded. 'Especially now in September. The summer tourists are gone. The locals are busy with the beginning of the new school year and settling back into their regular work routine. And it's too early for the autumn tourists to visit for the changing of the leaves.' She handed Hope a second tin that was even rustier than the first. 'Speaking of which, maybe we should have waited another couple of weeks before starting up the Wednesday afternoon tea for the season. What if no one shows up tomorrow?'

Summer had mentioned the concern more than once over the past few days, so Hope made an extra effort to sound positive on the subject. 'Turnout for the first week or two might naturally be a bit thin, but I'm confident that the group will steadily expand as it did last year. During the winter, your Wednesday afternoon teas were so popular that we never had enough seats for everyone. I remember that several of the ladies ended up bringing their own foldable camp chairs.'

'You're guaranteed to have at least one person in attendance tomorrow,' Megan added. 'I'll be at the tea.'

'That doesn't count. You don't have an option about being here. You're stuck in this place and can't leave.' Summer must have realized that her remark had an undue sharpness, because she immediately turned to Megan with an apology. 'I'm sorry. I didn't mean it the way that it sounded.'

'Oh, that's all right.' Megan shrugged. 'It's more or less true. I appreciate you letting me stay with you while my leg is healing. I'm afraid that I've been an inconvenience and an imposition.'

'Not in the least! We love having you with us,' Hope assured her. Next to Summer, Megan was her oldest and closest friend. 'Here in the brownstone you can access all of the necessities on one floor. The pull-out sofa in the study, the kitchen and the bath, even the back patio when you're in need of some fresh air. How could you possibly go up and down your apartment stairs while wearing that enormous plaster cast?'

'I couldn't.' Megan shrugged again, this time adding a slight smile. 'But that would have put me on a forced diet, and then I might finally have been able to squeeze back into that fabulous red dress which has been hanging in my closet since our college days.'

'Nonsense,' Summer scoffed. 'I wish that I had half as good

of a figure as you do. You definitely don't need to lose any weight. And if Daniel Drexler has been telling you otherwise, then he isn't worth one moment of your time.'

Megan shook her head. 'Daniel hasn't told me to lose weight – or for that matter, much of anything else. I've only gone on a total of two dates with the man, and I've barely spoken to him in the past week. He's still at that restaurateur convention in Atlanta.'

'But when he heard about your unfortunate accident at work,' Hope reminded her, 'he sent you the largest bouquet of flowers ever to be seen.'

In unison, they all turned toward the mammoth crystal vase that was sitting on top of the boutique's jewelry display case. It was the only space wide enough to accommodate the five dozen long-stem apricot roses.

Summer heaved a dreamy sigh. 'Such a beautiful, romantic gesture.'

Megan was silent.

'And the fragrance is heavenly,' Summer continued. 'Everyone who came into the shop yesterday commented on it.'

'They weren't admiring the scent or even the unusual shade of the flowers,' Megan rejoined. 'They were all only impressed with how big and showy the bouquet is.'

'You think that it's too big and showy?' Hope asked her.

She hesitated. 'Maybe. I'm not sure. Both of my dates with Daniel were at the Green Goat, and both times it was very splashy. The most expensive oysters flown in fresh that morning. The rarest bottle from the depths of the locked wine cabinet. The fanciest cuts of meat brought out personally by the chef for us to choose from.'

'That's understandable, though, isn't it?' Hope said. 'Daniel was trying to impress you, particularly because he owns the restaurant.'

Megan hesitated again. 'Maybe. I'm not sure. I had a strange feeling on both occasions, as though something was off.' A crease formed in her brow. 'Or maybe I'm overthinking it.'

'You aren't overthinking Daniel's interest in you. His interest is clear.' Summer motioned toward the roses.

The crease deepened. 'Except I know so little about him. That's what I meant before when I said that Daniel hasn't told me much of anything. He speaks well, but it's all been extremely vague. I'd like to find out what's below the surface.'

'My Tarot deck is lying right in front of you on the table,' Hope said. 'Pull a card and see what it shows you.'

Megan gave a short laugh. 'I may know almost nothing about Daniel Drexler, but I certainly know better than to touch those cards without you sitting here next to me. I might cast an unintended spell or open up a portal that lets in a snarling hellhound.'

Hope laughed with her. 'The sight of a hellhound bounding over the cobblestones would probably alarm the neighbors.'

'But I wouldn't object to a spell,' Megan amended after a moment. 'You can't cast one to stop my leg from itching, can you? It was driving me crazy last night. It woke me up at least half a dozen times.'

'Sadly, I'm not familiar with any anti-itch spells. But Summer might have a tincture that can help.'

'It would have to be topical, and that obviously isn't possible under the plaster.' Summer was thoughtful. 'Unless we try gold-enseal. The powdered root might work. I'm not sure whether I have any in stock. It would be up here . . .' She stretched for a chipped earthenware crock at the far end of the uppermost shelf, and the counter shook precariously beneath her.

'Be careful, Summer!' Megan cried in alarm.

'I'm fine. No worries.' Although she succeeded in retrieving the crock, it was evident that the wobbling counter had made Summer nervous, too, because instead of continuing to stand on it, she cautiously climbed down.

Megan exhaled with relief when Summer safely reached the ground. 'If you had gotten injured, there would have been two invalids. Then Hope might have thrown up her hands in disgust and gone off to the beach, leaving us in misery to fend for ourselves.'

Both Megan and Summer laughed. Hope frowned.

'Don't be angry,' Summer said to her sister. 'I didn't fall. Nothing bad happened.'

'I'm not angry. Although I do wish that you would use the stepladder. That's why Gram bought it for us. The counter isn't sturdy enough to support a person.'

'Next time I'll use the ladder. I promise.'

The frown remained.

Summer frowned back at her. 'You can't honestly be that upset about me climbing on the counter.'

'No, I was thinking about the neighbors,' Hope mused.

Megan – whose fingers had been inching toward the Tarot deck – pulled back her hand abruptly. 'I was only joking about the hellhound before. You don't mean that it's possible to actually summon . . .'

Hope shook her head absently. 'Of course not.'

'Regarding the neighbors,' Summer pursued after a minute when Hope didn't continue, 'are you referring to Miranda and Paul next door?'

'Yes. I was wondering if that man who Megan keeps seeing at the window is one of the new construction workers.'

'Construction workers?' Summer echoed in surprise. 'But I thought the Larsons' cellar problem had been resolved.'

'I thought so, too. They did also. But I saw Miranda yesterday evening in the garden, and she told me over the fence that to her and Paul's horror, the foundation of their brownstone has started leaking again. It was only a little seepage before. This time it's an actual flood. Following that heavy rain a couple of days ago, they have nearly a foot of water standing in their cellar. And it hasn't drained away, so the contractor can't even determine which side of the property it might be coming from until they pump it out.'

'What a nightmare.' Summer groaned. 'And now we – and all of our customers – are going to have to listen to that infernal drilling from the repairs again!'

Hope nodded. 'According to Miranda, the crew is expected to start work sometime this week, so it occurred to me that the man at the window could be connected to them.'

'He didn't look as though he was in the construction business,' Megan said. 'No hard hat or fluorescent safety vest.'

'He might only be doing an initial survey,' Summer replied. 'Or he could be from one of the utilities, marking the sewer and gas lines before any digging commences.'

'He didn't look as though he was from one of the utilities, either.'

'What did he look like?' Hope asked, her curiosity growing.

'Well, he . . .'

There was a pause. Having been reassured on the subject of hellhounds, Megan was unable to resist the siren song of the Tarot. She began to flip through the deck, one card after another with a flourish.

Summer rolled her eyes. 'You won't get any useful information that way. You can't select the card you like best and pretend that it applies to your situation. If you don't draw the card properly, it means nothing. Less than nothing, even. Isn't that right, Hope?'

Suddenly Megan stopped flipping. 'That's him.'

'Who? Daniel?' Summer retorted. 'I just explained that you can't pick the card you want and make believe it—'

'Not Daniel,' Megan cut her off impatiently. 'It's the man who was at the window.'

Both Hope and Summer moved toward the table for a better look.

Summer rolled her eyes a second time. 'That can't be the man.'

'It's him,' Megan insisted.

'He can't seriously have a long beard and a cloak and a lantern—'

It was Hope's turn to interject as she stared at the Tarot card in Megan's hand. 'You saw the Hermit?'

TWO

Megan was adamant. Hope was puzzled. Summer was point-blank incredulous.

'How much pain medication have you taken this morning?' Summer said to Megan, her tone pitying.

'I am not hallucinating from either pain or pills,' Megan returned tetchily. 'I know what I saw. The man at the window was the Hermit.'

'Then you should put Hope's Tarot cards away before you imagine seeing anything else, such as the Devil lurking in the fireplace or the Hanged Man swinging from the ceiling—'

The sentence was cut short by the sound of the wind chimes above the front door of the boutique. Startled, their collective gaze snapped toward the entrance to the shop. A man stepped across the threshold. He wasn't in possession of a beard, a cloak, or a lantern. On the contrary, his sandy hair was fashionably cut, his trousers were tailored, and he was carrying a mahogany leather satchel.

Summer gave a disappointed sigh. 'Oh, it's only you, Dylan.'

A frostiness glided over Dylan Henshaw's chiseled features. 'Always a pleasure to see you, too, Summer.'

'Is anyone else out there?' she asked him, hurrying toward the door. 'On the sidewalk or at the corner of the brownstone?'

The frostiness moved to Dylan's voice. 'Not that I noticed.'

Leaning through the open doorway, Summer looked along the sidewalk, first to the left and then to the right. The disappointed sigh repeated itself. 'No one,' she reported over her shoulder. 'Not a person in sight.'

'I wonder where he went,' Megan mused. 'And whether he'll come back.'

'Who are we referring to?' Dylan inquired.

Megan held up the Tarot card for him to see. Hope winced slightly in anticipation of his reaction. Dylan was an avowed skeptic. The Tarot, palmistry, and all other forms of divination were nothing more than superstitious nonsense to him. In the same vein, he viewed Summer's tinctures and teas as silly, ineffectual attempts at home-cooked cures. Age-old natural remedies conflicted with Dylan's modern, scientific medical training.

'*The Hermit*,' Dylan read aloud. The frostiness was replaced by amusement. 'The Hermit's been hanging around the boutique?'

'He has,' Megan told him. 'In the span of an hour, he passed by the front window at least three times that I saw.'

Dylan looked at the card again, more carefully. 'Vagrant or Sherpa?'

'Huh?' Megan said.

'Vagrant or Sherpa?' he repeated. 'His physical appearance – along with the title of the card – suggests homelessness or an extreme recluse. But the light shining in the lantern and the staff in his hand and his location on the summit of a snow-capped mountain imply a spiritual person or a seeker of wisdom.'

Megan took a closer look at the card herself, then she looked questioningly at Hope.

Hope was so surprised by the insightfulness of Dylan's remarks that it took her a moment to respond. He was correct in his interpretation of the card. As with all of the Tarot, the Hermit was representational, not literal. 'Sherpa,' she answered at last.

For the first time since entering the shop, Dylan turned toward her. 'Hello, Hope,' he said softly.

'Hello, Dylan.'

His pale blue eyes gazed at her intently, then his lips curled with the beginnings of a smile. 'So a Sherpa? When my dad told me that Megan had injured her leg, he failed to mention that it was from a climbing accident in Nepal where she had befriended a Tibetan guide, who then decided to return with her to Asheville because he had grown weary of the Himalayas and wanted to trek through the Appalachians instead.'

'You're hilarious,' Megan responded dryly.

The smile grew. 'Is that not right? Then why is a Sherpa here?'

It was Hope's turn for a dry reply. 'You know perfectly well that we're not talking about an actual Sherpa.'

'But you said . . .'

'Only because you said it first, and it's more accurate than calling him a vagrant. The Hermit seeks knowledge and enlightenment.

He values spiritual growth and the discovery of profound truths rather than material goods or social opportunities.'

'And this quest for truth and understanding is taking place in your boutique?'

'He hasn't been in the boutique,' Megan corrected Dylan. 'Up to this point, he's only been outside.'

'Well, he's not out there now,' Summer informed them as she returned to the shop, letting the door bang shut behind her. 'I've waited and watched, but there isn't any sign of him. Meanwhile, I've come up with an explanation for the cloak and the staff.'

'You have?' Hope and Megan said in unison.

'Yes. The sky is overcast with a definite chance of drizzle—'

'There were a few drops falling during my walk here from the office,' Dylan corroborated.

'So the cloak could have been a raincoat, and the staff could have been an umbrella,' Summer concluded.

'I suppose that's possible,' Megan responded slowly, not sounding entirely convinced.

'And the long beard and the lantern?' Hope asked her sister.

'Plenty of men have some form of a beard. Maybe it only appeared to be long because of the hood on the raincoat or a shadow from the window. As for the lantern . . .' Summer turned to Megan. 'Are you absolutely certain that there was a lantern? Could it have been a reflection from one of the lights in here against the gray background of the street?'

Again, Megan was slow to answer. She was beginning to look somewhat gray herself. Her baby-fine blond bangs were dampened against her forehead with perspiration.

Dylan's expression grew earnest as his medical training jumped to the fore. 'How are you feeling, Megan? How is your leg feeling? Are you experiencing any dizziness or pulsating sensations?'

With long, swift strides, he reached the table before Megan had managed to get out more than a word or two in reply. Dylan studied her briefly, then he opened his mahogany leather satchel, which was evidently his doctor bag. He pulled out several medications.

'Take two of these,' he instructed her. 'And this one also.'

Megan swallowed the pills without question or argument. It

was a clear indication to Hope that she really wasn't feeling well; Megan wasn't usually so compliant.

Dylan nodded his approval. 'That should help.'

He sat down on one of the matching coffee-brown chairs at the table and began a more thorough examination of Megan's injured leg, which was propped up on another of the chairs. When he had finished, he leaned back in his seat and nodded his approval once more.

'There's nothing to be concerned about. It all looks and feels fine. Whoever treated you in the emergency room did an excellent job with that cast. Plaster is a much better choice for a ligament tear such as yours than an air cast. It will heal faster and stronger. You'll have far fewer problems later on.'

'Your dad said the same thing,' Megan told him.

'Speaking of Morris,' Summer interjected. 'Since when do you deign to make house calls, Dylan? I thought your father was the last doctor left in the state – probably in the entire nation – who voluntarily visits his patients.'

Morris Henshaw – Dylan's father – was a family doctor from a different era. Instead of a glossy professional complex, his office was located in another old brownstone just down the street from the boutique. Morris considered every one of his patients to be a neighbor and a friend, and as such, he took pleasure and pride in making house calls to those who had a difficult time getting to him.

'My dad is swamped this morning,' Dylan responded. 'Too many walk-ins on top of his scheduled appointments. So I volunteered to come to the boutique and check on Megan in his stead.'

'Isn't that a nice story, Hope?' Megan winked at her. 'When we all know that Dylan really came here to check on you.'

Hope pretended not to understand her.

Megan winked again. 'He's got good hands, Hope. My leg just experienced their magical touch. Never be too quick to discount a man with good hands.'

Although she tried to restrain it, Hope couldn't help smiling. Whatever medication Dylan had dispensed was obviously working, because the gray had vanished from Megan's cheeks, and her usual verve had returned.

'If my hands were as good as Dylan's,' Megan continued

drolly, 'I wouldn't be in this mess. There would be no ligament tear or cast. But as my Aunt Diana so wisely says, you can only chase one pig through the village at a time.'

'Or in this case,' Hope added, 'through the hotel lobby.'

The three women burst out laughing.

'I've clearly missed the joke,' Dylan said.

'Should I tell him?' Megan asked Hope and Summer. Not waiting for their answer, she turned to Dylan. 'Your guess – although clever – was wrong. It wasn't a climbing accident in Nepal. It was a porcine accident in Amethyst.'

The trio laughed harder. Dylan did not laugh with them.

Struggling for breath, Megan began to explain, 'The injury to my leg happened at work last week . . .'

Megan was the Director of Activities at Amethyst, a luxury hotel and spa also located in the historic district of the city, only a few blocks from the boutique.

'Early Friday morning, a new guest arrived. The man – his name was Edward – must have been close to a hundred. Severe spinal curvature, two canes, and more age spots than identifiable skin. But he was cheerful and friendly, which was a refreshing change from the typical rich and pretentious clientele.'

Dylan raised an eyebrow. 'You seem to forget that I'm staying at the hotel.'

'I haven't forgotten.' Megan's pert nose twitched. 'Anyway, Edward had a large, opaque animal crate with his luggage. I told him right away that Amethyst has a strict policy prohibiting pets, and service animals have to be certified with the proper paperwork submitted to the hotel in advance, otherwise everybody would waltz in and claim that their pet was suddenly a service animal. Edward started to argue – politely, though – and I gave him the standard speech about the concern for other guests' allergies, noise and pet waste issues, and potentially dangerous animals.'

'You proved the last one,' Summer said.

'Unfortunately, yes,' Megan agreed. 'Although calling Sally a dangerous animal is somewhat unfair. After all, it wasn't her fault they were serving bacon at the breakfast buffet. One could contend that she was merely defending the honor of her species.'

The three women burst out laughing again. Dylan's eyebrow went higher.

Megan hiccupped, then continued, 'So Edward went on arguing, insisting that an exception be made for Sally on account of her being the sweetest, gentlest creature on earth. According to him, she didn't bark or bite; she had no dander that could cause allergies, and she was fastidious about her cleanliness. In an effort to convince me, Edward opened the crate. I leaned down to say hello to Sally, but just at that moment, the porter dropped a trunk next to us. The loud noise startled everyone, including Sally, who burst out of her crate like an exploding firecracker. She knocked me down, followed by the porter, three guests, and two floral arrangements on pedestals.'

Hiccupping once more, Megan grinned at Dylan. 'As you've probably guessed by now, Sally wasn't a standard Labrador or schnauzer. She turned out to be a pot-bellied pig. Kind of pretty, actually. Pink and black dappled, with a happy little face. Except the rest of her was far from little, and after her initial stampede through the lobby, Sally made a beeline straight for the main restaurant, which at that time of the day had the breakfast buffet in full swing. Not realizing then how badly my leg had been injured from being bowled over, I limped after her, as did Edward with his pair of canes. We were joined by nearly everyone from the lobby, employees and curious guests alike. First Sally charged through the bacon and sausage stations. Next she trampled the pastry table. And then came the destruction of the fresh fruit platters. Diners were screaming and jumping up on their chairs as though Sally was a marauding alligator, about to chomp off a stray foot or hand. The whole place was in a squealing, screeching, panic-stricken uproar.'

Even Dylan was grinning now.

'Half a dozen people were trying to catch Sally, all without success, because she was racing around in circles at top speed, the epitome of the slippery pig. Edward said the solution was easy: simply set a bowl of water on the floor for her. And would you believe that it worked? The instant Sally noticed the water, she skidded to a halt, trotted to the bowl, and peaceably began to drink. According to Edward, pot-bellied pigs only sweat from the bridge of their noses, so they need to consume a lot of water to help regulate their body temperature. And that,' Megan concluded with a final hiccup, 'is your porcine trivia for the day, along with the thrilling tale of how my leg ended up in a hot and itchy plaster cast.'

Dylan chuckled. 'I go away for a week, and I miss all of the excitement.'

'Except you were gone for more than a week,' Hope remarked under her breath.

And that was the crux of the problem. Dylan was mostly away. His permanent home and job were in California. He had originally come to Asheville to help out with his father's patients when Morris had undergone back surgery several months earlier. Now that Morris was almost fully recovered and was once again working nearly full-time, Dylan had started to return to his own patients. Although Hope would have preferred to pretend other-wise, the chemistry between her and Dylan was undeniable. But it was almost equally undeniable that beginning a relationship with someone who lived and worked thousands of miles across the country was not a wise idea.

Dylan was asking Megan some specifics about the physician who had treated her at the emergency room, while Hope continued to ruminate on the inadvisability of long-distance relationships, when Summer gave a little start and pointed toward the window.

'I think Miranda is coming here,' she said.

A moment later, Summer was proven correct. Miranda Larson appeared on the sidewalk in front of the boutique. She paused on the doorstep, as though deliberating whether to enter. Miranda didn't normally visit the shop, so Hope knew that something important must have brought her there.

Hope ushered her inside with a welcoming smile. 'It's nice to see you, Miranda.'

Miranda's smile in reply was thin and worried. She was a tall, square woman in her fifties with mousy brown hair and a regret-tably squeaky voice. Miranda and her husband, Paul, were good neighbors. Setting aside the recent construction noise, they were quiet. Their property was always clean and well maintained. And they kept a vigilant eye out for any potential trouble on the block.

'I'm sorry to hear that your cellar is leaking worse than before,' Summer sympathized. 'Will they be able to start work on it soon?'

'Today,' Miranda answered. 'They're supposed to start today,

at least with pumping out the water, possibly also some explora-
tory digging around the foundation. That's why I'm here, actually.
I was standing at the window, watching for them to arrive, and
I noticed something . . .' She hesitated.

'You noticed something?' Hope asked her when she didn't
continue.

'Yes. I don't want to be one of those meddling busybodies,
poking my nose into other people's business, but . . .' Miranda
hesitated again.

'But?' Summer pursued.

'But the man's appearance was so strange. He was wearing
this humongous cloak and—'

'A cloak!' Megan exclaimed. She threw Summer a triumphant
look that said, *I was right! The Hermit was outside!*

'It must have been a large raincoat,' Miranda mused. 'There
is a light mist falling. I hope that it doesn't get any heavier,
because then the contractor will decide not to come, and there
will be even more water in the cellar.'

'That wouldn't be good—' Hope began in commiseration.

'You were telling us about the man in the raincoat?' Summer
interjected.

Miranda nodded. 'Paul saw him, too. We were debating
whether or not to contact the police.'

Dylan turned to her with sudden interest. The Hermit may
have been a joke to him, but the police were not.

'I said to Paul that we shouldn't jump to any hasty conclusions,' Miranda continued. 'It would be embarrassing to everyone
if we contacted the police and then it turned out to be nothing.
So we decided that it would be best if I came over here and
mentioned it to you before doing anything else.'

'Mentioned what exactly?' Summer pressed her with
impatience.

Miranda's thin lips quivered. 'It looked as though the man was
trying to break into *your* cellar.'

THREE

'No doubt whatsoever,' the uniformed policeman declared. Having finished his inspection of the side of the brownstone that bordered the Larsons', he joined the little group standing at the head of the narrow strip of grass and shrubbery that separated the two properties. Megan had remained inside the boutique on account of her injured leg. Miranda had returned to her own brownstone the instant the much-anticipated contractor and his crew had appeared.

'There was definitely an attempt to gain entry,' the policeman confirmed, wiping dirt and bits of wet foliage off his hands with a paper towel from his pocket. He turned to Hope and Summer. 'You believe that you saw a man?'

'Yes,' Hope answered. 'Our friend watched him pass by on the sidewalk several times. And then our neighbor noticed the same man – or at least someone who was similarly dressed – come around the corner and—'

'But you didn't observe this man yourselves?' the policeman interrupted.

'No, we—'

He cut Hope short again. 'Unlikely,' he said, this time addressing Detective Nate Phillips. 'Highly unlikely to have been a man.'

Summer frowned. 'Are you suggesting that it isn't true? Our friend and our neighbor are lying about what they saw?'

'Not lying,' the policeman corrected her. 'Confused.'

'Confused?' Hope echoed, also frowning.

'Women are nervous creatures by nature,' he replied. 'They often fancy hearing noises and seeing shadows, and then they let their imaginations run wild, resulting in confused witness statements.'

Both Hope and Summer's gazes narrowed.

Dylan grinned. 'You had better be careful, officer. I've seen that look from them before. In another minute, they'll be discussing hexes and curses to put on you.'

Detective Nate laughed. 'Don't give them any ideas, Dylan.' He wrapped an affectionate arm around Summer's shoulders.

Although she didn't pull away, Summer also didn't lean into the embrace. 'If you're not going to take the matter seriously, then I shouldn't have called you,' she said to Nate, her tone chilly.

'You didn't call me,' he reminded her. 'Dylan did.'

The chilly tone was now directed toward Dylan. 'I don't know why you did that.'

'Because I was under the impression – perhaps in error – that you and Nate had recently started dating. If I was a detective and my girlfriend had a prowler attempting to break into her home, I'd want to know about it.'

'And I appreciate the heads-up,' Nate said, nodding at Dylan.

Dylan nodded back at him.

The uniformed policeman half suppressed a yawn. 'Well, in this case, it was a waste of everybody's time and energy. There hasn't been a crime. It's pointless to even write up an incident report. Yes, there was an attempt to gain entry, but it was clearly from some*thing* and not some*one*.'

Hope and Summer exchanged a startled glance.

Dylan's grin resurfaced. 'You two think that he's talking about something supernatural, don't you?'

Nate laughed again. 'Watch out, Dylan. Otherwise, the hexes and curses might be put on you next.'

He chortled. 'It will probably be in the form of a voodoo doll, with a needle stuck through my eye.'

'If I were you,' Summer sniped, 'I wouldn't be so eager to tempt Hope. She could take you up on it – and then you'd be missing an eye.'

There was another drowsy yawn from the policeman, which Hope was grateful for. It meant that he was only partly listening to the conversation. Nate must have been thinking something similar – or he didn't want to annoy Summer any further for fear that their fledgling relationship would come to an abrupt end before it had barely even begun – because he returned to the more pressing issue before them.

'So who exactly do you think attempted to gain entry here?' he questioned his colleague.

'A fox, in all likelihood. Or possibly a coyote.'

'Rubbish,' Summer muttered.

Nate agreed with her, albeit with more diplomacy. 'There have been no recorded sightings of either foxes or coyotes in the downtown area in recent memory.'

The policeman shrugged. 'Then it was a raccoon or a possum.'

'What are you basing that on?' Dylan asked him.

Motioning for them to follow, the policeman started back down the narrow border between the two properties. In a single file, the group headed after him. When they had squeezed past a pair of boxwoods that were wet from the morning's intermittent drizzle, they halted. The policeman pointed toward a short metal door that was set low in the wall of the brownstone, just above the ground. The door was no more than two feet in both height and width. Its pewter-colored paint was faded and flaking from age. There were also numerous scratches and abrasions on it.

'Claw marks,' the policeman said. 'Obviously claw marks.'

It wasn't obvious to Hope. She knew from her and Summer's considerable experience with the fencing around their vegetable patch at the rear of the garden that any animal interested in gaining entry would have clawed at the entire door – and possibly also the surrounding wall – leaving long, sharp, defined marks. But these marks were little chips and dents along only one edge of the door, predominantly at the latch, which had been painted shut many years earlier. Unless she was very much mistaken, they were pry marks. Somebody – was it the Hermit? – had been trying to pry open the door.

'But why?' she murmured.

Dylan turned to her. 'Where does the door lead?'

'The cellar.'

'That's the reason they're trying to gain access,' the policeman said, once again wiping his hands on the paper towel from his pocket. 'This is the time of year when animals are looking for a good place to hibernate.'

Summer shook her head. 'It's barely the beginning of autumn, and the nights are still plenty warm. No animals are hibernating yet – and even if they were, they wouldn't choose a cellar in a brownstone on a city street.'

'A cellar in a brownstone on a city street is an excellent spot for animals to find food,' the policeman responded.

'Not our cellar,' Summer countered. 'We don't keep any food in it.'

'What do you keep in it?' Nate asked her.

'Nothing.'

When her sister didn't elaborate, Hope explained, 'Our cellar isn't a finished basement; it's a dirt crawl space. It's difficult to access, so we don't store much down there. In fact, I don't think I've even been in the cellar for at least six months. Have you, Summer?'

Summer shook her head again.

'I don't understand why your cellar would have a door out here,' Dylan said.

'It's for the potato-coal chute,' Hope told him.

'The what?'

'The chute that was used for the brownstone's deliveries back in the olden days. That's why the door is so short and close to the ground. It was never intended as an entrance for people. There are no steps or stairs on the other side going down into the cellar – only the chute. It's how they originally brought in the wood for the fireplaces. Then later, the coal for the heaters. And also when they received a wagonload of potatoes or apples from a local farmer for the winter supply.'

'Up until a few years ago, my uncle used to get his bushels of turnips delivered that way,' the policeman remarked.

Hope nodded, although she couldn't help wondering what anyone in recent times would do with a wagonload of turnips.

'Our cellar still has the old bins that separated one family's coal and potatoes from another's,' Paul Larson said.

They all turned toward the unexpected voice. Paul was standing at the corner of his own brownstone, observing the group in the bordering strip of greenery. Similar to his wife, he was tall and square, but instead of her squeaky syllables, his were a booming baritone. He had a bright orange shock of hair.

'As far as I'm aware, your brownstone was never divided into apartments as ours used to be,' Paul continued, 'so you probably don't have the bins. But it's a good thing that Miranda and I don't store much in our cellar, either, because everything would be half submerged now. There is nothing worse than moldy, floating turnips.'

Hope smiled. 'Hello, Paul. I'm glad to see that your contractor has arrived. It's some progress, at least.'

'Yes. They're presently trying to decide which direction would be best to pump out the water. I'm afraid that it might get a bit noisy when the machinery starts, especially if they end up emptying it on this side of the property.'

There was a sigh from Summer.

'We understand,' Hope replied, swallowing her own sigh. 'But the sooner the work begins, the sooner it will be completed.'

'That's the theory. And also the reason that I came over to speak to you . . .' Paul hesitated just as his wife had done earlier in the boutique.

'Oh?' Hope said.

Paul shifted his weight from one foot to the other. 'I hate to be the bearer of potentially bad news, but . . .' He hesitated again.

Summer sighed a second time. 'But?'

'But after a closer inspection, the contractor indicated that the source of the problem might not be limited to our property. He strongly recommends that you examine your own cellar to make sure that it doesn't have water in it, too.'

Hope and Summer looked at each other with a mixture of surprise and concern. The possibility that their foundation might also be leaking had never occurred to them.

Nate pushed past one of the damp boxwoods to reach Summer. 'Not to worry,' he told her. 'Your cellar is probably as dry as a bone. We'll check it out. We need to go down there anyway, just to be certain that everything is all right.' He motioned toward the marks on the door.

'So it turned out to be nothing with that strange-looking fellow we saw earlier?' Paul asked.

'Nothing,' Hope confirmed, although she wasn't entirely convinced on that point. She had no doubt it was a person and not an animal that had made the marks, but she still didn't understand why the person had tried to pry open the door.

'Miranda will be relieved,' Paul said, sounding rather relieved himself. 'She was beginning to fret about burglaries and home invasions cropping up in the neighborhood. But it's good to know that sometimes a peculiar man in a peculiar raincoat is simply that, with no harm intended.'

'I hope you're right,' Summer mumbled, sounding no more convinced than her sister.

'We'll check it out,' Nate repeated. 'And if we need additional details from either you or your wife on what exactly you saw regarding the man, we'll be in touch. In the meantime, if you have any questions . . .' He handed Paul his business card.

Reading the card, Paul was visibly impressed. 'Thank you, detective. I have to stop complaining about the city's high taxes when a detective of your rank handles a minor matter such as this.'

Nate smiled politely. 'Just doing my job.'

Hope restrained her own smile. The detective was there solely because of his interest in Summer, but the neighbors didn't need to know that.

Any further conversation was cut short by the appearance of the construction crew with a large portable generator, a small backhoe, and a mound of rubber hoses. Apparently the water was going to be pumped out in their direction.

'Time for ear plugs,' Summer groaned.

With a nod in parting, Paul headed toward the crew. Nate, in turn, nodded at the uniformed policeman, who headed toward his vehicle. The remainder of the group headed toward the boutique.

'Wait.' Summer held Hope back from the others. 'Should we tell Gram?' she said in a low tone.

Their maternal grandmother, Olivia Bailey, was the legal owner of the brownstone and also an important confidante for the sisters.

'You mean about the marks on the door or the potential leakage in the cellar?' Hope asked her.

'Either, or both.'

Hope considered for a moment. 'At this point, Gram can't do anything more than we can. Let's hold off until we have some concrete information.'

Summer twisted her hands together anxiously, but she was forced to let the subject lapse, because they had reached the door of the shop.

'No customers came in while you were out,' Megan reported,

still sitting in her same chair at the table. 'But there were two phone calls. The first woman wanted a palm reading. I scheduled her for tomorrow morning.'

'Perfect. Thanks,' Hope said.

'Assuming you'll be able to hear each other over the construction noise,' Summer grumbled.

'And the second woman,' Megan continued, 'wanted to know if the boutique sells Ouija boards. She said that it was for a séance at her young daughter's birthday party.'

Summer's hazel eyes stretched wide. 'Good lord! Better to give the child a stick of dynamite to play with. It would be safer.'

Hope hastily tried to hush her sister, motioning toward Dylan and Nate. But it was too late. Dylan had already heard.

'Is it the séance or the Ouija board that's supposedly dangerous?' he inquired.

'Hope has some excellent Ouija board stories,' Megan told him. 'They're super scary. Definitely not appropriate for bedtime.'

'Is that so?' Dylan turned to Hope with a rakish grin. 'I'd be happy to tuck you into bed any time.'

She felt her cheeks warm. In an effort to conceal it, her response was dry. 'Without the requisite knowledge, conducting your own séance is about as effective as creating your own voodoo doll. And in the case of the Ouija board, you could lose a lot more than an eye if it goes wrong.'

The grin continued. 'Returning to the subject of your bed—'

To Hope's relief, he was interrupted by Nate, who was studying the mammoth collection of apricot roses on the jewelry display case. 'That is a really big bouquet.'

There was a distinct hint of apprehension in his voice, as though he feared that Summer might have another suitor, one who sent her extravagant floral arrangements. Hope was quick to reassure him.

'Aren't the flowers lovely? They were a gift from Daniel Drexler to cheer up Megan after she injured her leg.'

'Daniel has set the standard pretty high for the rest of us, hasn't he?' Dylan commented to Nate.

Megan's pert nose twitched. 'Have no fear, Dylan. If Hope ever has the misfortune to be trampled by a pig, you won't need to send roses. You've got those good hands to give her succor.'

The grin reappeared. 'Indeed I do. Now if you'll only manage to convince Hope of their value . . .'

Hope raised an eyebrow at Megan, then she turned and started toward the rear of the shop.

'Are you going to the cellar?' Summer said, and hurried to accompany her.

Dylan and Nate followed them. This time Megan didn't remain behind. With the assistance of a pair of crutches, she rose from her chair and hobbled slowly after the group.

Walking from the boutique into the living quarters of the brownstone, Hope and Summer headed down the main hallway.

'Where is the entrance to the cellar?' Nate asked.

'In the study,' Summer answered without stopping.

'Sorry about the mess,' Megan called out. 'I didn't realize that there would be visitors today and a surprise inspection of my unmentionables.'

The door to the study stood open. It was the brownstone's library. The walls consisted entirely of built-in oak bookcases that were stacked from floor to ceiling with thick, dusty tomes. There was an old barrister desk, an antique standing globe, a trio of scuffed leather armchairs with bronze nail heads, and the pull-out sofa that currently functioned as Megan's bed. As she had warned, the room was in disarray. Her bedding lay in a jumbled heap on the floor, and her clothes were strewn across the furniture, with several lacy undergarments hanging indecorously from the globe stand.

Together Hope and Summer went to the far end of the room, which contained a narrow corner bookcase. Standing on tiptoe, Hope stretched up to the top shelf and slowly ran her fingers underneath it.

'Can you reach the spot?' Summer asked her. 'Now would be a good time for that stepladder from Gram.'

'Give me a second. I think I've got it. Yes, there it is. You had better move back.'

She waited until Summer had retreated a pace, then Hope pushed the indentation that her fingers had found and immediately jumped back herself. The corner bookcase rotated noiselessly to one side, revealing a slim door in the wall.

'How very clever,' Dylan remarked. 'Are there secret passages throughout the brownstone?'

The sisters exchanged a glance, but neither one responded.

Nate's brow furrowed. 'It's an odd place for a cellar door.'

Summer nodded. 'The main door used to be adjacent to the pantry,' she explained. 'But it was sealed up when the kitchen was renovated some years back. Now this is the only way into the cellar.'

'Aside from the chute,' Hope clarified.

There was no knob or handle on the door. It simply swung inward over what appeared from their vantage point to be a large, black cavern. Reaching into the darkness, Hope felt around until she located the string for the lone lightbulb and pulled it. A dim yellow glow emerged, illuminating the top of a primitive wooden staircase.

'Watch your head and feet,' she cautioned the men as she started to descend. 'The ceiling slopes down quickly, and the steps are slippery from age and wear.'

'Really slippery,' Summer corroborated with a laugh. 'Hope, do you remember the time – we must have been five or six – when we tried to use an old piece of carpeting to sled to the bottom and . . .'

Hope didn't hear the conclusion of the reminiscence. She had stopped on the second step, because there was something lying in front of her on the third step. At first glance, it looked like a piece of torn black plastic that had gotten snagged on a protruding nail. Hope untangled the item from the nail and held it toward the light for a better view. It wasn't plastic; it was waxed canvas. And it wasn't black; it was olive green. She felt suddenly cold.

'Megan?' she called behind her. 'Are you there?'

'Yes, I'm here!' Megan and her crutches hobbled closer to the cellar door.

'What did the cloak from the man you saw look like?'

There was a slight pause. 'The fabric was heavy. Duck or canvas. And it was a dark shade of green. Maybe olive.'

Hope drew a shaky breath. The Hermit hadn't only been outside the brownstone. He had been inside, too.

FOUR

It didn't take the rest of the group long to reach the same unsettling conclusion that Hope had.

Nate immediately put his hand on his holster and moved past the others to take the lead on the stairs. 'Dylan,' he said, 'I'm going to need you to keep the sisters up here.'

'They'll stay up here,' Dylan confirmed, stepping in front of Hope – who was ahead of Summer – to block their way.

'But it's *our* cellar—' Summer began in protest.

'And *I'm* the one carrying a firearm,' Nate returned.

His tone brooked no dissent, and Summer didn't argue further.

Firearm or not, Nate was forced to proceed slowly, because the lightbulb offered him little assistance beyond the first few steps. The lower portion of the stairway was cast in heavy shadows, and the remainder of the cellar was impenetrably dark.

'There are eleven steps,' Hope told him. 'You're on the fifth one now. At the bottom of the stairs on the left side is a wicker basket. There should be several flashlights in it.'

He nodded.

'The batteries might be dead,' Summer said.

Hope frowned at her. 'Surely not all of them.'

'How about getting some candles from the boutique?' Summer suggested. 'Megan could—'

'What's happening?' Megan called from the cellar door, evidently catching the mention of her name. 'What do you need me to do?'

Nate gave a sharp cough in a command for silence.

With an indignant harrumph, Summer sat down on the nearest step. 'Bossy,' she muttered. 'I was just trying to help.'

'Nate knows that,' Hope began in a consolatory whisper. 'He—'

Dylan turned to her. 'What will it take to keep you quiet?'

His voice was low, and he was standing directly in front of her, so only Hope heard him. She felt a matching flash of indignation, but it was replaced a moment later by a flutter in her throat as Dylan leaned close to her.

'If I kiss you,' he said, 'will that work?'

Hope looked at him. In the dim light, Dylan's eyes were indigo. There was a yellow spark of fire in them, too. She didn't know if it was a reflection from the lightbulb – or a mischievous glint.

'It depends,' she answered with a mischievous spark of her own.

'On what?'

'On how good the kiss is.'

Dylan didn't blink. 'I accept the challenge.'

Whether he would have followed through right then and there, Hope was left to guess, because they were interrupted by a flashlight clicking on at the base of the stairway. Thankfully, Summer's concern had been needless; the batteries weren't dead. In conjunction with the firearm, the flashlight circled slowly around the interior of the cellar. From her position on the steps, Hope couldn't see far in any direction, but to her relief, the main portion of the floor appeared to be dry. The foundation of their brownstone wasn't leaking, at least not to the same extent as the Larsons'.

'All clear,' Nate announced after a minute. The flashlight moved to a relaxed position, and the firearm returned to its holster. 'We're alone in here.'

Summer rose from her seat and proceeded down the stairs. 'Of course we're alone in here. If you hadn't shushed me like an unruly child, I could have told you that almost immediately after we entered.'

'You could have?' Nate asked, sounding both surprised and doubtful at her claim.

'Yes,' Summer said. 'It's the smell.'

Following her down the steps, Dylan echoed Nate's skepticism. 'The smell?'

'The smell,' she repeated decisively.

In unison, the two men took an audible sniff.

'I smell nothing,' Nate said.

It was Summer's turn to express incredulity. 'I find that difficult to believe. Surely you smell *something*. The packed dirt beneath your feet and the earthen walls at your sides. The dust and must that come with the temperature variations of the seasons. Even the staleness of the still air. They all have an odor.'

The men sniffed again, more thoughtfully this time.

'While we're on the subject,' Summer said to Hope, who was the last to descend, 'I don't smell any moisture. With luck, that means we won't have to suffer through the same repairs as Miranda and Paul.'

As fate – or irony – would have it, the construction crew chose that moment to start up the generator to pump out the water next door. The ground trembled briefly, followed by a deep, continuous rumble. Mercifully, down in the cellar, the sound was more akin to distant rolling thunder than the migraine-inducing pounding of a jackhammer.

Nate's voice rose to accommodate the addition of the noise. 'I didn't see any sign of seepage when I was looking around. Even so, I would recommend that you have a qualified professional come in to conduct a thorough inspection of the place. In my experience, it's always better to get ahead of home repairs when they're comparatively small and easy to fix than to wait until they become enormous projects like what's happening to your neighbors.'

'That's probably true,' Summer acknowledged.

'I did see this, however,' Nate continued. He held a flat, rectangular object up to the beam of his flashlight.

They all looked at it. It was another piece of olive-green waxed canvas, slightly larger than the one Hope had discovered on the steps. By all appearances, it was also from the Hermit's cloak.

'Where did you find it?' Hope asked.

'Over there.' Nate pointed toward the far end of the cellar. 'Next to the potato-coal chute. Based on its ragged border, it most likely got caught on a rough edge of either the chute or the outside door and tore off.'

Taking a flashlight from the wicker basket, Dylan headed in the direction of the chute and the door.

Remaining where he was, Nate lifted the piece of canvas to his nose. 'It doesn't have much of a smell. Just a faint damp-fabric odor.' He turned to Hope. 'What does your piece smell like?'

'The same as yours. Damp fabric.'

Nate's brow furrowed at Summer. 'I don't understand. How could you know from the barely detectible scent of a scrap of damp canvas that we were alone in here?'

Summer shook her head. 'It wasn't the scent of the canvas. It was the opposite. There wasn't enough of a scent.'

The furrow deepened.

'You have a smell . . .' she began to explain.

Nate looked taken aback.

Summer half suppressed a laugh. 'It isn't only you. It's every-body. We *all* have a smell; some more pronounced than others. For what it's worth, your smell isn't bad. On the contrary, you smell quite nice. Your cologne has a distinct sandalwood base.'

'It-it does?'

'Yes. In comparison, Dylan's scent is lighter. My guess is that he uses an aftershave balm or lotion with a eucalyptus top note. That makes sense, considering he's a doctor. He might have patients with fragrance sensitivities.'

Nate glanced at Dylan for his reaction, but Dylan – who was examining the area around the chute and was thereby closer to the noise from the generator outside – didn't appear to have heard the sandalwood and eucalyptus remarks.

'As soon as I stepped on to the cellar stairs,' Summer continued, 'I could tell who was around me. There was the sandalwood from you. The eucalyptus from Dylan. And a lingering hint of damask rose from Megan up in the study. But that was it. There was nothing more, aside from – as I mentioned before – the natural odors of the surrounding earth and air. If someone else had been down here with us, I would have noticed right away. They didn't need to speak or make a noise by moving around. Their soap, or shampoo, or laundry detergent would have given them away.'

With his brow still furrowed, Nate was silent for several long seconds. 'What about Hope?' he asked.

'Oh, I don't notice Hope's scent,' Summer told him. 'I don't notice Gram's, either. Growing up together and living in the same house for such a long time, it's simply become part of the back-ground. I'm so familiar with it, I'll be able to identify both of them by smell in the next life, even when Gram returns as a raptor and Hope as a reptile.'

'I object!' Hope protested with a laugh. 'Why does Gram get to come back as a bird of prey while I'm stuck as a reptile?'

Summer grinned. 'How about a king cobra or a Komodo dragon? Both are venomous reptiles.'

'Being venomous would be pretty cool,' Hope acceded.

'Definitely. And don't you think that Gram would make an excellent bird of prey?'

'Without question. She—'

'I've always imagined coming back as a penguin on the outer Falkland Islands,' Nate interjected contemplatively.

Hope and Summer exchanged an amused glance. It wasn't unusual for some of their clients – particularly during a more expansive palm or Tarot reading – to share their varied beliefs regarding a possible next life. But it was the first time that either of them had heard anyone express a desire to return as a penguin. Large African cats were occasionally mentioned, along with oceanic dolphins and whales. The most common preference, of course, was for a gleaming heaven surrounded by loved ones, with the accompaniment of angel wings.

'If you come back as a penguin,' Dylan remarked drolly to Nate, 'then Summer and her super sniffer will be able to identify you in the next life, too. There is no way to conceal the smell – or, more accurately, stench – of a raw fish and squid diet.'

Nate laughed.

'And, no,' Dylan continued, leaning against the side of the potato-coal chute, 'just because I use a shower gel courtesy of the hotel that contains essence of eucalyptus does not mean that I want to be reincarnated as a koala.'

Nate laughed harder. Hope couldn't help smiling, as well. She also noted that Dylan's hearing was a lot better than he tended to let on.

Unlike the others, Summer was not entertained, perhaps due to the reference to her *super sniffer*. 'Reincarnation is *earned*,' she said tetchily. 'At this point, Dylan, I doubt that you merit anything more than earthworm status.'

He responded with a shrug. 'That may be correct, but you'll never know for certain, because if I end up as a lowly earthworm, you won't be able to smell me.'

Summer scowled and started to say something about squashing

a worm on the sidewalk with the heel of her boot, but Nate was quick to interrupt.

'As interesting as this discussion on the afterlife has become—'

There was a little chortle from Dylan.

'—my earlier question was either misspoken or misinterpreted,' Nate went on. 'I meant to ask whether Hope could also smell that we were alone down here in the cellar?'

Hope shook her head. 'No. I'm not blessed with Summer's olfactory gift. My nose only goes so far as to differentiate between peonies and hyacinths in the garden, and rosemary and basil in the kitchen. But if you give that basil to Summer, she can tell you with a single sniff the variety, country of origin, and length of time since harvest.'

'Truly?' Nate said.

'Truly,' Hope confirmed. 'That's why Summer is in charge of the boutique's herbs and teas. If they were left to my care, our customers would be sadly limited to bulk chamomile and hibiscus.'

Nate turned to Summer. 'That's an impressive talent you have. I'm not trying to steal you away from your shop, but if you're ever interested in branching out, the police department could find good use for your skills.'

Even in the dim light, a pair of pink spots was visible on Summer's cheeks. 'That's kind of you to say,' she replied softly.

'The morgue could probably also use a super sniffer,' Dylan commented in a low, wry tone.

Thankfully, Summer's ears were not nearly as proficient as her nose, so she didn't hear him. Hope did, however, and she shot Dylan a sharp look.

He chortled once more, then said in a louder voice, 'Considering what we've learned today, Nate, I would advise you to keep your consumption of such pungent foodstuffs as garlic and onions to a minimum on any future dinner dates.'

Nate grinned. 'A sage recommendation – no pun intended.'

The spots on Summer's cheeks grew larger. 'You can eat whatever you like when we're together. There's no need to worry about . . .' She broke off, embarrassed.

Hope's sharp look toward Dylan repeated itself.

He feigned innocence. 'I was merely pointing out the obvious.

No one wants a romantic evening to go awry because of too many leeks in the lamb stew.'

The sharp look became a roll of the eyes. 'You've had a lot of romantic evenings with lamb stew?'

'I make an outstanding lamb stew,' Dylan informed her. 'When you've had the pleasure of tasting it, you can apologize to me for your skepticism with a kiss. You do owe me a kiss, after all.'

'I do *not* owe you a kiss.'

'Yes, you do. I distinctly recall accepting your challenge on the cellar stairs a short while ago. Don't pretend that you don't remember. Are you trying to welch?'

Hope couldn't decide whether to laugh or throw up her hands in exasperation. The man was incorrigible.

A smile tugged at the corner of Dylan's mouth. 'So then we're in agreement? You owe me a kiss.' His expression grew suddenly serious. 'Is it just me, or does anyone else smell smoke?'

FIVE

Regardless of whether Dylan was in error about – or, most likely, embellishing – the quality of his lamb stew, he was certainly not wrong about the smoke. The moment that he mentioned it, Hope caught the smell also and immediately felt the instinctive urge to flee upstairs to safety. But she made it only half a step in the direction of the stairway before she realized that there was no fire in the cellar. In the dim lighting, any spark or flame would have been instantly visible, and there wasn't the slightest hint of a fiery glow around them. Furthermore, aside from the wicker basket with the flashlights and a couple of old wooden crates, there was nothing in the cellar that could even burn. There was plenty that could burn upstairs, however.

The same alarming thought must have occurred to Summer, because she gave a panicked cry. 'Smoke means fire! The study!'

As Summer started to dash toward the stairway, Nate reached out and grabbed her arm to stop her.

'But Megan is up there!' she protested, struggling to free herself. 'With her leg in the cast, she can't move quickly!'

Nate held her firm. 'Megan's not in danger. There is no fire in the study – or anywhere else in your house.'

Both his expression and his tone had the calm assurance of competent law enforcement, and Summer stopped trying to wrest her arm away. Her expression was less assured, however. 'If it isn't in the house, then where . . .'

'It's outdoors,' Dylan answered. 'See for yourself.'

They all turned in the direction that he indicated. Dylan and Nate were correct. The smoke was coming from outside the brownstone, not inside. It was a thin, lead-colored fog, seeping through the edges of the metal door and drifting down the rusty potato-coal chute like a wispy cloud being blown on a spring wind. As the smoke crept closer to them, it grew increasingly caustic.

Summer wrinkled her nose at the acrid aroma. 'How could

there be a fire outside? Everything is damp from the drizzle and—'

'The generator,' Hope interjected, suddenly noticing that they no longer needed to raise their voices to be heard over the rumbling noise. 'When did it stop running?'

'I was wondering that also,' Nate said. 'It might have short-circuited, which would explain the smoke and the burning smell.'

A flurry of shouts could be heard outside. The words were too muddled to understand, but it was clear from their volume and tenor that all was not well.

Releasing his hold on Summer, it was Nate's turn to head toward the stairs. 'I had better go out there and see what's happening. Dylan, you should probably have a look, too, just in case someone's been injured.'

Dylan nodded and was beginning to follow him, when Megan called down from the cellar door.

'Hope? Summer? Can you come back up? There's a problem.'

Although he continued to climb the steps, Nate's pace slowed, as though he was considering what Megan had said.

'Hope?' she called again after a moment. 'Summer? I think you should hurry. Your help is needed.'

Nate didn't increase his speed. Instead, he glanced down at the sisters, who had moved swiftly to the base of the stairway. There was a look of distinct annoyance on his face.

'There's a problem,' he grumbled. 'But you don't ask for help from the detective or the doctor.'

'Of course not,' Dylan responded with undisguised sarcasm. 'Why would anyone want the assistance of a decorated police officer and a board-certified physician when they can have the consummate wisdom of a fortune teller and a tea lady?'

Nate gave an amused snort.

Hope glared at the back of Dylan's head, while Summer glared at the back of Nate's. Several choice words bubbled on both their tongues, but they were interrupted by Megan's increasingly urgent entreaty.

'Hope!' she exclaimed. 'You have to get up here! It's bordering on an emergency!'

The decorated police officer and the board-certified physician still didn't rush.

'There is no such thing as *bordering on*,' Nate remarked sourly. 'Either it's an emergency or it's not.'

'And if they don't know the difference,' Dylan said, 'they should spend a couple of hours at a hospital or a police station. Then they'll see what real emergencies are.'

'You've got that right,' Nate agreed.

Megan must have caught some portion of their conversation, because she commented crisply, 'I don't know what you boys are blathering about, but it would be lovely if you could manage to move faster than a pair of arthritic turtles, so that Hope and Summer can get up the stairs behind you.' Before anyone was able to answer, she continued, 'Hope, I'm going outside. Come quickly!'

The sound of Megan's crutches could be heard as she hobbled out of the study and into the hall. A moment later, Nate and Dylan reached the top of the stairway, with Summer and Hope following on their heels. As soon as they had all stepped into the room, Hope pulled the string to switch off the cellar lightbulb, and Summer tried to slam the cellar door shut. The door wasn't heavy enough to make much noise, so she tried to slam the corner bookcase next. But it made even less of an impact by rotating closed and concealing the cellar door just as silently as it had first opened and revealed it.

'I'm still waiting to learn about all of the secret passages in this place,' Dylan said.

'A full guided tour would be nice,' Nate added.

'You'll both be waiting for a very long time,' Summer snapped.

'And you can forget about me owing you a kiss,' Hope muttered under her breath. 'I officially welch.'

She didn't know whether Dylan heard any of her words, and she didn't stay to find out. Megan was not by nature an unduly nervous or panicky sort of person, nor did she tend to exaggerate minor mishaps into full-blown crises. So if she said there was a problem and their help was needed, it meant that something was genuinely wrong and they should proceed with haste, not scoff and deliberately dawdle like Nate and Dylan.

Without further delay, Hope exited the study and headed down the hall toward the boutique. She paused as she entered the shop and noticed a collection of shopping bags that were sitting on the floor not far from the front door, which stood wide open.

Only a few paces behind her sister, Summer noticed the bags also. 'We must have had a visitor in our absence.'

'A visitor with luxury taste, apparently,' Hope said. 'Those are from some of Asheville's most expensive clothing stores.'

'I wonder who the person is.'

Hope responded with a small smile. 'Probably not the Hermit. Based on those pieces of waxed canvas that we found, together with Megan and Miranda's descriptions of the man, he appears to be more of a camping and outdoor enthusiast than a designer shoe and handbag aficionado.'

Summer nodded. 'That makes sense. What doesn't make sense is why he was in our cellar. There is absolutely nothing of interest or value down there, especially for a camping and outdoor enthusiast. And if his goal was to sneak upstairs into the brownstone, it still doesn't make sense. It's not as though we keep piles of cash lying around the living room. The jewelry in here has some worth, of course, but the case' – she gestured toward the display case that was still crowned by the mammoth crystal vase with its throng of apricot roses – 'is always locked. The only way that someone could steal from it is by distracting us with a potential purchase, the same as with any other attempt at shoplifting. A prospective thief wouldn't crawl through the shrubbery and the metal door, slide down the potato-coal chute, and then slink up the cellar stairs into the study. The possibility of being caught is too high. Plus, there's the issue of getting out again. Does the person return through the study and the cellar, or do they hope to leave through the boutique?'

'An excellent question. In the case of the Hermit, he must have climbed back up the chute and gone out the metal door, because we would have spotted him otherwise.' Hope considered for a moment. 'And from a timing standpoint, it works. Miranda saw him at the side of the property after Megan saw him in front of the window, so Miranda's sighting could have been when he was coming out of the cellar rather than entering it.'

Summer nodded again. 'That makes sense, too. But what doesn't make sense is why he was in front of the window at all. If you want to break into someone's cellar, don't you try to be as stealthy and invisible as possible? Miranda caught a glimpse of him by chance, because she was watching so closely for the arrival of the contractor and construction crew. But Megan saw him multiple times. Do you pace back and forth on the sidewalk in front of a building that you're planning on breaking into? It isn't smart.'

'It certainly isn't,' Hope agreed. 'And while we're on the subject, it also isn't smart to leave such obviously high-priced shopping bags sitting in an open doorway like this. Anybody passing by on the street could see them and simply reach inside to take them.'

'Which means that our visitor has more money than brains—'

Summer was interrupted by another flurry of loud shouts outside. Unlike when they had first heard them in the cellar, these were no longer muddled.

'What the devil is he doing?' yelled a man.

'Get him away from it!' hollered a booming baritone that resembled Paul Larson's.

Miranda's squeaky syllables came next. 'Stop him! Won't somebody stop him?'

Startled, Hope and Summer looked at each other. Were they talking about the Hermit? Before either one could react, Dylan and Nate appeared next to them, having finally made their way from the study into the boutique.

'What the hell is going on out there?' Dylan said.

'Nothing good. I can assure you of that,' Nate replied.

Grabbing his doctor bag, Dylan dashed out of the front door with Nate.

'Oh, sure,' Summer groused, as she and Hope followed the pair, albeit at a somewhat slower pace. 'When Megan says that help is needed and we should hurry, Nate and Dylan drag their feet and lecture us about the definition of an emergency. But when it's Miranda and Paul and whoever else bellowing for assistance, now suddenly it becomes a truly urgent situation.'

Hope was seconding the complaint, when she caught an odd sound coming between the continuing shouts. 'I wonder . . .' she mused to herself. Then she said to Summer, 'Hold on a second. I'll be right back.'

With quick steps, Hope returned to the boutique, pulled a bag from the drawer in the palm-and-Tarot-reading table, and then rejoined her sister, who had paused on the front walk. They were just turning the corner to the side of the brownstone when Nate's voice rose above the others.

'Do *not* touch the water!' he ordered.

'But we have to get him out!' Paul argued.

'If we don't, he'll be electrocuted!' Miranda shrieked.

'And if you touch the water, then you'll be electrocuted with him,' Dylan informed her sharply.

Hope and Summer rushed toward the commotion. The drizzle from that morning had recommenced as a fine mist. It thickened the smoke that spiraled up from the generator into a heavy black plume and further intensified the accompanying burning smell. Nate's guess in the cellar appeared to have been correct: the generator had short-circuited. To Hope's surprise, no one was attempting to repair it or was even standing near it. The entire group was clustered around what looked from a distance to be a large, inflatable swimming pool. The pool – together with a set of giant snaking hoses – took up nearly every inch of space between the two brownstones, flattening the bordering boxwoods and smothering the grass. As Hope got closer, she saw that it was a makeshift retention pool into which the water from the Larsons' cellar had evidently been pumped. Based on the shouts, she expected to find the Hermit with his olive-green canvas cloak wading confusedly in the middle of it. But there was no Hermit. Instead, there was Percy.

'My baby!' Rosemarie Potter cried. 'My poor, darling baby!'

Rosemarie was a gregarious woman in her fifties with blazing red-dyed hair that had been dampened to a slightly less eye-popping shade of cranberry by the mist. She was one of Hope's most loyal clients, regularly visiting the boutique every few days for a reading, which was almost invariably focused on her bumpy love life. Almost equally invariably, Rosemarie was accompanied to the boutique by her darling Percy. Except Percy wasn't a baby. He was a middle-aged, roly-poly pug with a similarly sociable disposition and a proclivity for ending up in places where he shouldn't be. In this case that meant taking an impromptu bath next to a visibly sparking frayed extension cord. Hope could only guess whether the cord had arrived at the Larsons' already damaged, or was the victim of Percy's sturdy, exploratory teeth. Either way, it was in all likelihood the cause of the generator's short-circuit. It was also the cause of everyone's shouting.

'Won't somebody do something!' Miranda implored.

'How is the cord getting power?' Nate asked her and Paul. 'Can we cut the supply?'

Paul nodded in the affirmative and pointed toward the rear of their brownstone. 'The contractor said that he would go to the main—'

Hope didn't hear the rest of the explanation, because Rosemarie gave an ear-splitting wail.

'Percy! You must get out of there right now!'

Percy didn't budge an inch. In his defense, Rosemarie's words were so garbled by her sobs that he probably had difficulty even recognizing his name.

'Get out right now!' Rosemarie repeated, more pleading than commanding. 'Please, Percy!'

The pug responded with a cheerful yip and continued to splash in the pool, which was brown and murky with sediment, as could be expected from water that had been standing for days in the Larsons' earthen cellar. As the spray hit the frayed cord, it sparked brightly. Everyone gasped, and Rosemarie wailed once more.

'He'll die! My poor, darling baby will die!'

In her distress, Rosemarie started to race toward the pool. Dylan pulled her back just in time.

'No,' he said firmly but calmly. 'You aren't going anywhere near that water.'

Rosemarie looked at him beseechingly. 'But Percy needs help!'

'And he'll get help,' he assured her.

'A solution is in the works . . .' Nate began.

As he reiterated what Paul had told him a minute earlier about the contractor cutting the power, Rosemarie clutched at Dylan's arm for support. It reminded Hope of the bag that she was holding under her own arm. In the general panic, she had forgotten all about it. She took the bag into her hands and opened its top with a deliberate crumpling noise.

Summer turned to her sister. She squinted at the bag for a

moment in confusion, and when she realized what it contained, she grinned. 'How on earth did you know to bring those out here?'

'I wasn't sure, but I thought that I heard Percy's yips between all of the yelling. That's why I went back into the shop before.' Hope shook the bag and its contents as loudly as she could.

Percy stopped splashing. His dripping face snapped in Hope's direction.

She shook the bag again and called in a low, clear voice, 'Percy, I've got your doggie cookies.'

In spite of all of the surrounding noises and distractions, Percy managed to catch some combination of the word *cookie*, the sound from the bag, and possibly even a hint of aroma from his favorite treats. Without an instant of hesitation, he sprang out of the pool and sprinted toward Hope. She had never seen his chubby little legs move with such speed.

Megan – who was standing to one side, leaning heavily on her crutches to relieve the pressure on her injured leg – burst out laughing. 'Apparently the old adage about a man's stomach being the way to his heart applies equally to canines. This is why I said that your help was needed, Hope. With as often as Percy is in the boutique, I knew that you would be able to think up a rescue plan for him.'

Percy slammed to a halt directly in front of Hope. Eager for his promised treat, he pushed his wet nose against her leg, leaving behind a glob of mud.

It was Hope's turn to laugh. 'That's the thanks I get, eh?' She took a cookie out of the bag and gave it to him.

Summer reached down to add a pat, but she pulled her hand back when she realized that he was coated with a film of dirt. 'Yuck. You need a bath, Percy. A real one this time, with a good shampoo. We have to make sure that he doesn't go into the shop today, Hope. We don't want wet-dog smell lingering tomorrow during the Wednesday afternoon tea.'

'Or a trail of muddy paw prints, which neither of us is interested in scrubbing from the floor.'

Ordinarily when he visited the boutique, Percy was limited to one treat, otherwise he grew greedy and continually demanded more. But Hope figured that an exception could be made on this occasion, considering that the poor chap had very nearly been electrocuted.

'Here's a second cookie. It's the last one for today, though,' she told him. 'So don't stare at me with those big, sad eyes as though you've been horribly deprived. We all know that Rosemarie spoils you rotten. Isn't that right, Rosemarie?'

Hope turned to Rosemarie with a smile, but she discovered that Rosemarie hadn't heard a single word. Nor had Rosemarie noticed that her darling Percy was safe and sound and merrily crunching on a bonus treat. She was too busy alternately sniffling into Dylan's shoulder and nodding earnestly at Nate. Both Paul and Miranda had disappeared from view, presumably to check on the contractor's progress regarding cutting the power to the frayed cord.

'How's that for irony,' Summer remarked dryly. 'The fortune teller is the one who solves the problem, while the decorated police officer and the board-certified physician stand around and discuss it.'

Hope's smile widened. 'Don't forget about the vital contribution from the tea lady. As I recall, you were the one who refilled Percy's treat bag last week.'

Summer laughed.

'Hello!' Megan called and waved at Rosemarie's group. 'The calamity has ended. The pug has been liberated. All is well.'

There was a momentary silence as the group glanced around in collective surprise, then came a cry of delight.

'Percy! Oh, my darling, darling Percy!'

Rosemarie rushed to the pug, who was finishing the last of his cookie while simultaneously depositing several more globs of mud on Hope's leg. As Rosemarie scooped him up in her arms, Percy shook himself, showering Rosemarie in myriad dirty droplets of water, but she didn't care. She just hugged him harder, tears of joy streaming down her face.

'Was it you who saved him?' Rosemarie looked back and forth between Hope and Summer, bobbing her red mop that was beginning to frizz from all of the moisture. Before either of them could reply, she continued, 'I don't know how to thank you! You're wonderful! Didn't I tell you how wonderful they are?'

As she posed the question, Rosemarie turned her head toward

the boutique. Hope followed her gaze and, to her astonishment, she saw a woman standing at the corner of the brownstone. She was wearing a slim, charcoal-colored dress that blended with the gray sky and the gray mist, making her appear nearly invisible. Hope didn't recognize the woman. But Rosemarie was apparently familiar with her, because she went on speaking to her.

'Didn't I tell you?' Rosemarie repeated enthusiastically. 'That's why I said you had to come with me to the boutique.'

Hope and Summer exchanged a curious glance. Did the shopping bags that had been left on the floor of the shop belong to the woman? Hope took a closer look at her. She was in her late thirties or possibly early forties, with silky black hair that was parted down the middle and tapered perfectly at the top of her shoulders. Both her dress and the coordinating high heels were chic – and definitely not designed for standing outdoors on the wet ground in the steadily increasing drizzle.

'Why don't we go inside?' Hope suggested, directing the remark and a friendly smile at the woman.

The smile was returned, and the woman took a step forward.

Rosemarie went on chattering. 'I'm sure that you and Hope and Summer will be the best of friends. You have so much in common.' She gave a little start as though a sudden realization had occurred to her, and she stared at Hope with wide eyes. 'Could you foresee the peril that would befall Percy? Did the Tarot cards show you what would happen? Is that how you knew to rescue him?'

There was a chortle behind Hope. She didn't need to turn around to know that it came from Dylan. Summer must have heard it, too, because she began to glower at him, but Rosemarie's next words stopped her short.

'How silly of me!' Rosemarie exclaimed with a giggle. 'I'm prattling away, and I haven't even properly introduced you. Hope, Summer . . . This is Madam Gina. She has the gift, the same as you. *And* she holds séances.'

SIX

'I don't like her,' Summer said.

'You don't even know her,' Megan responded.

'I don't have to know her. I can just tell.'

Megan looked up from her seat at the palm-and-Tarot-reading table, where she was decoratively arranging an assortment of snack platters in preparation for the imminent arrival of the Wednesday-afternoon-tea participants. 'Based on what?'

'That smile of hers yesterday. It was cold and stiff. She was obviously forcing it. Don't you think so, Hope?'

Hope – who was positioning small groups of chairs around the boutique to allow for natural movement and flow of conversation – hesitated a moment before answering. 'I'm not sure what I think of Gina.'

'Don't you mean *Madam Gina*?' Megan returned with a chuckle.

'That's precisely my point!' Summer exclaimed. 'It's impossible to like someone who uses such a ridiculous moniker. It's inane and insulting and—'

'Yes, we know,' Hope interrupted her sister gently. 'You've mentioned before that it makes it sound as though she's running a brothel.'

Summer nodded vigorously.

'But we don't know if she actually calls herself *Madam Gina*,' Hope said. 'It could be a flourish courtesy of Rosemarie. She can get a bit overly dramatic at times, especially when it involves the mystic arts.'

'Gina didn't correct Rosemarie when she introduced her to us that way,' Summer argued.

'That's true,' Hope conceded.

'And she also didn't correct Rosemarie regarding her supposed gift or that she holds séances.'

Hope couldn't dispute those points, either.

'I can tell you exactly what kind of séances Gina holds—' Summer continued.

'The kind that bring in lots of cash,' Megan concluded for her.

Summer nodded again. 'I have no doubt that she preys on the pocketbooks of the grieving. She probably combs the local obituaries in search of distraught relatives and friends who will eagerly hand over their last penny, desperate to see or speak with their deceased loved ones once more.'

Hope frowned at her sister. 'Aren't you taking it a little far? Rosemarie has never mentioned that she paid to attend a séance. We don't have any evidence that Gina is making money from—'

'We certainly do have evidence,' Summer cut her off. 'What about all those pricey shopping bags of hers that were sitting in here? Or the expensive dress and heels that she was wearing?'

'Her jewelry, too,' Megan added. 'I've gotten pretty good at judging the pieces worn by the swanky guests at the hotel, and the stones in Gina's necklace and earrings looked genuine to me.'

'Even if they're worth a small fortune,' Hope replied, 'it doesn't mean that she got them by swindling the bereaved. We have no idea where her money comes from. It could be family wealth, or a large settlement with an ex, or a lucrative former profession.'

Megan grinned. 'Such as running a brothel.'

Hope raised an eyebrow at her. 'That isn't helpful.'

'I don't know why you're defending Gina,' Summer said crossly.

'I'm not defending her. I'm merely pointing out that we don't know enough about her to reach a definitive conclusion – yet. You could be right that Gina is a classic charlatan trying to take advantage of people's sorrow by pretending to communicate with the dead in exchange for a generous sum. On the other hand, she might be nothing more than a silly, harmless woman who thinks it's terrific fun to imagine that she's in possession of vast magical powers and can summon spirits at will.'

'There is nothing harmless about summoning spirits,' Summer rejoined. 'It isn't an amusing parlor game or a birthday party sideshow. It can be extremely dangerous. You and I both know what can happen if things go wrong. We've witnessed firsthand what the consequences can be when foolish people attempt to play with things that they don't begin to comprehend. Not every spirit is some jolly old uncle who wants to chum around for an afternoon. Many spirits are angry, or mischievous, or downright nasty and vengeful. And they don't like to be summoned. They appear on their own schedule and of their own volition, not when—'

She was interrupted by a thud.

Startled, Megan turned toward the front window. 'Was that outside? I hope a bird didn't hit the pane. Maybe we should check the sidewalk in case it—'

As though in answer to her question, the thud repeated itself, louder this time and distinctly above them, inside the brownstone. They collectively looked up.

There was a third thud, followed by a fourth and then a fifth in steady succession. It sounded like the heavy, plodding footsteps of a gigantic creature marching across the ceiling. With each one, the walls of the shop shook progressively harder, the herb-and-tea counter rattled more violently, and several of Hope's newly positioned chairs tumbled backwards. The sisters exchanged a glance. It was definitely not a bird.

Megan's brow furrowed. 'Is that coming from . . .'

'It's the ghosts in the attic,' Hope confirmed.

'And they're demonstrating my point,' Summer said. 'The spirits aren't fond of being summoned. They choose when and how to make their presence known.'

A trio of especially strong thuds occurred next, shifting the snack platters in front of Megan. Hope rushed to the table and grabbed a blue-checkered dish just as it started to careen off the edge toward the floor.

With a quick hand, Megan steadied the remaining platters. 'That was awfully close to being a mess.'

'Too close,' Hope concurred. She raised her gaze toward the ceiling – and the occupants of the attic three floors beyond. 'Your message has been received. No one – Gina included – will be holding a séance in the boutique or the brownstone at any time in the foreseeable future. We would appreciate it if you would stop now, please.'

After a brief, deliberating pause, there came one final elephantine thud, and then silence followed.

'Thank you,' Hope said, before turning her attention to the blue-checkered dish, which she set safely back on the table. 'And my thanks to you also, Megan. This cheese platter is fabulous. You've made it wonderfully appetizing.'

Summer – who had been straightening the tumbled chairs – studied the variety of cheeses. 'Did you organize them by flavor?'

'No, country of origin. That's why the Dutch Edam is between the Swiss Gruyère and the English cave Cheddar.'

Hope smiled. 'Apparently all those four o'clock wine-and-cheeses at the hotel have left their mark.'

Megan responded with more of a grimace than a smile. 'Considering that I've been hosting them five days a week for the many years that I've worked there, something was bound to rub off eventually. It's a real show-stopper on my curriculum vitae: adept at gliding across a lobby or conference room while engaged in mindless small talk and simultaneously carrying two carafes of wine along with a variety of nibbles.'

As Hope and Summer laughed, they were joined by a sound from upstairs. It was different from the previous thuds. Instead of an elephant stomping across the ceiling, this one was more like the whinny of a horse.

'I think that's their version of a chuckle,' Summer said.

Now Megan did smile. 'Maybe they enjoy wine and nibbles just as much as the rest of us.' She hesitated a moment, then lowered her voice. 'I probably shouldn't mention this, because it might irritate them and make it worse this evening, but with all of their hullabaloo last night – in addition to my leg, which was itching like crazy again – I couldn't sleep a wink.'

'Were they noisy last night?' Summer asked in surprise. 'I didn't hear anything. Did you, Hope?'

'They were a little restless, as usual. There was some whimpering and whispers. A couple of doors opened and closed. It was nothing out of the ordinary.' Hope turned questioningly to Megan. 'You've overnighted here and heard them on countless occasions, since we were kids even. They've never disturbed or worried you before, at least not seriously.'

'It wasn't the ghosts that I was worried about,' Megan said. 'It was the Hermit. Every time a floorboard squeaked or a door creaked, I wondered if it was them or him making the noise. I kept turning on the lamp to check that the room was still empty and the Hermit hadn't crept up through the cellar.'

Summer shook her head. 'The Hermit couldn't creep up through the cellar. If the bookcase is closed, the cellar door can't be opened from inside the stairway. Plus, at this point, the Hermit can't even get into the cellar.'

'He can't?' Hope echoed doubtfully. 'But based on those pieces of canvas we found, we're pretty sure that he got into the cellar earlier.'

'That was *before* the contractor and construction crew arrived with their equipment. Now with the retention pool and those enormous hoses taking up every inch of space, it's impossible to reach the outside door. Didn't you see how tightly the boxwoods were pressed up against it? No one – neither the Hermit nor anybody else – could pry open the door and get down the potato-coal chute.'

Megan wasn't convinced. 'Even if the door and the chute aren't accessible now, they could become accessible later. The pool and hoses might be gone by this evening.'

'Highly unlikely,' Summer said. 'When I last looked outside no more than half an hour ago, the pool hadn't been emptied. It was just as full as when Percy decided to take his impromptu swim yesterday. They can't drain the pool or pump the water elsewhere until the generator has been repaired, and they're not able to work on that without first resolving the power issue. It must be causing them considerable difficulty, because two electric company trucks have been parked at the Larsons' all day.'

'There was a third one parked in the street in front of the boutique this morning,' Hope added. 'I noticed it when the lights in here kept flickering.'

Summer chortled. 'That flickering couldn't have been more perfectly timed if *you* were a charlatan and had chosen that exact moment to flip a hidden switch to make the lights turn off and on.'

Hope smiled. 'Jill was a little spooked by it.'

'A *little* spooked? Her eyes bulged out of her head like a cartoon insect, and she nearly fell from her chair at the table!'

The sisters shared a laugh.

'When was this?' Megan asked. 'I must have missed it.'

'It was during Jill Berg's palm-reading appointment,' Hope told her. 'I think you were taking your bath then.'

'Oh, yes, I remember the lights flickering while I was getting dressed. It takes me such an annoyingly long time to move around and do everything with this cast on. So what happened with Jill?'

'She'd never had anyone look at her palm before, so I started with a simple, introductory reading. When I got to her heart line, Jill was anxious to know how much it showed regarding any love affairs and dalliances. She kept shifting in her seat and blushing, so it wasn't hard to guess that she's either currently having an affair or seriously considering starting one. And just as she was inquiring whether someone such as her husband could also look at her hand and see how she might be spending her spare time, the lights in the boutique went dark. Jill gasped. The lights switched back on, and she gaped in awe. When the lights turned off again, Jill became absolutely convinced that the flickering was a message intended for her. The only problem was that she couldn't decide whether it was a sign for or against the affair.'

'That is a dilemma,' Megan agreed, laughing also.

'If Jill wants to keep her liaisons secret,' Summer remarked wryly, 'then she should worry less about her husband reading her palm and more about him reading her text messages and emails.'

The lights in the boutique flickered.

Megan laughed harder. 'The message definitely isn't for me. I'm barely even dating Daniel, so I can't possibly be cheating on him.'

The flickering repeated itself.

Looking at the clock on the wall, Summer's amusement faded. 'I hope it stops soon. The guests for the tea will be arriving at any moment.'

'It didn't last long this morning,' Hope reminded her. 'Only a couple of minutes.'

'But no one will want to stay if the power keeps going on and off. It'll be too dark to see their cups or the snack platters.'

A noticeable fretfulness had crept into Summer's tone, and Hope tried to reassure her. 'Everyone will be able to see fine, regardless of what happens with the power. There is plenty of natural light coming in through the windows. Granted, it's a little gloomy outside because of the thick clouds, but it's certainly not the pitch black of night.'

'We can always set up a whole bunch of candles,' Megan suggested.

'That's an excellent idea.' Hope gave her a grateful glance. 'It would be cheerful, and Rosemarie loves candles, so she'll instantly be in a good mood.'

'Rosemarie might not come to the tea,' Summer said.

'Of course she'll come! When has Rosemarie ever missed an event at the boutique? The only question is whether she'll have Percy on his lead, or if he'll try to make a dash for the pool and have another swim in that dirty water.'

The lights flickered again, and this time, they were joined by a pair of thuds on the ceiling.

Hope frowned. 'That's odd. Why would the spirits care about Percy swimming in the retention pool?'

A sharper set of thuds followed.

Summer groaned. 'Now in addition to the flashing lights, there will be thumping in the attic that we can't explain. And Rosemarie will probably make some ludicrous remark about—'

She was stopped by a series of thuds that were forceful enough to clatter the windows.

Hope's frown deepened. 'I don't understand. The spirits have never been troubled about Rosemarie. She's such a kind, inoffensive soul—'

It was her turn to be interrupted as the wind chimes rang out above the front door of the shop. A crowd of ladies bustled inside, with everybody talking at once. Even over the boisterous chatter, Hope could hear Summer's sigh of relief, and she smiled at her. All of the worry about no one showing up for the first tea of the season had been unnecessary. The group was large and enthusiastic. If only the lights and the occupants of the attic would cooperate . . .

'Hope! Summer!' Rosemarie rushed forward to hug them, with Percy racing alongside, no doubt in anticipation of receiving a treat. 'I'm so happy that the Wednesday afternoon teas have started up again. We've all been looking forward to it, haven't we?' She didn't wait for anyone to respond. 'And I've brought along a marvelous friend.'

'Percy is always welcome,' Summer replied convivially.

Hope began to move toward the drawer in the palm-and-Tarot-reading table to retrieve the bag of doggie cookies.

Rosemarie giggled and shook her scarlet mop, which matched the color of the poppies in her billowy crepe dress. 'What a funny misunderstanding! I didn't mean Percy. I was referring to Madam Gina, of course.'

With the air of making an entrance, Gina stepped out from behind Rosemarie. She was also wearing a dress, but the effect was starkly different from Rosemarie's. Instead of bright and breezy, Gina's garb was cool and refined. It was a narrow, linen sheath in a pewter shade that was slightly lighter than her charcoal choice from the day before. Gina evidently favored solid, neutral tones, perhaps because they accentuated the glossy black of her hair and the sparkling jewels around her throat and wrist. Whatever the source of her money, she was clearly not stingy about the amount that she spent on her wardrobe and accessories.

As Gina greeted the sisters with a smile, Hope felt an elbow nudge her in the ribs. She didn't have to look at Summer to understand her meaning. The smile was the same one that had been given to them previously. Summer thought it stiff and forced. Was it artificial? Hope still wasn't sure. It might have simply seemed that way in comparison with Rosemarie's overwhelming natural effusiveness. There was also the possibility that Summer held a bit of a grudge against Gina as a result of Nate audibly commenting to Dylan yesterday before their departure that he would be interested in attending one of her séances.

Gina must have sensed Summer's reserve, because she lengthened the smile and said politely, 'I hope it's all right that I've come this afternoon. I wasn't sure if an explicit invitation was required.'

'An explicit invitation?' Rosemarie exclaimed. 'What nonsense! You're as welcome here as Percy and I are. Isn't that right, Hope?'

Although Hope nodded and began to reply in the affirmative, Rosemarie continued without pause.

'The boutique and the tea are open to everyone. The more, the merrier! There is no restriction on who can attend. It's not like when you hold one of your séances, and you have to limit the number of people and make sure that they're all—'

A tremendous boom sounded above them as though a cannon

had been fired, and the entire shop reverberated. There was a short, startled silence, and then the ladies burst out with a flurry of excited questions and comments.

Nudging Hope again, Summer leaned close to her and whispered, 'You see? The spirits agree with me. They don't like Gina, either.'

SEVEN

Hope's mind moved fast. She needed an explanation for the strange noise and the accompanying tremor that not only seemed plausible but also wouldn't frighten anyone away from the boutique.

'There is construction at the Larsons',' she told the group, who continued to buzz excitedly.

'Our neighbors,' Summer said, gesturing in the direction of Miranda and Paul's brownstone.

'Their cellar has been leaking for some time,' Hope went on, 'and the water was pumped out yesterday.'

'Into a pool on the side lawn,' Rosemarie corroborated. 'When Percy saw it, he jumped straight in, and when he came back out, he was covered with a layer of muck. It took *two* shampoos to get him clean.'

No further account of the Larsons, their cellar, or the retention pool was necessary. The ladies now began to chime in, half of them recounting their own tale of woe regarding water seepage and related flooding, and the other half remarking on the exasperating tendency of dogs to explore where they shouldn't and emerging grubby.

For his part, Percy didn't appear the least bit interested in the chattering ladies or their narratives. He simply wanted his treat and conveyed that sentiment to Hope by staring at her with impatient eyes.

She smiled and gave him a doggie cookie. 'Apologies for the delay, Percy.'

The pug replied with a good-natured snort and promptly carried his treat beneath the palm-and-Tarot-reading table, where he could enjoy it at his leisure, safely removed from the many sharp heels and pointy-toed shoes moving around the shop.

Watching him, Hope smiled once more. At least one of their guests was happily settled. And it turned out that he had sought the protection of the table legs just in time, because the moment that Megan directed the ladies' attention to the snack platters on the table and the steaming cups that Summer had begun serving on the herb-and-tea counter, there was a stampede in both directions.

Even with her wounded leg, Megan proved to be a consummate hostess. It was no surprise that the hotel awarded her a substantial bonus every year for dealing so effectively with their difficult clientele. When handling a group, Megan had the natural ability to discern who was already acquainted and who needed introductions. She was also skilled at rekindling the conversation during a lull, although on this occasion no great wit or creativity was required as her cast became a source of universal interest and discussion, with everyone eager to share an injury story regarding some friend or relation.

'I don't know if I mentioned this yesterday, but I like the way that you've decorated your store. It has a certain charm.'

Hope gave a little start, not having realized that Gina was standing beside her. 'Thank you. That's kind of you to say.'

'Are there more rooms in the back?' Gina asked, motioning toward the doorway at the rear of the shop and simultaneously taking a step in that direction.

'No, the entire boutique is here before you. That door leads to the living quarters of the brownstone.'

Gina's gaze remained on the doorway for a moment, then she took a sip from the cup that she was holding. 'This tea is interesting.'

'Thank you,' Hope said again, although she wasn't entirely sure that the remark had been intended as a compliment. There was an ambiguousness to Gina's tone. There was an ambiguousness about her generally.

She took another drink, this one longer and more contemplative. 'I'm curious to know what sort of tea it is.'

'It's a proprietary blend of Summer's.'

Gina raised a sculpted eyebrow. 'I didn't realize that it was such a great secret.'

'Oh, I didn't mean it that way,' Hope responded hastily. 'I honestly don't know what the specific ingredients are. The boutique's teas are Summer's area of expertise. Some of her blends are intended for health and medicinal purposes, while others' – she gestured toward Gina's cup – 'are purely for taste and enjoyment. But Summer isn't at all cagey or secretive about it. She'll tell you exactly what's in them – and in her tinctures, too. She wants people to have confidence in her preparations, so she's completely open about their ingredients, their benefits, and also their limitations.'

'Except there are no limitations,' Rosemarie said, joining the conversation while munching on a handful of rye crackers. 'Not in my experience, at least. The tincture that Summer gave me last month for my ear stopped the ringing entirely. There hasn't been a bell, buzz, or whistle since. And Percy got one from her to help with his atrocious breath. Isn't that right, Percy? Aren't you as fresh as a daisy now?'

Percy neither confirmed nor denied his ostensible freshness. Having finished his cookie, he had curled up in a ball beneath the table for a peaceable snooze.

'He's as fresh as a daisy,' Rosemarie insisted. 'Even his veterinarian complimented him on it at his last appointment. She wanted to know what I had used that worked so well, and I told her about Summer's tincture. She was very impressed. I've often thought that Summer must have been an esteemed medicine woman in a former life.'

'That depends,' Gina replied. 'At some places and times in history, traditional healers were highly regarded, revered even. And at other times and locations, they were declared to be witches or sorcerers and strung up from trees or burned at the stake.'

Rosemarie choked on a cracker. 'Good heavens! Burned at the stake for providing tinctures and teas? That can't be right.'

Hope was also somewhat taken aback, but for a different reason than Rosemarie. She didn't doubt the veracity of Gina's statements; she and Summer were well familiar with the long and incendiary history of witches and sorcery. It was the little smirk that accompanied her words, as though Gina found a morbid delight in the grisly tales of the past. It was especially odd coming from someone who claimed to hold séances and could therefore potentially have been declared a witch herself.

'I assure you that it's true,' Gina told Rosemarie. 'The use of potions and herbs has led to the death of many a wise woman.

Numerous scholars have studied the subject and written books on it.'

'What gruesome bedtime reading that would be!' Rosemarie exclaimed. 'The whole thing is too horrible to even contemplate.' She coughed to clear the crumbs from her throat. 'Let's talk about something happier. It's the boutique's first tea of the season, and that means there should be only cheerful thoughts.'

'Indeed!' Hope swiftly agreed. 'It may be gray and gloomy outside, but that's no reason for us to be gloomy in here, too.'

Gina responded with another little smirk. It was clear that she thought Hope's remark to be insipidly trivial. Except that was exactly Hope's intent. She was even more eager to move off the topic than Rosemarie, but – again – for a different reason. A slight rumbling had commenced above them. Although thankfully not as loud or conspicuous as the previous cannon boom, it was nonetheless a marked sign of discontent from the occupants of the attic. Summer was correct: the spirits were not fond of Gina. Or, at the very least, the spirits were not fond of Gina's commentary on potions and wise women. In any case, the sooner the conversation shifted to a lighter, less mystical subject, the better and safer for all present.

'A wonderful idea just occurred to me—' Rosemarie began.

'That's a strange noise,' Gina interrupted her. 'Where is it coming from?'

Hope feigned ignorance. 'Which noise do you mean?'

'That sort of rumbling. It sounds like a train in the distance.'

'I don't think that there are any train tracks near here,' Rosemarie said. 'Oh but Percy loves to ride the train! Did I ever tell you about the trip that I took with him and my cousin Anastasia and her wire-haired dachshund Bella to—'

'I didn't say that it *was* a train,' Gina cut her off unceremoniously. 'I said that it sounded *like* a train.'

Rosemarie blinked and chewed on a rye cracker.

Gina cocked her head to listen. 'It's inside, isn't it?'

'There are so many voices and noises,' Hope murmured vaguely.

'Upstairs,' Gina determined. 'Toward the back.'

Just as she had earlier, Gina took a step in the direction of the doorway at the rear of the shop. Hope was no more inviting than previously.

'That area – the living quarters of the brownstone – isn't open to customers.'

Still chewing, Rosemarie said, 'I've been inside several times, and I've always admired how you and Summer and your grandmother have maintained the interior so beautifully. I'd like to see it again.'

Encouraged, Gina took another step toward the doorway. Hope was quick to nip the idea in the bud.

'That's awfully sweet of you, Rosemarie. Another day perhaps, but not now during the tea.' She added to herself, *And certainly not while the occupants of the attic are active and expressing an aversion toward Gina.*

'You have such marvelous antique furniture and paintings,' Rosemarie continued. 'And I love that big globe, together with all the old books in the library. It makes me feel as though I've walked into a museum.'

Gina advanced several more steps. Hope frowned.

'The place is filled with so much history. The positive energy radiates in every direction.' Rosemarie bobbed her head enthusiastically. 'And that brings me back to the wonderful idea I had a minute ago. Gina, I was going to suggest that you invite Hope and Summer to your next séance—'

Hope's jaw sagged. Gina froze in place.

'But instead of having it at your house as usual' – Rosemarie bobbed her head some more – 'you should have it *here*. The séance could be in the brownstone!'

'No!'

The declination came from Hope and Gina simultaneously, with nearly equal volume and vigor. It startled several of the ladies, as well as Summer. A cup clattered against one of the platters on the palm-and-Tarot-reading table. The teapot slipped from Summer's hands on to the herb-and-tea counter. Fortunately, the cup was almost empty, and the ceramic teapot didn't shatter.

The formerly mild rumbling above them strengthened to a degree that it became patently audible to everyone. Hope and Summer exchanged a pained look. What should they do? They could no longer simply ignore it.

A crease formed in Rosemarie's brow. 'Is that Percy snoring? He does tend to get congested.'

Despite her anxiety, Hope almost smiled. Leave it to Rosemarie to come up with the most innocent explanation for restless ghosts in the attic.

Gina did not share Rosemarie's naivety. 'I doubt that your dog's wheezing is enough to shake the walls of the store.'

'Is he wheezing?' Rosemarie exclaimed, the crease deepening to a worried furrow. 'Does he seem to be having difficulty breathing? I've been afraid since yesterday that he might have caught a cold from that chilly water in the pool.'

'Percy isn't wheezing,' Megan reassured her, while at the same time dabbing at the few spilt drops of tea on the table with a cocktail napkin. 'I'm standing right beside him, and I promise you that his breathing is absolutely fine.' She glanced at Gina with disdain. 'There's no need to be dramatic and make people fret unnecessarily.'

'I wasn't being dramatic,' Gina argued. 'I want to know where that noise is coming from, what is causing it, and why it's making the walls shake.'

Megan rolled her eyes. 'Nothing is shaking. You make it sound as though it's some gaudy mystery. It isn't the least bit mysterious; it's merely the construction going on next door at the Larsons'. We already discussed that earlier. There's no need to be dramatic,' she repeated sharply.

The sisters' pained expression melted into one of relief. Megan spoke with such confidence and purported authority that it succeeded in convincing the other ladies of the insignificance of the noise, and they promptly returned to their eating, drinking, and general chit-chatting. A pair of large red spots appeared on Gina's cheeks. She was clearly piqued by Megan's high-handedness toward her, but at that moment, Hope was far more concerned with keeping the group distracted from the ongoing activities in the attic than soothing Gina's wounded pride.

The chit-chat grew livelier. Fresh tea was poured. Additional snacks were sampled. Gina, however, did not participate in any of it. She stood alone to one side of the boutique, alternately studying the doorway at the rear of the shop and the ceiling, her interest in the continuing noises visibly undiminished. The rumbling subsided and was replaced by an intermittent clicking that resembled a loud clock ticking every few seconds. Hope also began to study the ceiling, trying to understand the meaning behind the change. She had the feeling that instead of being angry or irritated, the occupants of the attic wanted to tell her something. They had helped her on more than one occasion previously by finding things that she had been searching for and cautioning her about people. What message were they sending her now? She wished that she could pull out her Tarot cards and throw a quick spread. It might not have given her an exact answer, but at least it would have shown her the direction that the spirits were pointing toward.

All of the lights in the shop dimmed slightly. It was barely perceptible, and when Hope looked around, it didn't appear that any of the ladies or even Summer had noticed it. The lights dimmed again. Was it from the spirits, or due to the electrical problems at the Larsons'? The clicking overhead abruptly ceased, and to Hope's surprise, no new noise replaced it. Instead of being relieved at the sudden stillness, an apprehensive shiver crept along her spine. Something wasn't right. She looked around once more and, this time, she saw Gina looking around, too. How much did Gina understand or guess regarding the attic? Hope was beginning to wonder – and worry – what exactly she was able to sense. *Madam Gina*'s séances couldn't actually be real, could they?

The lights flickered several times in swift succession, as though someone was flipping the power switch off and on repeatedly for fun – or in warning. The wind chimes banged as the front door of the boutique slammed open. A man burst inside, perspiring heavily and swearing.

'There you are!' he shouted. 'You witch!'

EIGHT

There wasn't a sound in the brownstone, including from the attic. Although the man had bellowed the words at such a volume that it was impossible for anybody inside the shop not to have heard them, no one spoke, and the ladies all looked around in confusion as though they must have misunderstood.

The man broke the silence by panting for air after having apparently run – or at least walked with considerable speed – to the boutique. Aside from his profuse sweating, he was unremarkably average: middle height, middle weight, and youngish middle age, with the early stages of a receding hairline and slightly hunched shoulders. Hope had never seen the man before, and based on her sister's perplexed frown, Summer didn't appear to recognize him, either.

'You bloody witch!' the man hollered, still huffing from his exertions.

Out of the corner of her eye, Hope saw Gina flinch. It lasted only for an instant. When Hope turned to look at her more closely, Gina's face betrayed nothing. There were no red spots on her cheeks as when Megan had chastised her a few minutes prior, and her expression was placid. But the tiny wince that Hope had caught was enough to make her suspect that Gina might know the man.

'You bloody witch!' he cried again.

The ladies' initial bewilderment was becoming uneasiness. They shifted in place uncomfortably. Half-full cups of tea had been set down. The previously mobbed snack platters were now ignored. Even Percy was no longer enjoying his tranquil nap. After a yawn and a stretch, the pug had started to emerge from beneath the palm-and-Tarot-reading table, no doubt with the hope that a treat or two would be forthcoming. But he also must have sensed the sudden tension in the shop, because after only a few tentative paces, he swiftly returned to the safety of the table legs.

'If you thought that I wouldn't find you,' the man yelled, having at last fully regained his breath, 'you were wrong!'

Oddly, he didn't appear to be yelling at anyone in particular. Although it sounded as though he was referring to a specific person, his gaze moved around the group generally and wasn't focused on a single individual. It made Hope wonder whether the man himself might be confused. Perhaps he was in the wrong location or had received some sort of incorrect information.

'There must be a misunderstanding—' she began mildly.

'Hell, no!' the man cut her off. 'There is no *misunderstanding*, or mistake, or misinterpretation.'

There was so much fury and derision in his tone that it startled Hope. She and Summer had certainly dealt with their share of difficult and disgruntled customers over the years. Experience had taught her that in most instances, a client's anger or unhappiness had very little to do with the boutique and was instead related to a problem in their personal or professional life. But Hope could see that this man was different. He wasn't incensed by something outside the shop; the object of his rage was directly in front of him. Except she still couldn't tell who it was. She looked at Gina again for a possible signal or hint, but her expression remained phlegmatic. The earlier flinch did not repeat itself. If Gina was acquainted with the man, she kept it well concealed.

'You can pretend that you have no idea what I'm talking about,' the man seethed, 'but it's a lie. A damn filthy lie!' A string of profanities followed.

More than one lady gasped. Several murmured something about heading to the powder room. And quite a few sets of eyes began to glance toward the front door as a means to exit from the increasingly awkward and unpleasant situation. Up until that point, Summer had appeared too puzzled by the man and his unaccountable behavior to react, but the moment that it became clear that her first Wednesday afternoon tea of the season was being brought to an abrupt conclusion because of him, her own temper flared.

'Leave,' Summer demanded curtly.

The man snarled at her. 'Who are you to tell me to leave?'

She didn't shrink at his open hostility. 'I am Summer Bailey. Co-owner of this boutique. *Who* are you?'

'Austin Berg.'

He didn't elaborate, as though he fully expected the name to mean something to her. Hope thought that it sounded vaguely familiar, but she couldn't immediately place it. There was a slight hesitation before Summer responded, indicating that she was struggling to connect the name also.

'Thank you for visiting our shop, Mr Berg,' she said with stiff politeness. 'Now kindly get out.'

Austin didn't budge an inch. He folded his arms defiantly across his chest and locked his knees.

Summer's lips tightened. 'I won't ask you again—'

'Or what?' he challenged her in a mocking tone. 'What are you going to do? Beg? Plead? Cry?'

Although her lips tightened further, Summer managed to keep her cool. 'I will call the police.'

'I've done that already,' Megan informed them.

They turned toward her in surprise. Megan's energy had evidently been exhausted after standing for so long on her wounded leg in her self-appointed role as snack-platter hostess, because she was now half sitting, half reclining between two chairs at the palm-and-Tarot-reading table. Percy had jumped up to the seat of one of the chairs and was snuggled against the side of her elevated cast.

Megan waved the phone that she was holding to prove the truth of what she said. 'I've been talking to Detective Nate Phillips from the Asheville Police Department, and he is extremely concerned by what I've told him. He's coming to the boutique right now, so unless you' – she inclined her head at Austin – 'want to continue this discussion with a member of law enforcement, I suggest that you depart lickety-split.'

Rosemarie – who at the first sign of trouble had moved toward the table and her darling Percy – nodded in agreement. Several of the ladies took the opportunity to depart lickety-split themselves.

Austin still didn't move. 'I'll clear out of here as soon as you tell me where the other one is.'

Summer frowned, not understanding. 'The other one?'

'The other Bailey. Hope.'

He hissed her name as though it was bitter poison dripping

from his tongue. Hope was stunned. It had never occurred to her that *she* might be the object of his rage. For the man to have such a vicious hatred of her, there must be some concrete reason behind it, but as hard as Hope tried, she couldn't remember ever having had any previous encounters with Austin Berg. Although she certainly might have passed by him once on the sidewalk or in an aisle at the grocery store without realizing it, such a trivial event couldn't possibly create such strong emotions. The only other explanation that Hope could think of was that Austin had confused her with someone else.

Summer must have had the same idea, because she said to Austin, 'Are you sure that Hope is who you're looking for?'

'Of course I'm sure!' he snapped. 'Is she here?' His bloodshot eyes traveled around the shop. 'Which one is she?'

Neither Summer nor Megan answered him. Summer busied herself with covering a pair of teapots with crocheted cozies, while Megan straightened a stack of cocktail napkins. Industriously brushing cracker crumbs from the table, Rosemarie didn't reveal Hope's identity, either. But the rest of the group did. Almost in unison, the head of every lady remaining in the boutique turned toward Hope.

Austin's gaze instantly followed. For a long minute, he didn't speak. He just looked at her. He didn't appear to recognize her any more than she did him, which made Hope think that her guess had been correct, and he was indeed confusing her with someone else. A moment later, however, she learned that she was wrong. A gurgling emanated from Austin's throat. His neck flushed with deep red streaks, and his nostrils flared wide. Then the floodgates burst open, and a wave of wrath poured forth.

'You witch! You bloody witch!' Austin roared. 'What the hell did you tell my wife?'

There was such ferocity in his voice that everyone instinctively took a step backwards, as though trying to increase their distance from the man. Even Megan slipped lower in her seat, and she reached a protective hand toward Percy. Summer glanced anxiously at the row of windows that faced the street and then looked meaningfully at her sister. Hope responded with a slight nod. Nate would be there soon, and they needed to do whatever they could to keep the situation under some semblance of control until he arrived.

Hope took a breath to steady herself. 'Your wife?' she said to Austin with as much composure as she could muster. 'I'm not sure that I know who—'

'Stop pretending!' he barked. 'Stop lying! Do you think that I'm stupid? Do you think that if you keep acting as though you haven't a clue, I'll just walk away and all will be forgotten? Well, it won't be! I can promise you that. If it comes down to a battle of wills between us, then you'll be the one to flinch first, not me. I won't let anybody interfere with my . . .'

She didn't hear the conclusion of the sentence. At the word *flinch*, Hope was reminded of Gina and her wincing reaction to Austin when he had first arrived at the boutique. Maybe Gina really did know him. Perhaps she was even his wife! Hope looked hastily around the shop, but Gina was nowhere to be found. When had she left? Hope hadn't noticed her departure. For that matter, she couldn't recall when exactly she had last seen her.

Uncertain how best to proceed, Hope hesitated before interrupting Austin's continuing tirade. 'Is Gina your wife?' she said.

'Gina?' Austin squinted at her. 'No, she isn't, you miserable shrew! My wife's name is Jill!'

There was a brief hush, and then the whispering began. It wasn't in response to Austin calling Hope a miserable shrew. The few ladies who were still lingering from the tea – no doubt due to an irresistible curiosity to find out what would happen next – had started inquiring amongst themselves whether they knew a woman named Jill. None of them seemed to think of anyone immediately, but Hope did. And she realized why Austin's name had sounded familiar to her. Her palm-reading appointment that morning had been with Jill Berg.

'Your wife is Jill Berg?' she asked him, although she had little doubt of the answer.

He nodded and sneered. 'Didn't I say that you'd flinch first? I was right!'

Hope quickly thought back to the appointment. Jill had wanted to know how much her heart line showed regarding love affairs and dalliances. She had specifically asked what another person such as her husband would be able to see by looking at her hand.

Summer had joked afterwards that if Jill wanted to keep her liaisons secret, she should be more concerned with her husband reading her text messages and email than her palm. But it turned out that Austin Berg didn't need to read anything. Based on the fact that he was standing before them now, Jill had apparently run home and babbled about the appointment. The only question was what exactly she had shared with him.

Austin sneered some more. 'So now you're willing to admit it? You'll admit to what you told my wife?'

'No,' Hope replied.

The brevity of her answer seemed to surprise him. 'No?' he questioned, with a sharpness that showed he was not accustomed to being gainsaid.

'No,' she repeated firmly. 'As of this morning, Jill is one of my clients. Unless a client shows some indication of intending to harm themselves or someone else, all of my appointments with that client are confidential. So, no, I will not break the confidence and admit to telling Jill anything.'

It wasn't strictly true, of course. The confidence wasn't absolute. Summer had been present during Jill's reading and had overheard a substantial portion of it. And the sisters had told Megan about the part that related to the lights flickering in the shop. They also occasionally spoke to their grandmother about a client if they thought that she could offer some beneficial advice in a specific instance. But they never shared any intimate details with anyone outside of their little group. People came to the boutique in search of help and guidance. Hope had never violated their trust in the past, and she was not about to start now.

The red streaks reappeared on Austin's neck. They were joined by heavy beads of perspiration on his forehead. 'How dare you!' he spat. 'Jill is my *wife!*'

Hope didn't respond. The man's bluster was beginning to wear on her nerves. If she hadn't been so annoyed with Jill for being loose-lipped regarding the appointment – which had resulted in Austin storming into the boutique and ruining Summer's Wednesday afternoon tea – Hope would have felt sorry for her. Austin was obviously a bully, and it surely wasn't enjoyable to be married to a bully.

Her silence only provoked him further. 'My wife is having an affair because of you! It's your fault! You are responsible for—'

Hope cut him short. 'I met Jill for the first time this morning, so I hardly think that I could be responsible for anything she decided to do before then.'

Although it was accurate, she probably shouldn't have said it. Austin was clearly looking for someone to blame for his marital difficulties, and Hope was a much easier and more convenient target than holding himself or his wife accountable for their own behavior.

Hope saw her sister glance toward the front windows with increasing urgency. She shared Summer's impatience. Why was it taking Nate so long to arrive? Austin's anger and resentment were growing by the minute. His hands had curled into fists, and his inflamed eyes were bulging from their sockets.

'I'll get you for this, you bloody witch!' he thundered. 'I'll get you, and you'll be damn sorry for what you—'

The threat was left unfinished as all of the lights in the shop abruptly shut off. There was solid darkness and not a peep of sound. A moment later, the lights turned back on. Everybody – Austin included – looked around questioningly. Hope raised her gaze to the ceiling. Had the power failure been courtesy of the occupants of the attic?

The lights shut off again, and this time, they remained off. For several long seconds, it seemed impenetrably black. Then Hope's vision started to adjust. Although not sunny outside, the windows along the sidewalk allowed enough late afternoon light to filter into the boutique to turn the interior shadowy grey.

'Is everyone all right?' Hope asked, when she could begin to distinguish the outline of the people and objects around her.

There was an affirmative murmur from the group.

'I'll open the door,' Summer said, heading toward the front of the shop. 'We'll get more light inside that way.'

'Your poor neighbors.' Rosemarie clucked her tongue sympathetically. 'That construction of theirs is causing them some terrible electrical troubles.'

'It's not just the neighbors any more,' Megan replied with a touch of dryness. 'The troubles have apparently spread to us now also.'

'Oh, yes, I suppose that's true.' Rosemarie clucked her tongue again.

The wind chimes jingled as Summer propped open the front door. The boutique brightened perceptibly.

'That was a good idea, Summer,' Megan complimented her. 'I can see a lot better. Can you see better, too, Percy?'

Percy had lifted his head from its former resting position on Megan's cast. He sniffed the air demonstratively.

'Do you smell something?' Megan asked him. She gave a little sniff herself. 'I don't smell anything.'

'I don't, either,' Rosemarie agreed.

'But Percy sure does. Look at how alert he's gotten all of a sudden.'

The pug had risen to his feet and was standing on the edge of the chair. His nose was up, his ears were pricked, and his back was rigid.

'What are you sensing?' Hope said, genuinely curious. Percy spent a good deal of time at the boutique, and it mostly involved either eating or sleeping. He rarely showed any interest in the ebb and flow of customers or what might be happening in the street outside.

Percy cocked his head, as though listening closely to a noise that none of the rest of them could hear. He sniffed once more. Then in one swift motion, he jumped down from the chair and dashed toward the open door.

'Percy?' Rosemarie called after him. 'Wait, Percy.'

He paid no attention to her. After a slight pause on the threshold of the shop, he raced out to the sidewalk and disappeared from view.

'No, Percy, no!' Rosemarie cried. 'Stop! Come back!'

Not heeding her commands, Percy neither halted nor returned.

Rosemarie was instantly panicked. 'He'll get lost!' she wailed. 'He'll get hit by a car! His cold will turn into pneumonia!'

Megan shook her head. 'None of that will happen, Rosemarie. Don't worry. Percy knows his way around this place and won't run far away. He was on the side lawn with us yesterday, remember?'

'The side lawn and the pool are where he caught his cold to begin with,' Rosemarie responded, not the least bit comforted.

And she promptly hurried out of the boutique after her darling pug.

Hope, Summer and Megan all exchanged a look – and a sigh.

'I can't move fast,' Megan reminded them, motioning toward her leg.

Hope nodded at her, then she turned to Summer. 'You stay here with the remainder of our guests. I'll follow Rosemarie and help her find Percy.'

'I doubt that you'll have to go any great distance,' Megan remarked with a little chortle. 'Percy isn't exactly an endurance athlete. He probably petered out of gas at the corner of the brownstone and is currently begging for a treat from whomever happens to be passing by on the sidewalk.'

'Fingers crossed that you're right,' Summer said. 'Because Nate will be arriving at any second, and I don't think that he'll be very pleased if Rosemarie asks him to initiate a formal dog search.'

There was another little chortle from Megan.

As Hope started toward the door, she noticed that Austin was once again glaring at her. She debated whether to respond or simply ignore him. The decision was made for her a moment later when there came an ear-splitting scream.

NINE

The scream belonged to Rosemarie. There was no doubt about that. Hope did, however, have some doubt as to the urgency of the matter. Rosemarie had a tendency to over-react, and she occasionally indulged in a bit of histrionics. If, for example, she saw Percy approach a substantially larger dog in the park, she would shout in fear that the larger dog might suddenly attack, even though there had been no indication of aggression. Or if Rosemarie happened to catch sight of an old acquaintance in a café who she hadn't spoken to in a long time, she would give a great cry of excitement. So when her solitary scream wasn't followed by any further sound of alarm or distress, Hope wasn't immediately worried, and she didn't break into an automatic sprint to provide assistance.

Hope walked out of the boutique and looked down the side-walk. No Rosemarie and no Percy. She checked the opposite direction. It was similarly empty. The street was quiet. A delivery van turned at the nearby intersection. In the next block, two men adjusted the yellow-striped awning above the door of a beauty salon. Nothing appeared at all out of the ordinary. Except there was still no sign of Rosemarie. For a minute, Hope was puzzled, because Rosemarie in her ubiquitous strappy sandals didn't typi-cally move fast enough to disappear without a trace, but then it occurred to her where Rosemarie had most likely gone and what her scream most likely meant. Percy had probably run to the side lawn and jumped into the retention pool for another bracing swim, and Rosemarie had shrieked in terror, fearing that his cold would develop into pneumonia.

As she headed toward the side of the brownstone, Hope glanced through the front windows of the boutique. The interior remained dark, which meant that the power hadn't yet switched back on. She grumbled to herself. Although she knew that the Larsons weren't at fault for the ongoing seepage in their cellar, she couldn't help feeling increasingly frustrated that Miranda and Paul's problems had moved next door to her and Summer and the shop. There was the continual construction noise, the burning smell from the generator, the smothered grass and flattened shrubbery, and now the electrical outages. And if Percy really did come down with a bad cold from paddling around in the dirty drainage water, Rosemarie would be so distressed that she might end up making herself sick.

Still grumbling, Hope turned the corner to the lawn. As she had expected, Rosemarie was there. She was standing in front of the retention pool that was encircled by a tangle of rubber hoses like monstrous tentacles throttling its prey.

'Hi there,' Hope greeted her, making an effort to sound cheerful. Rosemarie didn't glance around.

'Did you find Percy?' Hope asked, walking toward her.

She didn't respond.

Hope frowned. It was usually much more difficult to get Rosemarie to stop talking than to make her start. 'That yell a minute ago was from you, wasn't it? Is everything all right?'

Rosemarie neither moved nor spoke. There was no indication that she even knew Hope was behind her.

'What's going on, Rosemarie? Are you . . .'

The sentence trailed away as Hope drew nearer and heard Rosemarie sobbing softly. Her shoulders were shaking, and her normally rosy face had paled to a stony white. And then Hope saw what had transfixed Rosemarie in horror.

The body lay motionless, face down. Its middle was draped over the edge of the retention pool, so that the bottom half stretched across the denuded ground and the top half was submerged in the cloudy water.

'Is he . . .' Rosemarie asked almost inaudibly. 'I think he must be . . .'

Although she didn't use the word *dead*, Hope knew it was what Rosemarie meant. For her part, Hope could do no more than nod in confirmation. The sudden shock of the scene had taken away her voice.

'But why?' Rosemarie whispered. 'How could – I don't understand . . . It doesn't make sense.'

She was right. It didn't make sense, and Hope didn't understand, either.

'Hey! You!'

In a slow-motion daze, Hope raised her head toward the shouts. A man was approaching them from the opposite end of the pool, walking purposefully with long strides. He was carrying something under his arm. To Hope's blurry vision, it looked like a mottled sack of potatoes.

'This is yours, isn't it?' the man demanded, holding out the sack.

Hope recognized the booming baritone, although she had never before heard him speak in such a caustic manner. She blinked, and the blurriness cleared. The man was Paul Larson, and the mottled sack of potatoes was Percy.

There was a joyous cry from Rosemarie. 'Oh, my baby!' She rushed to collect Percy from Paul and clutched him to her bosom. 'My poor, darling baby!'

Percy neither yipped in remonstrance at the snug hug nor struggled to free himself. On the contrary, he appeared rather relieved to be secure in Rosemarie's arms.

'That dog,' Paul said, 'is a nuisance.'

Rosemarie stared at him.

'A nuisance and a menace,' he declared.

While not nearly as staggered as Rosemarie, Hope was surprised by the remark. Certainly, some people had a greater affinity for dogs than others. And there were plenty of legitimate disagreements over breed preferences and suitability. But it was a considerable stretch for pug Percy to be deemed a menace. As far as Hope was aware, he had never bitten or nipped anyone. He barely ever even growled.

'If you can't control him,' Paul informed Rosemarie brusquely, 'I will be forced to contact Animal Control, and they will take possession of him.'

Rosemarie gasped and held Percy even tighter. 'They can't do that!' she protested. She turned to Hope. 'They can't do that, can they?'

Hope didn't know whether they could or not. The bigger question for her was why Paul wanted to contact Animal Control to begin with. 'I must have missed something,' she said to him. 'What has Percy done that would make you think he's a menace?'

It was Paul's turn to be surprised. 'What has he done?' he

echoed incredulously. 'You haven't missed anything. You've seen it in front of you with your own two eyes. This happened because of that damn dog!'

Rosemarie gasped again, aghast. Hope was also taken aback, but not because she was offended by the language used to describe Percy. With the sudden appearance of Paul and Percy, she had momentarily forgotten about the retention pool. But Paul's comment returned it to the front of her mind, and reluctantly, she looked down at the pool. The body was still there. It hadn't been a horrible illusion that had managed to magically disappear. Hope drew an uneven breath. Did Paul mean that it was Percy's fault? Percy was responsible for the body lying before them?

'That can't be,' she said, shaking her head. 'How could Percy possibly be responsible for—'

Paul didn't let her finish. 'How could he be responsible? Easily! He was in the pool yesterday, chewing on the extension cord. His teeth ripped it to shreds, and the result has been one cascading problem after another. And they're expensive problems, too! Additional rental costs for the generator, an endless string of electricians, repair fees from the utility company, overtime for the contractor and construction crew, and now Miranda and I have lost power at our brownstone completely. That blasted animal has been the cause of it all!'

Hope felt a sense of relief. Paul was blaming Percy for the electrical troubles. It had nothing to do with the body in the pool. But her relief faded a moment later when she realized that in Paul's huff and with his abrupt arrival, he may not have noticed the body, which was partially concealed amidst the tangle of rubber hoses.

'Paul,' she began awkwardly. 'There is . . .'

'Yes?' he asked with impatience.

Unsure how to continue, Hope looked at Rosemarie for assistance, but she was too busy worrying and fussing over Percy to focus on anything else. There was, however, no reason for Rosemarie to worry. Hope could see that Percy was in good health and spirits. He had clearly not gone for a swim that day. His coat was clean and dry. It was further proof that Percy didn't have any connection to the body.

At last, Hope simply motioned toward the pool. Paul glanced in its direction. He looked back at her and started to shrug, not understanding what she was referring to. Then his brain seemed to register what his eyes had seen. His gaze widened, and he turned again to the pool, this time slow and deliberate.

'Good God in heaven,' he exhaled. 'How did—'

His question was lost as Summer joined them on the lawn.

'We didn't know where you had gone,' Summer announced to her sister, 'so we came to find you.'

Hope's immediate reaction was consternation. Had the remaining ladies from the tea accompanied Summer outside? It would have been infinitely better if they had either remained in the shop or gone on their way. Now they would see the pool and the body. She could only imagine the shock and gossip that would follow.

'Nate is here,' Summer went on sunnily.

Although it should have been welcome news, Hope replied with an exasperated sigh. There was no question that Nate was interested in Summer, and Summer – although moving cautiously due to a bad previous relationship – was attracted to Nate. But the two never seemed to have a chance to be alone in a peaceful, mundane environment and genuinely get to know one another. Every time Nate was at their brownstone, it was on a professional basis. Dylan had called him yesterday because of the outside cellar door being broken into. Megan had called him today because of Austin Berg's aggressive behavior. And now – even though Nate and Summer didn't know it yet – there was a dead body on the property.

'Hello, Hope,' Nate greeted her in a friendly manner. 'Austin gave me his side of the story in the boutique, and it would be helpful if you could provide me with your interpretation of the events that led to—'

'That isn't at all accurate,' Austin interjected, marching alongside of Nate. 'You haven't heard even half of what I've got to say.'

Hope's exasperated sigh repeated itself. Austin's presence on the lawn was even worse than the ladies from the tea. 'This isn't a good time for rehashing old grievances,' she said to Nate, trying to keep the subject of Jill's palm reading from resurfacing.

'They aren't *old* grievances!' Austin shot back at her. 'It was today. This very morning. That is as fresh as it gets.'

As Austin's voice rose in agitation, Summer took several demonstrative steps away from him and Nate, closer to her sister.

The movement was not missed by Nate, who glanced after her regretfully. 'We all need to calm down,' he told Austin.

'Calm down?' Austin retorted. 'Are you married or engaged? Do you have a wife or a girlfriend?'

It was too faint to be readily noticed by the others, but Hope saw the tips of Nate's ears turn pink. He was thinking of Summer, no doubt.

'I'd like to see you stay calm,' Austin continued heatedly, 'when a fortune teller encourages your wife to have an affair!'

'A fortune teller encouraged your wife to have an affair?' Dylan said.

Hope's head snapped toward him in surprise. Dylan had arrived unannounced and was standing on the edge of the lawn, slightly apart from everyone else. Although his tone was impassive, Hope was pretty sure that the corner of Dylan's mouth was crooked with amusement.

'That fortune teller' – Austin pointed an accusatory finger at her – 'told my wife Jill that her palm said she should have an affair.'

Dylan raised an eyebrow at Hope.

'Rubbish. Absolute rubbish,' Summer disputed on her sister's behalf. 'I was present during Jill's palm reading this morning, and Hope said no such thing.' When Dylan's eyebrow remained elevated, she scowled at him. 'What are you doing here?'

'Megan called me,' he informed her, 'and reported that her leg had gone numb, which can be a dangerous sign—'

Hope's expression grew anxious.

'But in Megan's case,' Dylan continued, 'it's a result of standing too long and putting too much weight and pressure on her injury. I've advised you repeatedly that she needs to keep her leg elevated and rest,' he added sternly.

'I've been encouraging her to lie down and take frequent naps,' Hope told him.

'We really have tried to get Megan to rest,' Summer corroborated.

'Try harder,' he rebuked them. 'Resting means sleeping, reading, sitting quietly. It does not include playing merry tea party.'

Summer's scowl returned, redoubled. 'We have not been playing merry tea party!'

Dylan gave a cynical snort. 'I just finished examining Megan's leg, and throughout the shop, I saw teapots covered with cozies and flowered cups set in matching saucers. Frankly, at this hour, after an exhaustingly long day dealing with a number of very difficult patients, I would have been thrilled to find – and partake in – glasses and bottles containing something considerably stronger than tea.'

'Trust me,' Hope muttered, 'at this point, we could all use something considerably stronger than tea.'

Although she thought that she had spoken under her breath, Dylan must have heard it, because he looked at her curiously.

'I don't know who Megan is, and I don't care about her leg,' Austin remarked tersely. He addressed Nate. 'You're the police. I want to know what you are going to do about *her*.' The accusatory finger was aimed once more at Hope.

A shadow of irritation passed across Nate's face, but to his credit, his voice and bearing remained outwardly neutral. 'Based on the information that I have been given so far, there is nothing for me to do at present. I will remind you, however, that you are on Hope and Summer's property; they are not on yours. Before they choose to accuse you of trespassing – particularly since you are no longer in their public business, but on private land – I would urge you to consider leaving.'

It was clearly not the response that Austin had desired, and his lips quivered with anger. 'I will not leave. I will not turn my back and let her continue to interfere with my marriage. She's a homewrecker! The bloody witch is a homewrecker!'

Dylan's gaze turned to him sharply. 'Watch the language,' he warned.

'The bloody witch is a homewrecker!' Austin shouted again, and in a fit of unrestrained pique, he charged toward Hope.

With equal quickness, Dylan stepped forward and blocked his path. 'I said to watch the language.'

Austin sputtered and fumed, but Dylan was both taller and

visibly fitter, leaving little doubt as to who would win a physical confrontation between the two men.

Nate exerted his professional authority. 'I suggested politely before; this time, I will simply tell you. If you do not exit the premises of your own free will, I will be obligated to have you removed.'

Under other circumstances, Austin would have surely heeded the command. But in this case, he didn't appear to have heard it. As he had moved toward Hope, he had simultaneously moved toward the retention pool. Even with the obstructing hoses, he was now too close not to notice what was in the pool, and the finger that had been directed at Hope was redirected at the body.

'Hell's bells!' Austin exclaimed.

The group followed the shout and the finger. There was a collective gaping silence.

Even though he had already seen the body, Paul stared with the others. The only two who didn't turn toward it were Rosemarie – who was still cooing over Percy – and Hope. Dylan noticed the latter's lack of reaction, and his look of curiosity from earlier returned. A moment later, Summer looked at her sister, too.

'Hope' – Summer's voice quavered – 'do you see what he's wearing? That's him, isn't it?'

'Yes,' she answered. 'He's the Hermit.'

TEN

The man was as both Megan and Miranda Larson had described him. His cloak was a heavy, olive-green waxed canvas, faded and stained as though frequently used outdoors as a sturdy raincoat. The bottom hem was ragged and ripped in several places, by all appearances matching the torn pieces that Hope and Nate had found on the cellar steps and next to the potato-coal chute. Although the man was lying face down, the side of his beard was visible. There was no lantern, but the top of a large flashlight was protruding from the man's pocket.

'He's the Hermit,' Summer said, echoing her sister with a mixture of distress and confusion.

Hope saw Dylan and Nate exchange a troubled look.

'The Hermit?' Austin responded. 'What are you talking about? That's not a hermit. That's Carter Dalton.'

Everyone turned to Austin.

'Carter Dalton,' he repeated with assurance. 'He isn't a hermit. He lives – or lived,' Austin corrected himself, 'in a house up on Bent Mountain.'

For a minute, no one spoke.

'It's Carter!' Austin insisted. 'It's obvious from just one glance at him.' When there was still no response from the others, he became defensive. 'Don't you believe me? Well, then, I'll show you.'

And before anyone realized what Austin intended, he had rushed toward the pool. Dylan and Nate both yelled for him to stop. But it was too late. Austin had already reached his arms into the water and grasped hold of the body. For those who had seen the retention pool yesterday, with Percy splashing while the extension cord had been sparking next to him, there was a horrified intake of breath. They cringed, anticipating the worst. To their surprise – and immense relief – nothing happened. Austin didn't cry out. There was no sign of pain or shock from a jolt of electricity, only a grunt or two of exertion as he struggled with the weight of the body amidst the tangle of rubber hoses.

'Damn fool,' Dylan muttered.

'You've got that right,' Nate said. He added with irritation, 'Plus, he's contaminated the potential crime scene.'

Summer frowned. 'Potential crime scene?'

Disregarding her, Dylan continued in a low tone to Nate, 'It makes me wonder whether the contact might have been intentional, specifically to cover up any evidence.'

'I was thinking the same thing,' Nate agreed. 'On the other hand, it might have been nothing more than innocent stupidity. Unlike the rest of us, he may not have realized that the water could be charged. It wouldn't be automatically obvious or visible.'

'Unless for some reason, he already knew that there was no danger.'

Nate nodded. 'Which would make things rather interesting and possibly even give us a suspect. In any case, we need a cause of death.'

Dylan nodded back at him. 'I'll do a cursory examination. It won't be definitive, of course.'

'Noted. But anything you find would at least point us in a starting direction.'

As he headed to the pool, Dylan passed by Hope, and his hand brushed against hers. Her skin tingled. Had his touch been deliberate? Hope thought that it must have been. Dylan could have easily walked around her as he had the others. His eyes held hers for an instant before he continued onward.

'Potential crime scene?' Summer asked again, partly to Nate and partly to her sister. 'Does that mean . . .'

The question was left unfinished as Austin – with one final groaning effort – succeeded in turning over the body.

'You see?' he declared triumphantly. 'It's Carter Dalton.'

Hope was obligated to take his word for it because, prior to that day, she had never heard the name or seen the man who was lying in front of her. Carter was now face up, with his legs still stretched across the ground. As a result of Austin's labors, the upper half of his body was mostly out of the water, supported by the edge of the pool. Only one arm remained submerged,

ensnared in a pair of hoses. Based on Carter's physical appearance, Austin was correct about him not being a hermit, at least
in the conventional sense. His cloak was somewhat tattered, and
his shirt was nearly impossible to see beneath it, but the rest of
his apparel was relatively fashionable and in good condition,
albeit wet. Carter's loafers showed little wear, and his jeans were
nearly new. His beard was trim and tidy, and although his hair
was mussed and muddy from the water, it was cut short and had
evidently been recently styled. If Carter Dalton had indeed been
living in a house up on Bent Mountain as Austin had told them,
then in all likelihood, it wasn't a primitive little shack with no
access to modern amenities.

'You believe me now, right?' Austin said.

Whatever confirmation or recognition he was seeking, he didn't
get it. Dylan leaned over Carter to begin his examination. Nate
moved several steps closer to the pool to get a better look, as
well. The rest of the group watched the proceedings without
speaking.

Austin's tone grew belligerent. 'Why are you pretending that
you don't recognize him?' he snapped at Hope.

She had no answer to give him. She wasn't pretending, and
she couldn't understand why he would think that she was.

'I don't know what game you're playing,' Austin went on
angrily, 'but you can stop it, because I won't fall for your tricks.
You know perfectly well who Carter Dalton is. He's the one who
you told Jill to have an affair with!'

Hope's mouth opened, but not a syllable emerged. Everyone
had been staring at Carter; they were now staring at her. Even
Dylan glanced around for a moment. She noticed him and Nate
exchange another troubled look, similar to the one when Summer
had called Carter the Hermit. As Dylan returned to his examination, Nate addressed Austin.

'I'm going to need some clarification on what you just said.
Your wife, Jill, was having an affair with this man?' Nate
motioned toward Carter.

'Yes. And *she*' – Austin glared at Hope – 'encouraged them
in it.'

At that accusation, Hope found her voice. 'I certainly did not.'

'Liar!' Austin barked.

'Were you aware of this supposed affair between the two?' Nate asked her.

'No.'

'Double liar!'

Nate shot Austin such a stern and commanding look that he was momentarily silenced, although he continued to glare at Hope.

'I've only met Jill Berg one time,' Hope told Nate, 'this morning when she had an appointment with me for a palm reading. I've never had any encounters with Carter Dalton. Before I came outside and found him lying here, I hadn't ever talked to the man or talked to anyone about him, including,' she added firmly, 'Jill.'

Austin's glare intensified.

Happily for Hope, Nate showed little interest in delving further into the details of the palm reading. 'Why did you come outside?' he inquired.

'To find Rosemarie,' she explained, 'who had gone to find Percy, who had raced out of the boutique when Summer had opened the front door to let in more light after the power went off.'

'The power is off in the boutique?'

'The whole brownstone,' Hope clarified.

'The power is out at our brownstone, too,' Paul said.

Nate was thoughtful. 'How long was it exactly from the time that your brownstone lost power to the time that you found Carter?' he asked Hope.

She considered for a moment. 'Maybe fifteen minutes. It wasn't more than that, and it might have been a bit less.' She looked at her sister. 'Does that sound accurate?'

Summer nodded in confirmation.

Nate turned to Paul. 'And why did you come outside?'

'We've been having difficulties with the electricity ever since yesterday, when that dog' – Paul cast a resentful glance at Percy – 'was in the retention pool and chewed on the extension cord that connected to the generator.'

For his part, Percy didn't notice the cross look. He was too busy snoozing in Rosemarie's arms. Hope was a little surprised that Rosemarie had managed to hold the chubby pug for so long without her arms growing fatigued. She probably didn't want to take the chance of setting him down on the ground. He might decide to either jump into the pool beside Carter or start chewing on more extension cords.

'When we lost power completely a short while ago,' Paul continued to Nate, 'Miranda got pretty upset, and I said that I would take a look around outside to see if there was an obvious cause. That was when I caught him' – he cast another resentful glance toward Percy – 'bolting from Hope and Summer's lawn to ours.'

Rosemarie sniffled and said meekly, 'Oh, but you can't blame Percy. It's not his fault. He's been active and energetic ever since he was a puppy. He doesn't mean to do anything harmful. He isn't a bad dog.'

She sounded so sad and remorseful that Hope felt compelled to try to lift her spirits. 'Of course Percy isn't a bad dog, Rosemarie. He's as sweet as can be. We all know that.'

There was a disputative harrumph from Paul.

'Hope and I sympathize with your and Miranda's cellar and electrical problems,' Summer said to him. 'We truly do, because the ongoing construction and power glitches are far from ideal for us and our shop, too. But blaming Percy really isn't fair. Yes, he chewed on the extension cord yesterday, and yes, it might have interfered with the proper functioning of the generator, but Percy has been under strict supervision today. He was with us in the boutique almost the entire afternoon. He was only outside on his own for a couple of minutes at the most, which must have been when you caught him dashing between the lawns. You didn't see him chewing on anything during that time, did you?'

'Well, no, I didn't,' Paul acknowledged.

'That settles it.' Summer gave a satisfied nod. 'Percy isn't responsible for today's troubles.'

There was an exasperated sigh from Nate, as though the conversation had steered far from his desired course. 'Yes,' he remarked impatiently, 'we can all agree that the pug is not guilty of electrocuting Carter Dalton.'

Summer drew a sharp breath. Rosemarie gave a startled little yelp. Both Paul and Austin looked at Nate in surprise.

'So that's what you meant before about a potential crime scene?'

Summer's hazel eyes were stretched wide. 'You think this was intentional? What happened to Carter wasn't an accident?'

Nate's sigh repeated itself, but Hope could see that this time the frustration was with himself and not with them. It was clear that he hadn't intended to speak so bluntly. Hope found herself less taken aback at the possibility of a crime having been committed than the others. She didn't know why Carter Dalton had been at her and Summer's brownstone on the previous day, or why he had returned to the property today, but it seemed improbable to her that a man who was apparently determined and clever enough to break into their cellar would somehow be inadvertently electrocuted in a retention pool filled with dirty drainage water between the two lawns. Why anybody would want to deliberately electrocute Carter was equally incomprehensible to her.

'Could this have been the cause of the power outages at our brownstone and the Larsons'?' Hope asked Nate.

He seemed relieved at not having to reply directly to Summer's string of queries. 'I think that it's a safe assumption. Regardless of any electrical issues resulting from the damage to the extension cord or the generator yesterday, it would take a substantial surge to knock out the power to both properties simultaneously for a prolonged period this afternoon. Such a surge' – Nate motioned toward Carter and the pool – 'would in all likelihood be strong enough.'

That resolved one of Hope's lingering questions. She had wondered if the occupants of the attic were responsible for the power failure. The flickering, yes. The complete blackout, no. The flickering had been especially active immediately before Austin's appearance at the boutique. The spirits must have been trying to warn her about him. It was easy to understand why. Austin had been nothing but a problem for her since his arrival. And the more she thought about it, Hope realized that the flickering had also occurred immediately preceding Gina's arrival. Was it another indication – in addition to Gina's suspicious wincing reaction to Austin – that the two were acquainted?

Hope looked at Austin curiously. Was there a way – surreptitiously, preferably – to find out if he and Gina were connected somehow?

Summer must have noticed her sister's questioning gaze, because she also turned her attention to Austin, although her focus took a significantly different direction. 'If it wasn't an accident, was it you?' she asked him.

Austin squinted at her, not understanding. 'Me?'

'*You*,' Summer repeated with emphasis. 'You said that your wife was having an affair with him. You're clearly angry about it. You were hollering at Hope and calling her names, even though she had never even met Carter. But *you* identified Carter immediately. You didn't hesitate or need to deliberate for even a second. And you didn't seem terribly upset by the sight of him lying dead in the pool. All of which makes me wonder if you were the one who put him there. Was it you who electrocuted Carter?'

Austin gaped at her. For the first time since he'd barged into the boutique, he appeared to be at an utter loss for words.

'Summer,' Nate reproved her, earnestly but not severely, 'you can't go around accusing people of criminal acts – particularly something as serious as murder – based on a whim.'

Summer offered no apology. 'There is no whim,' she rejoined. 'Everything that I said is true. All afternoon Austin has been thundering furiously about the affair. The question is: was he furious enough to kill Carter?'

Austin made an aggrieved gurgling noise. His face and neck had turned a ripe plum shade of purple.

'Summer,' Nate began again, his manner somewhat sterner, 'you are jumping to a considerable number of conclusions that haven't been verified or even—'

He was interrupted by the gurgling noise as it rose in volume until it became almost a howl.

'Have you lost your mind?' Austin bellowed at Summer. 'It wasn't me!'

She responded with a dubious expression.

'It wasn't me!' Austin asserted a second time, now also looking at Nate.

Nate looked back at him thoughtfully.

'I couldn't have done it,' Austin argued.

Hope noted with interest that Austin's tone had become more entreating than antagonistic. She wasn't sure if that helped or hurt his case.

'I was in the store with you two' – Austin gestured between Summer and Hope – 'when the power went out. If the power went out from a surge due to Carter being electrocuted, then I couldn't have done it, because I wasn't on the lawn or near the pool at that time.'

'Is that correct?' Nate asked the sisters. 'Was Austin in the boutique with you when the brownstone lost power?'

Although Hope began to reply in the affirmative, Summer interjected.

'That doesn't prove anything,' she said defiantly.

'Yes, it does,' Austin countered, his purple nostrils flaring.

'No, it doesn't,' Summer retorted. 'When you first came into the boutique, you were breathing hard and sweating heavily. I originally thought that it was because you had been running to the shop. But now I realize that you weren't running *to* the shop. You were running to get *away* from the pool and what you did to Carter!'

Austin started to protest, but Summer cut him short.

'And I was wrong about your sweating,' she went on briskly. 'It wasn't sweat. It was water from the pool. That's also why you were panting for air. You fought with Carter in the pool or next to the pool, and then you pretended to be upset and agitated toward Hope to conceal that you planned to kill Carter!'

'That's absurd!' Austin shouted. 'I didn't plan to kill Carter! I couldn't have. How could I set up an electrocution to occur later? That's absurd!' he cried once more. 'I wouldn't know how to do something like that even if I wanted to.'

'You wouldn't have needed to know how to do it,' Dylan said.

They all turned to him in surprise. Dylan had been working so quietly and diligently in his examination of the body that he had momentarily slipped from everyone's mind during the voluble discussion with Austin.

'You wouldn't have needed to know how to do it,' Dylan repeated, 'or plan anything in advance, because this man,' he indicated Carter, 'wasn't electrocuted.'

ELEVEN

There was a contemplative silence, as though they all needed a moment to digest what Dylan had told them.

Summer was the first to speak. 'So it isn't a crime scene, after all? The death wasn't intentional? What happened to Carter was an accident?'

Rosemarie exhaled with relief and hugged Percy. 'Oh, thank heaven. It would have been awful if someone had deliberately committed such a terrible act.' She shook her scarlet mop at Hope. 'And in your backyard of all the places in the world.'

Technically, it was the side yard – both theirs and the Larsons' – but Hope saw no purpose in correcting the point.

Austin cast an angry eye toward Summer. 'And you were trying to blame me for it,' he snarled. 'How dare you! I won't forget the accusations you made. Mark my word, you'll pay for them.'

Summer scowled at him.

He turned to Nate. 'Are her lies considered to be a crime? Can you charge her with something?' Before Nate could reply, the angry eye snapped back to Summer. 'I should sue you. That would teach you a lesson. You can't drag my name through the mud by calling me a murderer when he' – Austin motioned toward Dylan – 'said that I couldn't possibly have done it.'

'I didn't say that.'

As they had a minute earlier, everyone looked at Dylan.

Austin frowned. 'Yes, you did. You said that Carter wasn't electrocuted.'

'That's correct,' Dylan confirmed matter-of-factly. 'You couldn't have electrocuted him, because he wasn't electrocuted. I never said, however, that you didn't kill him in a different manner.'

At the inference that the death had indeed involved foul play, there was a dismayed mewing from Rosemarie. It sounded like a cowed kitten compared to the enraged roar that emanated from Austin.

'So now you're trying to blame me, too!' Austin exploded. 'Why? What do you have against me?'

Dylan didn't raise his voice or grow heated in return. Both his tone and expression remained placid. 'I have nothing what-soever against you as it relates to the deceased. As it relates to Hope and Summer, I believe that you owe them an apology for your inappropriate choice of language and irrational amount of yelling. To tell the truth, I'm surprised that one of them hasn't waggled a finger and slapped a curse on you by now.'

Summer twitched her nose and smiled.

There was also a hint of a smile from Nate, although he kept it commendably restrained.

Rosemarie's dismayed mewing was replaced by nodding approval. 'Isn't Dylan gallant?' she cooed to Percy. 'He's defending the sisters' honor.'

Anyone who wasn't well familiar with Rosemarie might have thought that she was being facetious, but Hope knew that she meant it in earnest. Rosemarie – aside from having a sizeable soft spot for Dylan – was an incurable romantic and, regardless of the fact that she had been divorced twice and had additionally suffered through several other failed relationships, she still whole-heartedly believed in quixotic fairy tales and chivalrous heroes riding to the rescue in dreamy storybook endings.

Austin apparently didn't share Rosemarie's tender, starry-eyed notions, because he responded to the criticism of his yelling by yelling some more. 'That proves it!' he shouted at Dylan. 'You're in cahoots with them! I've seen how you and that one' – it was Hope's turn to receive his angry eye – 'look at each other. You're in her bed, aren't you?'

Dylan's lips curled with amusement. 'I wish.'

This time Nate's smile wasn't suppressed. Even Paul gave a chuckle.

Their laughter only added to Austin's irritation. 'You're all against me!' he fumed. 'You're setting me up to take the fall! You're corrupt and crooked and—'

His agitation was so great that his speech rose in pitch and became almost incomprehensible. When combined with the smiles that she had evidently witnessed from her husband and Dylan and Nate, Miranda Larson mistook it for merriment.

'I heard your voices and watched from the window at how much fun you were having,' Miranda said, as she approached them from the side of her brownstone, 'so I decided to head out and join you. It's much better than sitting indoors, alone in the semi-dark, waiting for the electric company to call me back with a further update. Am I correct in assuming that you've lost power, too?' she asked Hope and Summer.

Summer nodded and started to inquire if she had received any useful information from the electric company up to that point, but the subject was forgotten the moment Miranda got close enough to the pool to see the body.

'Gracious, that isn't fun at all,' Miranda corrected herself gravely. 'Poor Carter. What on earth happened to him?'

Nate instantly resumed his professional demeanor. 'You know this man?'

'Certainly I do. Why wouldn't I?' Miranda responded, as though the question was more astonishing to her than the discovery of Carter Dalton lying dead on the lawn. 'Carter is a member of my book group.' Her brow furrowed. 'Although I don't know why he would come here. We don't usually meet in the city. We most often get together at his place up on the mountain.'

'Ha!' Austin cried with an air of vindication. 'I told you he wasn't a hermit and had a house on Bent Mountain.'

Continuing her own thoughts, Miranda took no notice of Austin. 'And lately, a lot of our meetings have been at Gina's.'

There was a collective exclamation of surprise from Hope, Summer and Rosemarie.

'Gina?' Summer immediately asked Miranda. 'Which Gina are you talking about?'

'Which Gina?' she echoed, the furrow deepening. 'Gina Zaffer, of course. How many Ginas are there in the area?'

That was precisely what Hope and Summer wanted to know. They turned questioningly to Rosemarie. She sniffled.

'Is Gina Zaffer *Madam Gina*?' Summer pressed Rosemarie when she didn't offer any further response.

The sniffle repeated itself. It sounded disappointed and also slightly aggrieved. 'Gina never mentioned a book group to me. I would have joined it if she had.' Rosemarie frowned down at

Percy, who looked up at her and yawned. 'I don't know why she didn't tell us about it. I'm sure that I've told her how much we enjoy going to the library and choosing between the new arrivals.'

Although it wasn't a direct answer, Hope and Summer took it as sufficient confirmation that the two Ginas were in fact one and the same. The sisters exchanged a glance. What an odd coincidence that Gina would be in the same book group as both their neighbor and the man who had broken into their cellar.

'Wait a minute,' Hope said, with a sudden realization. 'Why didn't you recognize him yesterday, Miranda?'

'Recognize who?' she asked.

'Carter.'

Miranda blinked at her, puzzled.

'Yesterday you came to the boutique and told Summer and me that it looked as though a man was trying to break into our cellar.' Hope pointed at Carter. '*That* man.'

Miranda turned to Carter and studied him more closely. 'The raincoat seems familiar,' she mused.

'You mentioned the man's large coat – or cloak – to us,' Hope reminded her, 'as part of his overall strange appearance. But I'm wondering why you didn't realize then that you knew him, especially considering that you were thinking about contacting the police to report his suspicious behavior?'

The furrow reappeared in Miranda's brow, the more so as she looked up from Carter and found everyone looking intently back at her, including Nate, who had taken a small notepad out of his pocket and begun jotting down information.

'Well, I don't know,' Miranda murmured. 'It's rather confusing.' Her voice grew flustered and increasingly squeaky. 'Maybe it was the drizzle and mist that interfered with my view. I remember seeing the man from the window of our brownstone as I was watching for the contractor to arrive. I was worried that with the rain, the construction crew wouldn't come, and then there would be even more water in our cellar. I must have gotten distracted by everything that was happening and didn't match the man with Carter.' She added a touch defensively, 'It's a substantial distance from our brownstone to yours, particularly in poor weather.' She turned to her husband for support. 'Wouldn't you agree, Paul?'

'It is a substantial distance,' he concurred. 'Plus, there are the boxwoods along the side of the property, which obstruct a clear line of sight.'

Miranda nodded at him. 'Don't forget that you saw him yesterday, too, and you didn't recognize him, either.'

'But I wouldn't have recognized him,' Paul replied, 'regardless of the distance or weather conditions, because I never met Carter.'

'You never met him? I thought you had. Weren't you with me at Gina's when she had that get-together?'

Paul shook his head.

Miranda blinked at him with the same puzzlement that she had at Hope a minute earlier. 'I could have sworn that you and I went as a couple. It was a large group of people. I distinctly recall Carter being there. Others, as well . . .'

Out of the corner of her eye, Hope saw Austin shift his weight. She looked at him. Austin's furtive gaze was on the ground as he moved restlessly from one foot to the other. He had a pained expression, and he was peculiarly silent. Either his shoes were pinching his toes and causing him significant discomfort, or – more likely in Hope's opinion – Austin had also been at Gina's for the get-together that Miranda was referring to. Hope wasn't startled by the discovery. On the contrary, it simply confirmed her previous suspicions that Gina and Austin knew each other. She did wonder, however, why Austin – and similarly Gina when they were in the boutique – seemed to want to keep their acquaintance a secret.

'You really must not have been at her house,' Miranda continued to Paul, 'because it isn't one that you would easily forget. It's absolutely stunning! I can only imagine what Gina paid for it. She must have a good deal of money in the bank.'

Summer gave a little cough.

Hope understood its meaning. Summer was convinced that *Madam Gina* had made her wealth by swindling the bereaved with her supposed séances.

Miranda misinterpreted the cough and turned to Summer excitedly. 'Have you seen her house, too? It's spectacular, isn't it? All glass and stone. Everything so new and modern and bright and polished.' She heaved a wistful sigh. 'I wish that Paul and I could have a place that nice.'

It was Paul's turn to cough, except his was noticeably cross.

'More than a few people in this world would eagerly leave their homeland and give up every last one of their possessions for the opportunity to live in this splendid city in our splendid brownstone.'

'Oh, I know. I know,' Miranda responded quickly. 'We're extremely lucky. Of course I realize that. But Gina's house – on the edge of that magnificent mountain, overlooking that gorgeous valley – is something else entirely.' There was another wistful sigh. 'And she has no trouble with any of it, because none of it is old or broken. Her pipes don't clank and drip. Her heating and cooling aren't temperamental with every change of the season. Her cellar doesn't flood; she probably doesn't have a cellar at all! I'm quite sure,' Miranda added somewhat dryly, 'that electricity is currently running through Gina's lines, and the contents of her freezer aren't in any danger of spoiling.'

'I predict,' Paul said, 'that our power will come back on shortly, as will Hope and Summer's. And the contents of everybody's freezer will be fine as long as you don't keep opening the door to check on them.' There was now a weariness in his tone, as though it wasn't the first time that his wife had complained about their home's ostensible deficiencies. 'While we're on the subject of a home constructed of all glass and stone, can you imagine what the annual fuel costs for a place like that must be? We would probably need to earn double what we presently do to afford the utility bills alone.'

'That may be true, but at the same time,' Miranda countered, 'we wouldn't have to pay such outrageous sums for contractors, generators or construction crews.'

In an effort to broker a truce, Dylan offered a compliment to both sides. 'A modern megalith certainly has its visual and architectural appeal. Personally, I prefer an older house with history and character.'

'Percy and I are partial to Hope and Summer's brownstone, too,' Rosemarie agreed with him. 'Gina herself wanted a tour of it after I told her about the beautiful interior, and all the marvelous antique furniture and paintings, and the wonderful globe and old books that are in the—'

'And what was her verdict?' Dylan interrupted, smiling. 'Did their brownstone meet with *Madam Gina*'s approval?'

Hope gave him a sharp – and slightly surprised – look. Dylan had apparently taken note of how Rosemarie had introduced Gina to them.

'Unfortunately,' Rosemarie answered, 'there was no chance for a tour with the tea going on. Hope couldn't leave the boutique and go into the rest of the house while so many guests were in the shop.'

'Speaking of leaving,' Hope said, 'I'm not sure when exactly Gina departed from the tea. Do you happen to remember, Rosemarie?'

Rosemarie was thoughtful. 'I'm not sure, either. Perhaps it was when the power went out?'

'No, it was definitely before then—'

Miranda broke in, 'Gina was at the boutique today?'

'Yes,' Rosemarie started to reply. 'I invited her to join me for—'

It was Nate's turn to interject as he lifted his gaze from his notepad to Miranda. 'Does it surprise you that Gina was at the sisters' brownstone?'

There was a pause as Miranda considered the question.

'No,' she responded after a moment. 'I'm not surprised about Gina. I was surprised about Carter. I didn't understand before – I think I even said that to you – why he would come here. But it makes more sense now that I know Gina was here, too.'

Hope and Summer looked at each other, and they both listened with increased interest.

Nate also showed interest in Miranda's remark. 'How does it make more sense?' he asked her.

'Well, it's not a great secret or anything terribly scandalous, but . . .' Miranda hesitated, then she glanced around and lowered her voice as though it was a secret, after all. 'Carter was always running after Gina.'

'Running after her?' Nate said. 'In what way?'

'The usual way, I suppose.'

'Romantically, you mean?'

Miranda nodded. 'From what I heard, Carter was constantly calling Gina and skulking around her house at odd hours.'

Hope and Summer looked at each other again. Carter had been skulking around their house, too – not to mention breaking into their cellar – but in their case, there hadn't been any indication of a romantic element.

'You shouldn't gossip, Miranda,' Paul objected. 'Isn't right to speak ill of' – he gestured awkwardly in the direction of Carter – 'the deceased.'

'I'm not gossiping or speaking ill of him,' Miranda rejoined. 'I'm merely answering a few informational questions.' She turned back to Nate. 'I can't confirm whether or not there was ever an actual relationship between the two, but it really isn't shocking that Carter would be attracted to Gina. She has that phenomenal house, plus plenty of money to go with it, presumably. And she's obviously a very attractive woman.'

Nate inclined his head. In his defense, it wasn't clear whether he was assenting to Miranda's comments generally or to the specific observation regarding Gina's beauty, but Summer made no allowances in either event. She promptly glowered at him.

'Summer . . .' Nate began, in an effort to exculpate himself.

But there was little that he could say that would be appropriate under the circumstances, considering that he was a police detective on official duty with both a dead body and a mixed audience in front of him. In the end, it was Rosemarie who – more or less – came to Nate's rescue by changing the subject.

'Percy and I predict,' Rosemarie said, as both she and the pug looked up at the dismal sky, 'that there won't be any more rain or drizzle today, and by tomorrow, all the clouds will have cleared away from the city.'

TWELVE

I t was too early to judge the accuracy of Rosemarie and Percy's weather forecast, but Paul's prediction as to the electricity soon proved to be wrong. The power did not come back on shortly. The windows in both brownstones remained dark, and they became even darker as the afternoon slipped into evening and the daylight began to fade with it.

The group on the side lawn gradually dispersed, some more willingly than others. Miranda grew increasingly worried about the contents of her freezer, and she and Paul returned home to monitor the condition of their melting perishables, vigorously debating along the way the efficacy of packing the items into coolers filled with ice. Rosemarie departed with Percy – who was growing cranky for his overdue dinner – saying that she would drop by the boutique tomorrow for an update. Austin lingered the longest, resuming his complaints to Nate about Hope and Summer until a large contingent of police and related officials arrived and started to block off the area, effectively throwing him out of it. At last, only Dylan remained at the pool. He and Nate and several of Nate's colleagues huddled over Carter, discussing the findings from Dylan's examination of the body.

With slow steps, Hope and Summer headed back to the boutique. Having departed during the tail end of the tea, they expected to enter a gloomy and disordered shop, but to their surprise, they found it spick and span and cheerfully illuminated by half a dozen candles. The dirty cups and saucers had been loaded into the dishwasher in anticipation of the eventual return of the electricity. The teapots had been rinsed and stacked on the counter to dry. And all of the leftovers from the snack platters had been neatly wrapped and set aside, although not in the refrigerator, because Megan had demonstrated more restraint than Miranda and didn't open the doors while the power was off.

Unhappily, the power was going to stay off. Between her industrious cleaning and organizational activities, Megan had contacted the electric company. Either she'd had the good fortune to reach someone in the customer service department who was especially helpful, or she had used her indomitable hotel charm and cajolery to successful effect, because unlike Miranda, Megan had come away with significant useful information.

The electricity was not expected to be restored until the following day at the earliest. The current estimate was in the neighborhood of noon, but that was only a rough guess, because none of the repair crews had as of yet managed to pinpoint the exact source of the trouble. There was some thought that it might be a worn-out transformer, or it could involve a malfunctioning toggle switch on one of the branch lines. In any case, the outage was not an isolated incident. Some of the other houses on Hope and Summer's block were also experiencing problems, as were some of the other blocks in the city. To the sisters' relief, there appeared to be no direct connection to the retention pool or what had happened to Carter. While it wasn't good news for Miranda and her freezer, Rosemarie would certainly be elated when she learned of it. Now Percy could no longer be blamed – at least not to such a degree – for having chewed on the extension cord the day before.

Megan's next call in Hope and Summer's absence had been to their grandmother to find out if she and Morris Henshaw still had power. Although Olivia Bailey's driver's license listed the brownstone as her legal address with her granddaughters, and the post office continued to deliver her mail there, she spent an increasing number of days and nights at Morris's house. From Morris's viewpoint, it was a substantial victory. He had been sweet on Olivia for as long as Hope and Summer could remember, and he had never made any secret of the fact that his ultimate goal was to marry her. For her part, Olivia was less transparent as to her wishes for the future.

With regard to the electricity, Olivia had told Megan that she and Morris hadn't experienced any sort of an outage, and then she had immediately invited them all to come over for the night. Morris had apparently been so enthusiastic about the idea that he had started shouting out food and drink options in the background. In addition to his estimable skills as a physician, Morris was an avid cook and never missed the opportunity to show off his culinary talents. Megan had taken the liberty of agreeing to the visit on the sisters' behalf and, aside from throwing a few necessities into an overnight bag, snuffing the candles, and locking the front door, everything was arranged for the trio to depart the brownstone.

Although Hope and Summer were grateful to Megan for accomplishing so much while they had been outside, they also remembered Dylan's admonishment with regard to her resting. During all of Megan's assiduous tidying and telephoning, there didn't appear to have been much of an opportunity for her to sit quietly with her cast elevated or lie down. In response to their concerns, Megan merely shrugged and said that she would take it easy at Olivia and Morris's. Dylan's medical advice to her had evidently had the opposite effect of that which he had intended. Once reassured that the numbness in her leg was a result of too much strain and overactivity rather than sepsis, nerve damage, or impending paralysis, Megan had promptly gone about her business without another thought to her injury. She had never been good at slowing down or sitting still, and the concept of resting and a lazy day – unless it involved a chilled cocktail and a sandy beach – wasn't in her vocabulary.

There was no use in chastising Megan after the fact, so Hope simply thanked her for all of her efforts and quietly crossed her fingers that Morris and Gram would be more successful at keeping Megan stationary and off her feet than she and Summer had been. Hope knew that at a minimum Megan would be prohibited from hobbling around Morris's kitchen, because Morris was rather possessive of his kitchen, particularly when playing host. But when they finally reached the house, it turned out that Megan wasn't allowed to hobble through any of the rooms – and neither, for that matter, were the sisters. The moment their car pulled into the driveway, Morris hurried outside to greet them, and then just as quickly, he started to herd them toward the back garden.

'Hullo, hullo!' he cried. 'So glad that you've arrived safe and sound. Olivia and I were beginning to worry about the delay. We didn't know what might be holding you up. But there's no time to talk about that now. We mustn't dawdle! Leave your bags in the car for later. The cornbread is almost done.'

It was more zeal than Morris usually exhibited. He was an

earnest, contemplative man with a generous heart and a warm laugh, but he tended toward the somber, and the laugh didn't make an especially frequent appearance.

'How is the leg doing?' he asked Megan, immediately growing anxious at the sight of her cast. 'Dylan has checked on it, hasn't he? He assured me that he would.'

'Yes. Twice over the last two days. And all is well,' Megan told him.

'Good. That's excellent news.' Morris watched her move with considerable proficiency on her crutches, and his worried expression relaxed somewhat. 'Good,' he repeated, directing them up the elegant flagstone path that led to the rear of the house. 'You can't be too careful with fractures and sprains. They have a sneaky way of causing trouble down the road if you don't take proper care of them early on. Heed the experience of your wizened elders: you have to look after your health, so that it can look after you.'

'While we're on the subject of health,' Hope said, 'Megan has been exerting herself far more than she should today—'

'And now she needs to sit down for a long rest,' Summer chimed in.

'Tattletales,' Megan grumbled.

'Instead of complaining, you should be thanking us for our concern,' Summer rejoined. 'If you don't rest, your leg won't heal. If your leg doesn't heal, you won't get out of that cast. And if you don't get out of that cast, how will you be able to go on your next splashy dinner date with Daniel Drexler?'

Megan laughed. 'Touché.'

'You'll get plenty of rest here,' Morris promised her. 'Olivia has the guest rooms ready, and we have the patio all set up, too. There is a lounger for you to properly elevate your leg, and extra cushions to reduce the pressure on the cast, and . . .'

As he continued to enumerate the careful arrangements that had been made for Megan on the patio that evening, Hope noticed that Morris was hobbling a bit himself.

'Are you feeling all right, Morris?' she interjected. 'Has your back started to cause you more problems?'

'It's stiff,' he answered. 'But it's always stiff. And I don't like to grouse about it, because on the whole, the surgery was a greater success for me than it is for many other people. My range of motion has improved, and I have much less pain than I used to. Summer's teas have been extremely helpful, as well.'

'Any time that you need a fresh batch,' Summer said, 'just let me know.'

'I appreciate the offer. I'll certainly take you up on it when—'

Summer made a sniffing noise. 'I hate to interrupt you, Morris, but if you have anything cooking, I think that it might be getting a tad charred.'

'Do you smell something burning? It must be the cornbread!' Morris shouted in dismay. And with as much speed as his stiff back and hobbling gait allowed, he hastened around the corner of the house.

They followed after him slowly, letting Megan and her crutches set the pace. A minute later, they also turned the corner and promptly gave a collective exclamation of delight. The flagstone path had broadened to a spacious, beautifully appointed flagstone patio. It was bordered on opposite sides by two arching, burnished arbors decorated with intricate scrolling ironwork. The arbors were strung with numerous strands of glittering silver lights. In the center of the patio was a red brick firepit that flamed orange and gold. It was surrounded by an array of large, comfortable furniture, including the promised lounger with the extra cushions for Megan. A matching brick oven stood at the far end of the space, adjoined by a multi-tiered food preparation table and a stainless-steel wet bar.

'It's fabulous,' Megan said. 'Completely fabulous. With a convivial beverage in my hand, I could rest here for days without moving a muscle.' She added after a moment, 'It might be because I haven't seen the patio for a while, but I don't remember it being quite so fancy and luxurious.'

Hope nodded. 'The arbors are new to me, too. Morris and Gram keep renovating and updating.'

'I think,' Summer remarked in a low tone, 'that Morris is encouraging the continual makeovers as another way to tie Gram to the house.'

'Tsk-tsk. It isn't polite to whisper about your grandmother, my dears.'

They jumped in surprise. Olivia had come up behind them noiselessly and unseen in the impending dusk.

'Hi, Gram.'

'Hello, my dears. I'm so happy that you're here, as always.'

A bevy of kisses and hugs followed.

There was a clattering noise from Morris as he removed a round earthenware dish from the brick oven and deposited it heavily on the adjoining table.

'The cornbread didn't burn,' he reported with relief. 'Only a few crumbs singed along one edge.'

Everyone agreed that it was good news.

Using a pastry brush and a ready bowl, Morris began to spread a layer of melted butter on the crown of the bread. 'The key to a superior cornbread,' he informed them, 'is a heavy-bottomed pan.'

'If you slather any more butter on that bread, Morris,' Gram said, '*I* will become heavy-bottomed.

'Fiddle-faddle.' He went on slathering. 'Your bottom is perfect, Olivia. Nothing could ever alter that fact.'

The sisters and Megan exchanged a grin.

'They're giggling at my expense, Olivia. I can hear it.'

'Don't mind them, dear.' Gram winked at the trio. 'They're just envious that we – at our advanced age – have more of a love life than they currently do.'

The trio laughed, but they also sighed a little – and felt somewhat sorry for themselves – because it was the truth. None of them could claim to have any sort of a steady relationship, let alone the deep connection that Morris and Gram shared.

Megan's sigh must have been more pronounced than that of the others, because looking at her, Gram's own laughter faded and was replaced by the same worried expression that Morris had shown earlier.

'You're pale, Megan. Much too pale. You've pushed yourself too hard. Come over here and sit down.' Gram led her and her crutches to the waiting lounger. When she had gotten Megan comfortably settled and had properly adjusted the plethora of cushions around her leg and under her cast, she turned to Morris. 'Stop fussing with the cornbread, dear. I'm sure that it's perfect already, and we'll greatly enjoy it later. What Megan needs now is a liquid bolster for her spirits.'

'Well, of course. Without question! Why didn't anyone say so sooner?' Morris promptly set down the pastry brush and stepped toward the beverage cooler that was incorporated into the wet bar.

'Wow. That is a swanky new wine refrigerator you have,' Summer complimented him. 'How many bottles does it hold?'

'Sixty,' Morris answered proudly. 'It has dual zone temperature control with beechwood shelves and UV protectant glass. But I haven't filled it completely yet.'

Summer smiled. 'So there's room for Miranda to bring over a few things from her place during the freezer crisis?'

Hope chuckled with her sister.

Morris frowned, not understanding the joke or the question.

'Never mind. It isn't important.' Summer returned to the matter at hand. 'What are our wine options for the evening?'

Gram's response was dry. 'There are no options. You're looking at four dozen identical bottles.'

'Huh?'

'*Four dozen*,' Gram repeated with emphasis.

'It isn't four dozen any more,' Morris corrected her. 'We already drank two of the bottles, and then we gave one to the Fraziers after they so kindly offered to water the begonias for us when—'

Gram stopped him. 'An exact accounting isn't necessary, dear. The relevant point is that there aren't any choices in the cooler. It's either the white Bordeaux or nothing.'

'White Bordeaux?' Summer asked. 'I didn't know they made a white Bordeaux. I thought it was all red.'

She and Hope turned to Megan. After hosting countless wine-and-cheeses as part of her duties at the hotel, Megan was their go-to informational source for wine.

Megan shook her head. 'I'm not familiar with it. The only thing I can tell you is that it must be reasonably good and relatively pricey, because the hotel only provides inexpensive and mediocre selections for the four o'clock assemblage.'

'There is nothing at all mediocre about this white Bordeaux. It's outstanding!' Morris declared.

The dryness returned to Gram's tone. 'You only think that, dear, because you didn't have to pay for it.'

'Fiddle-faddle.' Morris withdrew one of the bottles from the cooler and started the process of opening it. 'We'll let the girls judge for themselves. I wager that they'll agree with me as to the quality of the wine.'

'And *our* agreement,' Gram reminded him,' was that there would be no further wagering, since that's how we ended up with so many bottles in the first place.'

'You won them in a bet?' Hope couldn't conceal her surprise. 'I never thought that you were a betting man, Morris.'

Gram chortled. 'Tell them what the bet was, dear.'

'Oh, yes.' Having successfully removed the cork, Morris began to fill a line of waiting glasses. 'It was rather interesting – and lucky for me. There's a colleague of mine who is an otolaryngologist specializing in the ear, nose, and throat . . .'

It was evidently a lengthy story that she had already heard on more than one previous occasion, because Gram wasted no time in seating herself. Keeping a motherly eye on Megan, she took the chair closest to the lounger. Gram gestured encouragingly for Hope and Summer to sit down, as well.

'He heads an international research committee that focuses on sinusitis . . .'

Summer chose a chair near the firepit. Hope settled herself in the rocking settee.

'Ordinarily, a pair of studies on the deviated septum wouldn't attract that much attention, but in this instance . . .'

The glasses were distributed to the group.

'The committee was convinced that the paper would never be accepted in such a prestigious peer-reviewed journal. I wagered with them that it would be. Perhaps it was unfair of me not to have mentioned at the time that I happened to know the managing editor of the journal from my days at the . . .'

Swirling the wine, Summer inhaled its bouquet. 'Peaches and lemon,' she murmured. 'With a hint of hazelnut.'

'And it was published in the latest edition! With a special mention to follow in the annual compendium! The committee was thrilled. Not only did they pay up immediately, but they quadrupled our original wager on their own generous initiative. Four cases of white Bordeaux were delivered to the house last week.'

'Well done, Morris. A superb accomplishment all around.'

Hope took a drink from her glass. 'And you're right. There isn't anything at all mediocre about it, gratis or not. It's a very nice wine.'

Megan nodded. 'I like that it's crisp and not overly sweet.'

'It's been too long of a day for a sweet wine,' Summer agreed. 'This is refreshing and hits the spot.'

Visibly pleased with their praises, Morris took a seat himself, not far away from Gram. 'When you go back home tomorrow or later on in the week, you can take as many bottles with you as you want.'

'As many as you want,' Gram confirmed with a smile. 'It's not as though we're about to run out and need to ration them for an emergency.' After a pause, she added more earnestly, 'And now that we've all gotten comfortable and have a full glass, why don't you tell us what happened at the brownstone today?'

It was Hope and Summer's turn to pause. They looked at each other, unsure where to begin.

'Well,' Hope said at last, 'the whole thing started yesterday morning when Megan saw a man at the front window of the boutique—'

She was interrupted by an unexpected voice.

'Ah, so this is where the homewrecker disappeared to.'

THIRTEEN

Hope's stomach sank with dread. How did Austin Berg find them at Morris's house? And why would he come there that evening instead of waiting until the next morning at the boutique if he wanted to harangue her – and in all likelihood Summer – again?

'Homewrecker?' Morris echoed with a mixture of surprise and disapprobation. 'What an unseemly thing to say, Dylan.'

Dylan? Hope turned in her seat toward the figure that had appeared in the back garden. He was tall and lean, standing at the edge of the flagstone path in the encroaching darkness. It was indeed Dylan and not Austin. Hope breathed a sigh of relief. She didn't have the energy for another confrontation with Austin that day. Her fatigue must have been why she didn't properly identify the voice and instead jumped to a faulty conclusion.

Either Dylan saw the weariness in her face, or he didn't want to risk further censure from his father, because he made little effort to defend himself.

'You're right,' he said. 'I meant it as a joke, but it is unseemly. Forgive me.'

Although Morris accepted the apology with a nod, he wasn't entirely satisfied. 'I don't understand how you could have intended the remark to be humorous.'

Dylan looked at Hope questioningly. She shook her head.

Gram – who had an observant eye – must have noticed the exchange and correctly guessed that it related to whether she and Morris had been apprised of the day's events, because she said, 'Pour yourself a drink, Dylan, and sit down with us. Hope was just beginning to tell your father and me about what happened at the brownstone.'

'Thank you, Olivia,' Dylan replied gratefully. He gestured at the glasses that they were all holding. 'What is tonight's feature?'

'You'll find the cooking sherry and some plastic cups on the lower shelf beside the oven,' Morris said.

Hope and Gram exchanged a glance. If Morris was offering the cooking sherry rather than the bonded bourbon or single-malt whiskey to his son, then he really wasn't pleased with him.

'Don't be nonsensical, dear,' Gram reproved Morris gently. She turned to Dylan. 'We're having wine. There is an open bottle on the table. The crystal tumblers and liquor bottles are in the bar cabinet next to it. Please help yourself to whatever you'd prefer.' And before either Dylan or Morris could respond, she addressed Hope. 'Now go on with your story. You have my complete attention.'

After taking a substantial drink of her wine, Hope gave an account as best as she could. Summer and Megan chimed in occasionally with supplemental details and relevant observations. When the narrative had been concluded, they sat in silence for a long moment, each perusing their own thoughts. Then Dylan – who had remained standing – spoke.

'Carter Dalton drowned.'

'Drowned?' Morris leaned forward in his chair with interest, any lingering disapproval of his son's earlier remark vanishing. Morris invariably showed a high regard for Dylan's medical knowledge and opinions. 'You're certain?'

Dylan inclined his head in the affirmative. 'I am. There will be an autopsy, of course. It will determine definitively – and legally, for Nate's purposes – whether there is in fact water in his lungs. But my examination left little doubt. I've seen drowning victims before, and Carter exhibited all of the classic signs. The manner in which his body was submerged. The immersion of the face, covering both the nose and the mouth. The larynx had plainly relaxed, indicating that water had been allowed to enter the lungs, which wouldn't have occurred if there had been a different cause of death.'

There was another silence. This time it was Summer who broke it.

'Could it have been an accident?' she asked Dylan. 'Could Carter have accidentally drowned in the retentional pool, even when it's so shallow that Percy was able to splash around in it without any difficulty?'

'In theory, yes,' he answered. 'I was once called to a camping ground in California where a man had drowned in a stream that

barely reached my knees. He was on a group canoeing trip without
any prior experience or proper instruction. Another person in the
canoe apparently became nervous and tried to stand up when
they hit some rough water. The balance of the boat shifted, and
the man fell out. The current pulled him under the canoe. He
couldn't swim well, panicked, and quickly became disoriented
in the cold water, and no one was able to reach him in time. It
was a tragedy and an accident.'

Gram clucked her tongue. 'How awful.'

'But that isn't what happened to Carter,' Dylan continued. 'His
drowning wasn't an accident.'

'How can you be sure?' Hope questioned.

'Because of the bruising on his upper body. Carter was trapped
beneath the drainage hoses. They were holding him down.'

Summer frowned. 'But why didn't he move the hoses, or move
out from under them? Was he unconscious, or had he been hit
in the head and was dazed?'

'I saw no indication of a significant head wound,' Dylan told
her. 'And based on the numerous abrasions across his fingers and
palms, Carter undoubtedly tried with every ounce of his strength
and energy to move the hoses. You seem to think that it would
have been easy for him to simply climb out of the pool at his
leisure, but when those drainage hoses are filled, they're tremen-
dously heavy and difficult to lift or shift. You saw how hard
Austin had to work to turn Carter over, and even with all his
effort, he still couldn't get him completely out of the water.'

Gram clucked her tongue again. 'Awful.'

'Now imagine,' Dylan went on, 'that you are Carter Dalton,
and for whatever reason, you're standing by the retention pool.
Somebody – with or without warning – pushes you into it. You
land in the water and immediately become entangled in the hoses.
No one needs to fight you and hold you under to kill you. All
they have to do is put a firm hand or foot on one or two of the
hoses, and those hoses will do the work for them. The hoses will
keep you weighted down until you tire and can no longer struggle.
That's when you drown. The hoses become a murder weapon.'

Hope shivered, remembering when she had first walked from
the boutique to the side lawn that day in search of Rosemarie
and Percy; how the tangle of hoses encircling the pool had seemed

like monstrous tentacles throttling its prey. She hadn't known then that the prey was Carter.

'Cold?' Dylan asked her.

She looked up and found him standing directly in front of the settee.

'No.' Her voice wasn't quite steady. 'I was thinking back to this afternoon.'

Dylan's gaze held hers for a moment, his eyes reflecting the orange and gold flames from the firepit. Then he turned and paced across the patio, drink in hand. Hope hadn't seen which bottle he had ended up selecting from, but considering that it was a copper liquid in a crystal tumbler, it definitely wasn't the white Bordeaux.

Summer shifted restlessly in her chair. 'But why? It doesn't make any sense. Why would somebody push Carter into the pool and then make sure that the hoses held him down? Yes, Carter may have looked a little peculiar or even suspicious in his big cloak. And yes, it's possible that he broke into our cellar through the potato-coal chute. But those are reasons to call the police, just as Miranda and Paul thought about doing when they first noticed him lurking at the side of our brownstone. Those aren't reasons to drown the man!'

Hope nodded. 'I agree with you, except there doesn't seem to be any real question that Carter was the one who broke into the cellar. It doesn't justify killing him, of course,' she added quickly.

'Which is another thing that doesn't make any sense,' Summer responded with growing frustration. 'We talked about it before, and we couldn't see a reason behind it. And I still don't see a reason behind it! What would Carter want in our cellar? There is absolutely nothing of value down there. According to Miranda and Austin, Carter had a house up on Bent Mountain, was a member of a book group, and might have been having an affair with Jill Berg. All of which means that he wasn't a down-on-his-luck vagrant looking for a safe place to shelter. So why was he in the cellar?'

'I may be able to answer that,' Dylan said.

They looked at him in surprise.

'It appears that Carter was in your cellar to get this.' Dylan retrieved an item from the edge of the flagstone path, having apparently deposited it there unnoticed in the shadows when he had first arrived. He held the item up, so that the silver lights from the nearby arbor could illuminate it.

It was a bag. A large, clear plastic evidence bag. Inside the bag, there was a visibly old, leather-bound book. The book's spine was nearly bare. Its corners were bent and scuffed. And its cover was so heavily worn that only a few patches of the original camel color remained. The book looked vaguely familiar to Hope, and then all of a sudden, she realized why.

'Is that . . .' Hope hesitated. 'Is that from the brownstone's library?'

Dylan's lips curled with a trace of a smile. 'I'm glad that you're willing to admit it. Nate and I had a little debate as to whether you and your sister would claim the book or deny all knowledge instead.'

'So Nate has seen it?' Summer said, with an uneasiness that indicated she recognized the book also.

The smile grew. 'Nate was the one who found it.'

'Where?' Hope asked.

'Inside Carter's cloak. It had been zippered into one of the many interior pockets, some of which are remarkably big. Other pockets contained a utility knife, two additional flashlights, and several helpful implements generally used in the art of breaking and entering. Fortunately, the waxed canvas is reasonably water-proof, and the book was on the side of the cloak that wasn't fully immersed in the pool, so it got a little damp in spots but not saturated. The pages remain legible.'

Megan – who had no connection to the book and didn't under-stand its import the same as Hope and Summer – focused on the cloak. 'That's probably why Carter chose the cloak. It's only logical that if you're intending to commit a burglary, you need a convenient way to hold your tools and, assuming that you're ultimately successful, your loot.'

Hope responded with an absent nod. She was still looking at the book.

'In addition to concealing what you've taken,' Megan continued, 'the cloak also conceals you. That could be another reason Carter wore it. He might have believed that it would help to hide or distort his identity. And it worked in that regard. When I first saw him in front of the boutique window, I thought that his beard was much longer than it actually was, and I mistook his large flashlight for a lantern. Plus, Miranda personally knows Carter, and instead of recognizing him yesterday, she only noticed his cloak.'

There was another absent nod from Hope.

'You've made a number of excellent points, Megan,' Dylan complimented her. 'But I think that at the present moment, the Baileys are considerably more concerned with this book than they are with the stratagem behind Carter's cloak. Shall we ask them why?' Not waiting for an answer to his rhetorical question, he began to open the evidence bag.

'I'm not sure you should be doing that, Dylan,' Morris cautioned anxiously. 'If the item is from a crime scene, then you don't want to be accused by the police of tampering with essential evidence.'

'The book has been officially cleared by the police's forensics team,' Dylan assured him. 'They found nothing on it that is of interest to them, legally speaking. There are no useable fingerprints or unidentified fibers or the like. Nate and I, on the other hand' – his hint of a smile resurfaced – 'found the book quite interesting. The more so because it confirms your original statement, Megan. Carter was indeed the Hermit.'

'You mean the Hermit from the Tarot?' she said. 'But I called him that based on his appearance at the window, not when we saw him later in the retention pool.'

'I'm not basing it on his appearance in either instance,' Dylan replied. 'I'm basing it on the book. Why else would Carter take the book if not to seek knowledge and enlightenment? He must have valued spiritual growth and the discovery of profound truths. Is that not how you described the Hermit to me, Hope?'

Hope gave him a wary look.

'What sort of a book is it?' Morris inquired curiously.

'It is a book written in Latin,' Dylan told him.

'Oh, my Latin is poor.' Morris shook his head with regret. 'Very poor. I can only muster a few medical terms at most, I'm afraid.'

Gram – who up to that point hadn't betrayed any emotion with regard to the book – exhaled quietly. Hope knew that it was a sigh of relief at Morris's lack of proficiency with Latin. Hope would have been relieved, too, if it hadn't been for Morris's next question and Dylan's subsequent answer.

'But you have some Latin, don't you, Dylan?'

'Yes, I do. Two inattentive semesters at boarding school.'

There was a muffled groan from Summer. Hope silently echoed the sentiment. Two semesters at boarding school – inattentive or not – were more than enough to cause them a heap of trouble.

'I'm admittedly rusty,' Dylan went on, removing the book from the evidence bag and letting the bag flutter down to the ground. 'But I have no doubt that someone here can correct me or assist me, as needed.'

Morris's brow furrowed. 'Someone here can assist you? But I just told you that my Latin is woefully inadequate.'

'I was referring to the others,' Dylan said.

The furrow deepened, as though Morris wasn't sure whether he'd heard his son correctly, or if he had, who the purported others might be.

Without providing any further explanation, Dylan shifted his attention to the book. To his credit, he handled the book with great care, as was appropriate for its august age and deteriorating condition. He gently opened the tattered cover. The pages inside were yellowed and heavily foxed with brown spots. There was the distinct smell of mildew, which was only going to grow worse now that the book had gotten damp in the retention pool.

Dylan turned to the brittle title page. He read aloud, slowly but clearly, *'Cornix cornici numquam oculos effodit.'*

There was a tense stillness. None of the Baileys uttered a word. Megan – who had no difficulty grasping the implication of their silence – sank somewhat lower in her lounger and sedulously studied her wine glass.

'Well?' Morris asked impatiently after a minute. 'What does the Latin translate to, Dylan?'

'Roughly,' he answered, 'one crow does not peck another's eye.'

Morris blinked in surprise. 'And what does that mean?'

'In Nate's view, it's akin to honor among thieves.'

Both Summer and Hope winced. It was bad enough that Nate had discovered the book and connected it to them. It was even worse that he – with the aid of Dylan – was interpreting the book's contents.

'Or more fittingly in this case,' Dylan said, 'a witch doesn't hex a fellow witch.'

FOURTEEN

'Crows and witches,' Morris mused. 'What an odd subject for a book.'

Dylan concurred with a chortle.

'And this book came from the brownstone's library?' Morris said.

Gram's response was both quick and quick-witted. 'Well, dear, the previous owner of the property left behind so many things. Aside from a mountain of books and assorted papers, there was also a good deal of artwork and furniture.'

'We found the old pine table and matching set of chairs that I currently use in the boutique up in the attic,' Hope corroborated.

'That's quite right.' Gram gave her a grateful glance before turning back to Morris. 'It probably would have behooved me to take a complete inventory when we first moved in, but time passed by, and there were always so many other things to think about between keeping the shop afloat and raising the girls that I simply never got around to it. Now that everything has been carried back and forth from one room to another and used in all sorts of different ways over the years – just as Hope said – it's difficult to remember what came from where originally or from whom.'

Morris nodded. 'That's entirely understandable, Olivia. Even though you and the girls have been in the brownstone for so long, I wouldn't be the least bit surprised if you suddenly stumbled over something that you had never seen – or really noticed – before. With three floors and the attic and the cellar, it's bound to happen. That's especially true with smaller items, such as the books and papers that you mentioned.'

Gram nodded back at him earnestly.

'The brownstone has such a large library,' Megan said, contributing her support to the Bailey explanation for the book in Dylan's hands. 'As you know, Morris, I've been sleeping in the study because of my leg, and every time that I'm in the room, I marvel at how the bookcases are bursting with so much history and information.'

There was another chortle from Dylan. 'Yes, you esteem the history and information to such a degree that you hang your underwear from it.'

Megan shot Dylan an irritated – and somewhat chagrined – look, but she couldn't dispute the actual point, because when they had gone into the study to inspect the cellar the day before, her unmentionables had indeed been strewn about.

Not understanding the reference to undergarments, Morris chose to ignore it. 'Knowledge can never be too highly valued,' he told Megan. 'I'm glad that a young woman such as yourself recognizes that fact.'

Dylan shook his head at him. 'You aren't honestly swallowing the story that they're feeding you?'

Morris was perplexed. 'What story?'

Although he shook his head again, Dylan didn't argue with his father. He must have realized the same as Hope that Morris's credence in the tale was due in large part to his fondness for Gram, and there was no quarreling with that.

Having Morris on their side at least temporarily, Hope figured that now would be the best time to try to regain custody. 'May we have our book back, please?'

'But you just said that it wasn't your book,' Dylan reminded her. 'You claimed that it had been left behind by the brownstone's previous owner.'

'That's precisely why it should be returned to its long-term home in the study,' Hope responded, and she extended her hand to receive the book.

Dylan made no movement toward her.

'I wonder,' Morris pondered, 'what else the book talks about. Can you translate some other parts of it for us, Dylan?'

'So late in the evening, dear?' Gram interjected hastily. 'And in the dim lighting out here on the patio? Dylan could damage his vision.'

'Oh, I hadn't thought of that.' Morris's expression grew faintly anxious. 'That's an excellent point, Olivia, especially with the ink on the paper being so old and faint. Reading it tomorrow in the natural light would be much wiser.'

Gram murmured in agreement.

Dylan smiled. 'I greatly appreciate Olivia's concern with regard to' – he halted for a second, indicating that he was fully aware of the difference between her professed and actual concern – 'the health of my eyes. In deference to her wishes, I won't translate any more of the book.'

The Baileys visibly relaxed.

'But in the limited time that I was able to study some of its pages earlier,' Dylan went on, 'I came across several intriguing passages.'

The Baileys tensed once more.

Morris turned to Dylan with interest. 'What did the passages say?'

Still smiling, he answered, 'I confess that I didn't completely understand them. There was something about mermaids. If they weep, they lose their magic nature.'

Dylan glanced around the group in anticipation of a response. No one spoke.

'And witches,' he continued after the pause, 'are not able to weep at all. Which reminds me' – this time, he looked pointedly at Hope – 'I've never seen *you* cry.'

'I will shed tears of joy,' she replied dryly, 'when you give me the book.'

Hope extended her hand again. There was a brief hesitation, then Dylan walked over to her and deposited it in her palm.

'Thank you,' she said. And without delay, Hope tucked the book safely between the seat cushion and the arm of the settee where no one could reach it but her.

A moment later – without invitation – Dylan deposited himself on the settee next to her. Annoyed at his presumptuousness, Hope would have moved demonstratively away from him, but there wasn't enough room on the snug rocker, which had been designed to fit a cozy couple. All she could do was shift slightly toward her corner and raise an eyebrow at Dylan.

He pleaded innocence. 'I thought that after being so generous in returning the book, you surely wouldn't deny me a seat.'

'There are plenty of *other* seats on the patio.'

'But this one is especially comfortable.' Dylan leaned back on the cushion. 'And it rocks so nicely.' He pushed against the flagstone with his foot, causing the settee to sway back and forth gently.

Although her eyebrow remained raised, Hope didn't make any further objection. She knew that she had achieved a tremendous victory by regaining possession of the book, and she had no intention of jeopardizing it by squabbling over seating arrangements.

'Mermaids?' Morris questioned, having apparently puzzled over the matter without reaching a satisfactory conclusion. 'And more witches? I don't understand what kind of a strange book that is.'

Hope's answer was swift. 'Folklore.'

'Folklore,' Summer concurred with equal speed.

'*Old* folklore,' Hope further elucidated, 'hence the Latin.'

'Hence the Latin,' Summer reiterated.

Morris was thoughtful and rubbed one of his ears, mussing his wispy white hair in the process. 'Folklore . . .' he ruminated. 'In Latin . . .'

Dylan gave a quiet laugh that only Hope could hear. 'The Baileys have all of their stories and explanations worked out in advance, don't they?'

Hope ignored him and focused on Morris, trying to sound sufficiently convincing so that they could close the subject of the book permanently. 'Before we in more recent times learned the science behind natural phenomena such as tides and eclipses, people created their own narratives to help decipher the otherwise inexplicable world around them. Dangerous shoals were bewitching sirens attempting to lure sailors to their death. Twinkling stars in the heavens were departed souls watching over their loved ones left behind on the earth. Most of the folklore was transmitted orally from one generation to the next, but some of it was eventually put down in written form and—'

'And it became our book that Nate found in Carter's cloak,' Summer concluded.

After rubbing his other ear, Morris gave a nod, persuaded at last. 'I retract what I said earlier. It isn't a strange book at all. On the contrary, from an anthropological perspective, it's really rather fascinating.'

There was more quiet laughter from Dylan. He stretched in his seat and draped an arm across the back of the settee. Hope shifted a little further toward her corner.

'Don't be afraid,' Dylan drawled. 'Haven't you just demonstrated to us that you are a renowned expert on folklore? If so, you should know that I'm not the Big Bad Wolf sidling up to Little Red Riding Hood.'

Hope rolled her eyes. 'That's a fairy tale, not folklore.'

Dylan responded by lowering his arm on to her shoulders. Hope promptly pushed it back up to the settee.

'Instead of proving yourself to be an inveterate troublemaker,' she remarked crisply, 'you could help us.'

'I like helping you.' The arm returned to her shoulders. 'What is it that you want me to do?'

Again, she pushed the arm up to the settee. 'For starters, you can support us when we ask Nate to take down the yellow crime scene tape from the side lawn. When we left the brownstone to come here, the police had just finished adding a second layer.'

Summer pursed her lips. 'That tape is bad. Very bad.'

'All right. I'll support you,' Dylan agreed, his arm once more sliding down to Hope's shoulders. 'But I have my doubts that Nate will remove the tape regardless of our requests. He's fairly consistent at following police regulations.'

'We know he is' – Hope surrendered and allowed the arm to remain in place – 'but we still have to try.'

'Why?' Dylan asked curiously. 'Do you think the tape will discourage customers from coming to the boutique?'

'Exactly the opposite,' Summer replied, pursing her lips harder. 'We're going to be besieged by folklore.'

Dylan looked at her with amusement. 'You're going to be besieged by mermaids and sirens?'

'Not magical creature folklore,' she corrected him tetchily. 'The folklore of conspiracy theorists.'

He shook his head, not understanding.

'Sasquatch, Mothman, Area 51.'

Still not understanding, Dylan turned to Hope.

'The boutique is well known in certain unconventional circles,' she explained. 'The moment the police tape went up, the tongues began wagging and the news started to spread through the extended grapevine. *Murder at – or adjacent to – the mystic shop.* It will bring out every conspiracy theorist with a camper van or a pop-up tent on the East Coast. And probably some from the West Coast, too. It invariably does. That's why we want Nate to take down the tape as soon as he reasonably can. If the tape disappears before the gossip has been widely circulated, then we won't have to deal with as many visitors later on.'

'This has happened before?' Dylan said.

'Yes. Not the murder, of course. But because of the boutique, whenever something quirky or mysterious occurs in the area, the conspiracy theorists appear. Some show up immediately; others trickle in over time.'

'They've been coming ever since I first opened the shop,' Gram told Dylan. 'Except there never used to be such a large number, and they were all friendly and intelligent and well mannered. I would invite them into the brownstone for nightly dinners, and the girls would play with their children on the tree swing in the garden. We never had any problems whatsoever. Back then, they were simply people who didn't believe the official government explanations for particular types of events and wanted to uncover the truth for themselves. Now, however, they are people who have no interest in any sort of truth, and their sole goal is to make as much money from each incident as they can. They record endless videos – including through house windows and on private property – and trample over everything and everyone in their way. Many get quite aggressive.'

Morris stiffened in his chair, and he looked at Gram with concern. 'Why haven't you mentioned this before, Olivia?'

'Because there was no reason to mention it, dear. As I said, we never had any problems back then. But now it's different, which is why the girls – as do I – would prefer to keep the boutique under the radar and not draw extra attention to it with superfluous police tape, if possible.'

'Of course it's possible!' Morris declared solicitously. 'The tape should only be necessary to protect and preserve the crime scene initially.' He turned to his son. 'You were at the brownstone, weren't you? Have Detective Nate and his colleagues completed their work on the lawn?'

'I believe they have,' Dylan answered.

'That settles it.' Morris stood up with authority. 'I will call the police chief. As you may recall, he was on the committee that I co-chaired for the charity festival this past summer. When I explain to him the gravity of the situation, he'll send someone to take that tape down as fast as you can snap your fingers. Come dawn tomorrow, the police tape will be gone!'

It was Summer's turn to stiffen in her chair. 'I'm not sure that calling the chief is such a good idea, Morris. Nate won't be happy if we go above him to his superior officer and ask to have the tape removed without his knowledge.'

But her argument was in vain. Morris had already decided that the best way to safeguard the precious Bailey flock was to contact his fellow charity festival committee member for a favor. And without any further discussion or deliberation on the matter, Morris marched from the patio toward the house.

As he disappeared through the sliding doors, Summer groaned. 'Nate is going to be so irritated at us. *At me.*'

Megan shook her head. 'Nate likes you far too much to be irritated for long. He'll understand, or at least shrug it off. Isn't that right, Dylan?'

'Nate will be fine,' Dylan assured Summer. 'He's got more than enough to worry about with Carter Dalton. He isn't going to lose any sleep over the quantity or distribution of yellow tape. In fact, Nate will probably wish that no tape had been put up at the brownstone at all when he learns about these conspiracy theorists. Speaking of which, I've heard of Sasquatch and Bigfoot, of course. And Area 51 is the secret UFO spot in the Nevada desert. But who – or what – is Mothman?'

'Big bug,' Hope said.

Dylan laughed, and his arm drew more closely around her shoulders.

'Mothman is a seven-foot-tall humanoid creature with immense wings and glowing red eyes. Repeated sightings occurred for slightly over a year between 1966 and 1967 in Point Pleasant, West Virginia. One theory is that it was a visiting alien or interdimensional being. Another theory is that it was a sandhill crane that had flown away from its usual migration route. The crane apparently has a similarly large wingspan and a red crown that includes the skin around the eyes.' In response to their surprised looks, Megan explained, 'We sometimes get tourists at the hotel who ask about Mothman when they're heading up the Appalachians. You've now heard my abbreviated travel guide.'

Dylan laughed again, and his hand slid casually into Hope's hair. 'Now tell us about the Abominable Snowman.'

'Well, once upon a time,' Megan began, laughing also, 'there was a Yeti, and he grew tired of everybody climbing Mount Everest in an attempt to locate him and take photos of his foot-prints and collect samples of his hair and scat, so he decided to take a vacation to—'

'How did he get in from the cellar?' Summer interrupted her.

Megan grinned, still playing the game. 'The Yeti went on vacation to the cellar?'

Summer wasn't entertained. 'Not the Yeti,' she said with agita-tion. 'Carter! How did Carter get into the study from the cellar to take the book?'

Gram threw an apprehensive glance toward the house and the sliding doors. Hope shared her uneasiness. Morris's interest in the book had been effectively sated, and they didn't want to rekindle it.

Either Summer didn't notice their anxiety, or she assumed that Morris wouldn't return to the patio any time soon, because she continued to Dylan, 'It's been bothering me ever since you told us that Carter had the book in his cloak. There's no ques-tion that the book is from the brownstone's library. But Carter couldn't get to it from the cellar. If the bookcase in the study is closed, the cellar door can't be opened from inside the stairway.'

Megan – who had grown solemn – said, 'I told you and Hope this morning that I'd had trouble sleeping for exactly that reason. All through the night, I was worried that the Hermit would creep up through the cellar.'

'And I told you,' Summer responded, 'that the Hermit couldn't creep up through the cellar.'

There was a little cough from Gram. They looked at her.

'That isn't strictly accurate,' she said.

'What isn't?' Hope asked.

Gram hesitated, as though she would have preferred not to elaborate on her previous statement.

Summer didn't have the patience to wait her out. 'How is what I said *not strictly accurate*? Are you implying that the Hermit – or Carter – could have crept up through the cellar?'

After another hesitation, Gram gave a small acknowledging nod.

Megan's eyes stretched wide. 'What! You mean those noises that I heard were actually Carter? One of the times that there was a creak or a squeak and I decided not to turn on the light, he was in the study? While I was lying on the sofa in the dark, Carter was sneaking around next to me and stealing the book?'

The nod – even smaller – repeated itself.

There was an indignant snort from Megan. 'That's the last time you'll see me there.' She folded her arms peevishly across her chest. 'And it doesn't matter one bit that Carter is now dead. Somebody else could come creeping in next! I am never again spending the night in that room.'

'And there isn't any need for you to do so,' Gram replied apologetically. 'You can stay here at the house until your leg is fully healed and your cast has been removed. Morris can check on its progress twice a day. You'll have healthful meals, and plenty of rest, and—'

'Stop trying to bribe Megan into forgiving you for not telling us the truth,' Summer interrupted sourly. 'So the cellar door can in fact be opened from inside the stairway?'

'Yes,' Gram admitted.

'Even when the bookcase in the study is closed?'

'Yes.'

Summer threw up her hands in frustration. 'Then why have you spent the last thirty years saying the complete opposite?'

'Because I was worried about your safety. When you and Hope were little, you got into the habit of playing on the cellar stairs. You would use an old piece of carpeting to sled down the steps. One time, you crashed hard at the bottom and cut your chin badly. It's how you got that scar, even though it's barely visible now. I decided that the cellar was too dangerous at your age, so to stop you from going down there alone, I told you that the cellar door couldn't be opened from inside the stairway. I should have corrected it later, but I never thought of it. And it never occurred to me,' Gram added, with a touch of dryness, 'that someday a man who resembled the Hermit would wriggle down the potato-coal chute into the cellar and then climb up into the study to filch one of our books.'

Megan unfolded her arms. Summer gave a little sniffle. It was hard to remain cross with someone who had told an innocent fib to protect young children from getting injured.

Gram rose to her feet. 'I had better go inside and check on Morris. If he can't reach the police chief as quickly as he would like, he might contact the Fire Department or the National Guard next.'

They all chuckled, but not too heartily, because although Gram was joking, it wasn't especially far-fetched. Morris could easily have been on the telephone with the mayor's office by that point.

With a pat on Megan's arm and a smile to her granddaughters, Gram headed toward the sliding doors and the house. Megan yawned and snuggled contentedly against her lounger. Summer curled her legs up on her chair and muttered some more – mostly to herself – about whether Nate would be angry regarding the removal of the police tape. Hope watched the flames bob on the firepit. The orange and gold tips blended together in a hypnotic dance.

'Hope?' Dylan said.

His voice was low. His fingers caressed the back of her neck.

'Hmm?' she murmured.

'About the book . . .'

Under other circumstances, Hope would have been instantly on alert and preparing her defensive wits. But the book was still tucked safely next to her, and she was too drowsy to think any more about it that evening.

'Hmm?' she repeated.

'When I was translating it earlier . . .'

She only heard half of his words. It was so peaceful on the settee as it rocked slowly in the cool night air. Dylan's fingers felt warm on her skin. And his shoulder – against which she was now leaning – was growing increasingly comfortable.

'I might be mistaken, because as I told you before, my Latin is rusty . . .'

Her eyes fluttered closed.

'But the title page appeared to say that it was Volume I. Is there a Volume II?'

Hope didn't answer. She had fallen fast asleep.

FIFTEEN

The night gradually faded, and a faint tint of pink appeared along the eastern edge of the horizon. A mourning dove cooed from its roosting spot in a magnolia. It cooed again, this time joined in harmony by its perching brethren, and Hope stirred at the sound. Stiff from lack of movement, she sat up slowly and rigidly. A thin paisley quilt dropped from her legs to the ground. Hope blinked at it in confusion. She had slept so hard that for a moment, she had no idea where she was or how she had gotten there.

She looked around. She was outside on the patio at Morris's house. A wine bottle stood open on the table. Empty glasses had been set down on the flagstones. A pair of flies buzzed around the bowl and pastry brush that had been used to butter the cornbread the previous evening. The cornbread in its earthenware dish was gone, presumably removed to the house. The chairs were all empty, but the lounger was not. Megan was sleeping amid a heap of cushions with a matching paisley quilt spread over her.

The sky continued to lighten. The pink deepened to lilac, followed by the beginnings of a pale baby blue. It appeared that Rosemarie's prediction as to the weather had been correct. The rain and drizzle from the preceding days had ended, and all the clouds had cleared away from the city. There was a light breeze. It carried the perfume of a late blooming rose – and also the unmistakable scent of freshly brewed coffee.

Hope turned toward the aroma and saw Summer approaching from the sliding doors. She was carrying a breakfast tray that held a small French press and a set of mugs.

'You are the . . .' Hope began, before quickly stopping herself, remembering that Megan was still asleep. She glanced at the lounger, found Megan undisturbed, and dropped her voice to a whisper. 'You are the best sister ever.'

'I am your only sister,' Summer whispered in return.

'Your timing is impeccable. I was desperately craving a cup of coffee. How did you know that I was awake?'

'I didn't.' Summer set the tray down on the table next to the wine bottle and began to fill the mugs. 'The coffee was ready, so I brought it out. If you had been sleeping, I would have made a loud noise or splashed leftover wine on your face to wake you.'

'Then you are most certainly *not* the best sister ever.'

Summer smiled. She added a teaspoon of sugar to her own mug but not to Hope's, who typically preferred her coffee black.

'Thanks.' Hope accepted the mug with eager hands and took a generous drink. Her face crinkled.

'Too bitter? Do you want some sweetener after all?

'No, the coffee is excellent. Gram can always be relied on to buy good beans, even at Morris's.'

Summer nodded in agreement, and to keep their conversation as quiet as possible, she drew a chair close to her sister.

'The problem is my neck.' Hope stretched her shoulders and upper back. 'It has a bad crick.'

'That is the price you pay for spending the night curled up on a settee,' Summer replied drolly. 'And before that, curled up on Dylan's chest.'

'Seriously?' Hope's face crinkled some more, except this time, it was not because of her neck. 'I was curled up on his chest?'

'Yup. Super cute and cozy.'

'Oh lord. What was Dylan's reaction?'

Summer's smile widened. 'He seemed to be quite pleased with the situation.'

Hope groaned.

'If it's any consolation, Megan fell asleep, too. Dylan suggested that since it was such a nice night – the temperature was good, and it was dry – we should leave her on the lounger instead of waking her to go inside to bed. There would be less stress and strain on her leg that way. Morris seconded the plan, and Gram brought out a quilt for each of you. Then she and Morris retired to the house, and I followed shortly thereafter. Dylan said that he would stay outside on the patio for a while longer. As I was leaving, he was tucking the quilt very thoroughly around you.'

Hope groaned again – and also blushed slightly. She had no recollection of that portion of the evening. The last thing that she remembered was rocking on the settee, watching the flames dance in the firepit as Dylan's fingers caressed her neck. It had felt awfully good, certainly much better than the crick did now.

'So if Morris seconded the plan with regard to Megan,' Hope asked, keen to focus on something other than the pleasure of Dylan's touch, 'does that mean he returned to the patio? Did he have any success with the police tape?'

'He said that he did. According to Morris, the police chief was highly sympathetic and obliging, and the tape would be removed from the side lawn immediately. But we can't be sure that it actually happened until we get back to the brownstone. Their conversation was pretty late in the day, and the chief's order might not have been so swiftly followed by his subordinates.' Summer frowned.

'You're not still worried about how Nate will react, are you? I honestly don't think that he'll care about the tape.'

'No, it's not the tape. It's the potato-coal chute.'

It was Hope's turn to frown. 'The potato-coal chute?'

'After Morris announced his triumph with the crime scene tape, he moved on to his next issue of concern: the potato-coal chute. He declared that it was a safety hazard and a security risk and that it ought to be sealed up forthwith.'

'Not so long ago,' Hope recalled, 'he made the same proclamation about the attic. When Gram slipped on the rickety stairs last year, Morris was so apprehensive that she might fall and break her hip, he wanted to shut off the attic permanently.'

'Which Gram refused to do, of course. We can't ever seal up the attic – and thereby its occupants.'

'Good heavens, no. Imagine the wrath and retribution if we even tried!'

The sisters looked at each other and shuddered.

'But Morris,' Hope remarked after a moment, 'may have a point about the chute. We aren't obligated to keep it open like the attic. It's not as though the brownstone is receiving deliveries of coal and potatoes. How did Gram feel about sealing it up?'

'She was undecided. I had the impression that she wasn't against the idea in theory, but she didn't want to launch into any hasty actions, especially in the middle of the night and without conferring first with us, privately. Her only comment was that prior to Carter Dalton, no one had crawled through the chute in thirty years, and there didn't seem to be much reason to think that anybody would crawl through again for the next thirty.'

Hope smiled at their grandmother's wryness. 'Am I correct in assuming that Morris didn't agree with her relaxed attitude?'

'He was astounded – and a little distressed – by it. As was Dylan. The Henshaws then teamed up to argue that the Baileys weren't taking the situation seriously enough. Gram just let them talk and, as she usually does, she murmured polite responses at appropriate intervals. But it made me wonder . . .'

'About?'

'Well, Gram is right that prior to Carter, no one – at least no one who we're aware of,' Summer amended, 'had crawled through the chute in thirty years. So why did somebody crawl through it now? How did Carter know about the chute?'

'That's a good question.' Taking a drink of her coffee, Hope considered for a minute. 'As far as I'm aware, all of the houses on our street have similar chutes. Even Paul commented on it yesterday – or perhaps it was the day before – saying that his and Miranda's cellar still had the old bins that separated one family's coal and potatoes from another's dating back to when their brownstone had been divided into apartments. Most of the surrounding streets have brownstones that were constructed during approximately the same time period as ours, so they presumably have the chutes, too. Which means that anybody who either lives in the area, or is acquainted with and visits someone who lives in the area, would know about the existence of the chutes. Carter was acquainted with Miranda through their book group. He could have noticed the chute while visiting her one time. Miranda said that they didn't usually meet in the city, but she didn't say that they *never* met in the city.'

Summer was hesitant. 'Let's suppose all of that is correct. Carter noticed a chute during a meeting of his book group at Miranda's or while visiting one of the local shops on an adjacent street, and he decided that it was his way into our brownstone.'

Hope nodded.

'But how did Carter know about the study? How did he know about the brownstone's library?'

'Tittle-tattle,' Hope answered.

'Huh?

'Word of mouth. A lot of people – neighbors, workmen, customers and clients from the boutique, assorted friends – have seen the study over the years. They always comment on it afterwards. They're impressed by the globe, the walls of built-in bookcases, the antique furnishings. Rosemarie has only been inside a couple of times briefly, and she's constantly talking about it. To us, to Dylan, to Gina Zaffer, to whomever she might cross paths with on her Sunday afternoon stroll in the park with Percy . . .'

Summer laughed.

'Carter could have heard about the study and the brownstone's library through the local chit-chat. Even though he didn't know the exact layout of the rooms, it would have been only natural for him to assume that he could get to the ground floor from the cellar. Based on the piece of cloak that Nate found, Carter obviously had some difficulty squeezing through the potato-coal chute. And based on the piece of cloak that I found, he must have also had some difficulty traversing the narrow cellar stairs with only a flashlight to guide him. The cellar door probably stumped him for a minute or two, but once he managed to swing the bookcase open, it was as simple as could be for him. Instead of needing to search through the entire house as he no doubt expected that he would have to, Carter was standing directly in the study, staring straight at the library.'

'And staring at poor Megan lying on the sofa,' Summer added.

They turned to Megan. Regardless of the rising sun, and the chirping birds, and the whispering sisters, she was still sound asleep. She had barely even shifted her position on the lounger. It was an indication to Hope of how utterly exhausted Megan's body was. It also helped her to better understand why Megan hadn't woken up when Carter had climbed from the cellar into the study.

'Although Megan would have gotten a terrible shock if she had found Carter slinking next to her in the middle of the night,' Summer said, 'I'm certain that she would have stopped him in his tracks. She would have hit him on the head with the nearest knick-knack; he would have dropped to the floor like a stone; we would have called the police to arrest him for breaking and entering . . .' She drew a sudden sharp breath. 'If that had happened, he would probably still be alive.'

Hope looked at her, startled. 'That never occurred to me. But you're right. If Carter had been arrested, he wouldn't have drowned in the retention pool.'

Summer drew another breath, this one long and melancholy. 'And all because he wanted that book.'

'The book? You think that's the reason . . .' Hope broke off abruptly. In her daze upon waking that morning, she had forgotten all about the book. Instantly panicked, she spun in her seat and jerked up the edge of the cushion. A wave of relief washed over her. The book was still there, wedged next to the arm of the settee. She pulled the book out and held it tightly in her hand. 'He didn't take it,' she exhaled.

'Who didn't take it? Are you talking about Dylan?'

'Yes. He saw where I put the book last night for safekeeping, and you said that he was tucking the quilt very thoroughly around me. He could have easily helped himself to the book in the process.'

'Dylan did show a great deal of interest in the book,' Summer agreed, 'certainly enough that he could want to take another look at it.' She added with a sigh, 'And I had the impression from Dylan's remarks that Nate was awfully interested in the book, too.'

'I'm afraid so.'

Summer sighed again. 'Well, there isn't much that can be done about it now. We can't put the cat back in the bag, so to speak. We can only try to limit the damage as much as possible by not letting either Nate or Dylan have any more contact with the book. The real damage, of course, is what happened to Carter.'

'That's what you meant before?' Hope asked her. 'You think the book is the reason that Carter died?'

'Don't you think so?' Summer returned. 'Is there any other explanation for why someone would kill him?'

'There was the affair with Jill Berg.'

She shook her head. 'That hasn't even been confirmed. We only have Austin's word for it. Maybe there was an affair between Jill and Carter, or maybe the affair involved someone else entirely. Either way, it's too weak to build a murder case on.'

'Except you were the one who directly accused Austin of being the murderer because of his anger over the affair,' Hope reminded her.

Summer shrugged. 'That was yesterday afternoon. We thought Carter had been electrocuted then. Now we know that he was drowned with the hoses. And now we also know that he had the book hidden in his cloak.'

'But if the murderer wanted the book from him, wouldn't they have simply taken it out of his cloak?'

'Not necessarily. They might not have known that Carter had the book in his possession. Or they might not have been able to reach it in the pool because of the water and the hoses. Or they might have had to make an unexpectedly quick getaway because you and Rosemarie came outside to look for Percy.'

Hope was thoughtful. 'There's no question that the book has value – but only to the right person. Plus, that person needs to translate it from Latin.'

'Which is difficult but not impossible,' Summer responded. 'With enough time and energy and patience, anybody could translate it eventually using a combination of a dictionary, grammar book, and the internet. But because Latin lacks the capitalization and punctuation that we're familiar with today in our modern languages, a novice would make a lot of mistakes along the way. And with this particular book, those mistakes would significantly alter its meaning. So I think that a person serious enough to want to steal the book either already has the necessary skills and training to translate it themselves, or they specifically know someone who is able to do it for them.'

'How many people in Asheville and the surrounding area can that include?'

'Perhaps a professor at the university who teaches classical languages? Or someone like Dylan?'

'Speaking of Dylan,' Hope said, 'we need to keep our fingers crossed that his proficiency in Latin is even rustier than he claims and that he only understood a few words and phrases of what he read yesterday. It was precarious enough with the mermaid tears and crow eyes. Imagine if he were able to study the book more thoroughly. Or if he got his hands on the other volume, which is the one that contains all of the incantations and . . .'

She sat bolt upright. 'Good God. I just remembered. Last night, as I was drifting off to sleep, Dylan told me that he knew it was the first volume. He saw it on the title page. And then he asked me if there was a second volume.'

Hope and Summer stared at each other, both coming to the same alarming realization.

'What if this book' – Hope's grip on Volume I tightened – 'wasn't the only one that Carter took?'

Summer swallowed hard. 'What if he also stole Volume II?'

SIXTEEN

Depositing their empty coffee mugs next to their empty wine glasses from the previous evening, Hope and Summer hurried from the patio to the flagstone path around the house and toward the driveway. They didn't worry about leaving Megan behind on the lounger. Between Morris and Gram, Megan was in the best hands possible. In Hope's hands was the book, held in an iron clasp. After spending the night outside in the fresh air, the book was no longer damp from its swim in the retention pool, and the former mildew smell was now almost imperceptible. But Hope was far less concerned with the spread of the foxing on the pages or the leather peeling from the cover than whether the book's companion remained amongst the rest of the brownstone's library in the study.

The sisters drove as fast as safety allowed. It was relatively early, so the traffic heading into the historic district was thin. When they reached their block, they looked down the row of buildings expectantly.

'Can you tell whether the power is still off?' Summer asked.

'No. The streetlamps are dark, except that's normal at this hour of the morning. The windows are also dark, but it's bright enough outside that we might not be able to see any lights on regardless.'

They parked the car in its usual spot in the alley behind their property. As they walked along the sidewalk toward their brownstone, they studied the Larsons'.

'The windows are dark there, too,' Summer observed. 'No sign at all of Miranda and Paul. Or their contractor.'

'I can't imagine that the contractor or construction crew would be allowed to come back here for at least the next day or two after what happened,' Hope remarked, 'both from a safety and an investigative standpoint.'

'If I were on that crew, and I heard that there had been a murder on the site, I wouldn't ever return.'

'Fair enough. But unless the Larsons tell them, I'm not sure that the crew will specifically hear about the murder.'

'Why do you say that?'

'Because the tape is gone. Take a look.'

Summer followed Hope's gesture toward the side lawn. Morris's conversation with the police chief had indeed been successful, and the chief's order had apparently been acted on without delay. Not one band of yellow crime scene tape remained visible. The retention pool was still there, as were the rubber hoses, which were now even more tangled than before, no doubt as a result of the police extricating the body from the water.

The sisters stood for a moment on the edge of the sidewalk, gazing contemplatively at the place where Carter had died.

'We didn't know him at all,' Hope said, 'but I still feel as though we should pay our respects somehow.'

Summer nodded in agreement. 'Thief or not, he didn't deserve to lose his life in that pool.'

'It was so cruel and so—'

She was interrupted by the rustling of vegetation. Turning toward the noise, Hope was startled to see a man on the side of their brownstone, pushing through the boxwoods along the wall with a sack of tools slung over his shoulder.

'Who is that!' Summer exclaimed.

The man was wearing a white T-shirt stained with dark streaks of paint or grease. Beneath an equally soiled baseball cap, his hair hung limply to his shoulders. It seemed to be a safe assumption that he was not a member of law enforcement.

'Hello!' Summer called to him, more inquisitorial than friendly. 'What are you doing at our house?'

He looked at the sisters with little expression. Then he looked down at a sheet of paper that he was holding. 'Henkin?'

'Huh?' Summer said.

'Henkin?' the man repeated. When he didn't receive a reply, he studied the sheet more closely. 'No, it's Henshaw. Are you Henshaw?'

Hope and Summer exchanged a glance.

'Which Henshaw?' Hope asked.

Once again, the man looked at the sheet. 'I don't know. There's only a first initial. I can't make it out. It might be an *M*. Whoever

answered the call and took down the instructions in the office
wrote too fast.'

'What call and instructions?' Summer said.

'The call and instructions for the job.' There was a hint of
annoyance in his tone, as though the answer should have been
obvious to them.

'What job?' Summer pressed him.

Now there was distinct annoyance. 'To seal up the door in this
wall.'

Hope and Summer exchanged another glance. Morris –
possibly in conjunction with Dylan – had evidently determined
that regardless of any opinion from the Baileys to the contrary,
the potato-coal chute was too great of a safety hazard and a
security risk and could no longer be allowed to remain accessible
from the outside.

'Gram is not going to be pleased,' Hope remarked to her
sister.

Summer shook her head. 'She explicitly didn't agree to
Morris's suggestion last night. She was still undecided.'

'I was told that this was a rush job.' The man waved the sheet
of paper at them. 'It had to be completed first thing this morning.
There was an emergency.' He frowned at the short metal door
set low in the wall. 'What kind of an emergency is it anyway?
Have you got rats coming in?'

'Something like that,' Summer muttered.

When no further response was forthcoming, the man grew
increasingly impatient. 'So do you want me to continue or not?
Seal it up, yes or no? I've got a full schedule today, and I need
to keep moving.'

There was a pause. Hope shrugged at Summer, uncertain how
to answer. Summer shrugged back at her.

'Yes,' Hope told the man at last. 'Go ahead with the job. Thank
you.'

His reply was limited to a grunt that clearly indicated his
irritation at having been stopped in the first place. He turned
back toward the wall and began to push through the boxwoods
once more. When he had found a position that seemed to suit
him, he dropped his sack of tools on the ground and crouched
down in front of the door to commence his work.

Watching him, Hope said to Summer, 'I think he's proven you wrong.'

'How so?' she asked in surprise.

'Well, it hardly matters now, considering that Megan is no longer sleeping in the study and the door is in the process of being shut permanently, but you told Megan yesterday that with the boxwoods pressed up so tightly against the wall due to the pool and the hoses, the Hermit wouldn't be able to pry open the door and climb down the chute to the cellar. Although it required some shoving and breaking of branches, that man with his tools has been able to both get to the door and open it without substantial difficulty.'

'Not only has he proven me wrong,' Summer admitted grudgingly, 'he's proven the Henshaws right. If the potato-coal chute can be reached with so little effort – even when the boxwoods are blocking the way – then we're much better off with it sealed.'

Hope nodded in agreement.

'And while we're on the subject of proving people right or wrong,' Summer continued, 'that man has also proven Miranda right. Looking at him from here, you can see someone moving along the side of the brownstone, but from a greater distance, if he was wearing a big cloak and there's drizzle and mist, it's easy to understand why Miranda didn't recognize the figure as Carter.'

Hope nodded again. Then she looked at the Larsons' brownstone. 'I still can't tell if they have power or not.'

'Me, either. We'd better check ours.'

'And check on the other book.'

They shared a sigh and headed toward the front door of the boutique. Unlocking it, they found the brownstone still without electricity.

'There isn't much point in opening for business when the lights aren't working,' Summer remarked. 'Not unless we want our customers to stumble into everything and possibly hurt themselves. Do you have any appointments scheduled for today?'

'None. We can use candles and lanterns later on if necessary, but let's at least wait until noon. That was the time estimate the electric company gave to Megan.'

'Good plan.'

The sisters lingered in the middle of the shop, neither one

moving toward the interior of the brownstone. They weren't eager to go to the study, apprehensive of what they would find – or not find.

'Standing in this spot,' Hope mused, 'makes me think of Gina.'

'Gina?' Summer gave a little snort. 'How does it make you think of her? She didn't leave any of her fancy shopping bags behind again, did she?'

'No, it's more serious than that.'

Summer looked at her curiously.

'When Gina was here yesterday during the tea,' Hope explained, 'she was standing right about where we are now, and her gaze was repeatedly focused on the doorway at the rear of the shop. She asked about it several times and continued to step toward it. She was really interested in seeing the rest of the brownstone.'

'You think that she knows about the study?'

'Without question. As we discussed earlier on the patio, due to Rosemarie's chattiness, everybody could know about the study. But in Gina's case, Rosemarie told her about it directly in front of me, including specifically mentioning *old books in the library*. And I had the impression that it wasn't the first time Gina had heard of it, because she didn't ask any questions; she just kept inching toward the door.'

'But you didn't let her go through it, did you?'

'Of course not. There were too many ladies here for the tea, and the occupants of the attic were growing increasingly restless. Then Austin burst in with his tirade, and that took everyone's attention. At some point after Austin's arrival but before the lights went out completely, Gina disappeared. I didn't see her leave. Rosemarie said that she didn't, either. Now it occurs to me that maybe Gina didn't actually leave. Maybe while we were all distracted by Austin, she went through the door on her own.'

'And presumably into the study?'

'I don't know. I suppose it doesn't really matter after the fact. Carter was the one who took the book, not Gina.'

Summer considered for a moment. 'No, I don't think Gina went through the door and into the study. She's certainly capable of doing it. She isn't an honest, upstanding person who wouldn't enter someone's home without their permission. She's an avaricious charlatan who pretends to talk to the dead for money. But if Gina had gone into the rest of the brownstone, Megan would have noticed her come back out. Unlike us, Megan stayed in the boutique the entire time, and she never mentioned seeing Gina later.'

'That's true. I'm glad you pointed that out. I feel better somehow.'

'Enjoy it while it lasts, because what I'm going to point out next will make you feel worse. If Gina left the boutique between Austin's arrival and the power outage, then she could have killed Carter.'

Hope stared at her.

'Don't look so shocked,' Summer said. 'It's possible, isn't it?' She didn't wait for an answer. 'I know you'll think that I'm accusing Gina simply because I don't like her.'

'You don't like that Nate expressed an interest in attending one of her séances,' Hope responded.

Summer grimaced. 'He better not attend one of her séances. Would you be happy if Dylan attended one of *Madam Gina*'s séances?'

She sidestepped the question. 'Let's get back to Carter. Yes, from a timing perspective, it's technically possible that Gina could have killed him. But why would she do that? Because they both lived on Bent Mountain? Because they were in the same book group? What motive could she have?'

'Maybe Gina was having an affair with Carter,' Summer proposed.

'I thought the affair was with Jill.'

'Maybe or maybe not. As I said on the patio, we only have Austin's word for it. It could have been Gina instead of Jill. We know from Miranda that Carter was always running after Gina, and constantly calling her, and skulking around her house at odd hours. He could have been stalking her.'

Hope's expression was doubtful.

'Carter might have followed Gina to our brownstone,' Summer hypothesized. 'Don't forget, Miranda became less surprised that Carter was there after learning that Gina had also been there. So, Gina got tired of Carter tracking her movements, she confronted him, they had an altercation, and he ended up dead.'

The doubt grew. 'Gina – in her flawless linen sheath and sparkling jewels – fought Carter on the side lawn, pushed him into the retention pool, and then took the chance of damaging her expensive designer heels in the dirty drainage water by holding a hose or two on top of him until he drowned?'

For a moment, it appeared that Summer wanted to argue. Then she frowned instead. 'You're probably right. Gina wouldn't risk ruining her shoes.'

Hope nodded. 'It's a grotesque way to explain a person's innocence. In her case, however, it seems pretty accurate.'

Summer frowned some more. 'But if we set the shoes aside, Gina is by far the best suspect.'

'She is? How so?'

'Because of the book. If the theory is that somebody killed Carter because of the book, who would be the most interested in it? Gina, naturally. That could be the reason she was so eager to see the study. She may have wanted to steal the book the same as Carter.'

Hope didn't immediately respond.

'You said before that to the right person,' Summer continued, 'the book is valuable. And Gina could very well imagine herself to be one of those right people. She's clearly trying to pass herself off as a spiritualist with magical abilities. An old book dealing with the occult is perfect for her pretensions.'

'Except the book is in Latin,' Hope countered. 'Do you honestly believe that Gina is a Latin scholar?'

'She may not have known that it was in Latin. Or she may have thought that Latin was as reasonably straightforward to translate as French or Italian. Or she may have planned on selling the book to someone. That could be another way in which Gina has been accumulating her wealth. Aside from her fraudulent séances, maybe she also deals in stolen art and antiques. There is a lot of money in the rare book trade.'

Hope shook her head at her sister. 'Don't you think that's a bit too much conjecture?'

'I don't think that you're conjecturing enough,' Summer returned.

'We don't have any evidence for what you're saying. It's all speculation.'

'No, it's not. You agreed only a minute ago that from a timing perspective, Gina could have killed Carter.'

'Yes, but if we start accusing people of murder based solely on incidental timing, then we might as well accuse Paul Larson next.'

'Why Paul?' Summer asked with instant interest.

'He appeared on the side lawn just after Rosemarie and I discovered Carter's body. He could have already been there, and Rosemarie and I just didn't see him. So – the same as with Gina – it's technically possible that Paul could be guilty of murder. But he obviously isn't guilty.'

'How can you be sure?' Summer rejoined.

'For starters, Paul didn't even know Carter. He had never met him.'

'Paul *claims* that he didn't know Carter and had never met him. Miranda thought that Paul did meet Carter at the get-together at Gina's house.'

'Either way,' Hope said, 'it's more speculation. But here's something that isn't speculation: when Paul appeared on the side lawn, he was carrying Percy. I specifically noticed that Percy's coat was clean and dry, and he hadn't been swimming in the pool that day. I would have noticed at the same time if Paul's shirt or shoes were wet, which they weren't. It's hard to imagine that whoever killed Carter didn't get at least somewhat splashed with water. You thought so, too, when you accused Austin of being the murderer and said that his profuse sweating was actually water from the pool and fighting with Carter.'

Summer couldn't dispute that.

'Plus,' Hope went on, 'when Paul saw Carter lying in the pool, he was seriously startled.' She added without pausing, 'I know you're going to contend that it could have been an act, but if it was, then it was really convincing. Paul stared at the body for a long while. I'm inclined to think that someone who is guilty of murder would look away sooner, perhaps even immediately. Although, once again, that's purely speculation.'

Summer was thoughtful. 'I don't suppose that there's any reason for Paul to have killed Carter.'

'Not unless Miranda was the one having an affair with him, and Paul found out about it. Miranda is certainly enamored with the idea of living on Bent Mountain. I don't know if Carter's house is as new and fancy as Gina's, but it probably has some sort of a nice view. Maybe Miranda was hoping to move in with Carter up there.'

'Miranda cheat on Paul and leave him?' Summer blinked at her in disbelief. 'Paul is the nicest guy in the world. Nobody would cheat on Paul and leave him.'

Hope replied with a cynical smile. 'That settles it. The *nicest guy in the world* – and our trusted neighbor – will turn out to be the murderer.'

SEVENTEEN

'I don't see it.'

'I don't, either.'

'Maybe we should start from the beginning,' Summer proposed, 'and do the whole thing over again.'

Hope climbed down from the stepladder that she had been standing on and seated herself on a metal rung. 'We've searched through this room for more than an hour. We've combed every corner, every shelf, every potential nook and cranny. We've examined the top of the bookcases, between the bookcases, and behind the bookcases. We've checked under the sofa, in all the drawers of the desk, even inside the bends of the globe stand, which couldn't possibly hold anything. There is nowhere left to look.'

'If the power were on and there was more light . . .'

'Inadequate lighting isn't our issue. We have two lanterns, plus that high beam flashlight you're holding, which is singlehandedly brighter than all of the electric lamps in here combined. We have to face the truth.'

Summer switched off the flashlight and sank into one of the scuffed leather armchairs with bronze nail heads. 'And the truth is that Volume II is gone.'

'Volume II is gone,' Hope echoed.

'On the positive side,' Summer said, not sounding particularly positive, 'at least we've recovered Volume I.'

They turned toward the book that Hope had carefully set on the blotter of the barrister desk when they had first entered the study.

'After what's happened,' Summer continued, 'I would say that it's too risky to leave the book in here in the future, but now that the potato-coal chute has been sealed up, it's probably safe.'

Hope shook her head. 'It isn't safe. Even though the cellar will no longer be a potential entry point into the room, the boutique still is. It never occurred to me until we discussed how Gina might have slipped from the shop into the rest of the brownstone unnoticed, but now I realize that anybody who is sufficiently motivated can get to the study by distracting us or waiting for our backs to be turned long enough to slink inside.'

'But we don't want to put a deadbolt on every door in the place and keep locking and unlocking them all day long to go from one room to another!'

'Definitely not. So in the alternative, we have to remove everything from the library that could generate too much interest and be too tempting to a prospective thief. Volume I is at the top of the list, obviously, and this weekend, we'll go through the other books and related matter to pull out any item that might be a cause for concern or would provide information that shouldn't be generally disseminated.'

'That's an excellent idea,' Summer agreed. 'If we had done it sooner, we wouldn't be in this mess now.'

'We didn't have any reason to do it sooner. Gram let the books sit in plain view on these shelves for decades, and not a single one was ever taken. During all the time that the conspiracy theorists had dinner here – and I remember some of them spending the night in the guest rooms, too – nothing was stolen or even borrowed temporarily without permission. No nosey friend or inquisitive workman walked away with anything over the years, either.'

'It's a sign that people's moral code used to be higher, or it's an unusual piece of bad luck.' Summer frowned at the ceiling. 'Aren't the occupants of the attic supposed to warn us about these things? They can thump and bump, whisper and whimper, slam doors and play with the lights at their whim, but they can't alert us that our books – books on the occult that certainly include information relating to them – are being filched?'

Hope raised an eyebrow at her. 'Leaving Volume I in here in the future isn't half as risky as what you just said about the spirits.'

Summer grumbled an acknowledgement, followed by a half-hearted apology toward the ceiling.

There was a pause as the sisters listened. No sound came from above them.

'I have the feeling that the spirits did try to warn us,' Hope said after a moment, her voice low. 'Both about the books and what would happen to Carter. They were restless in the night when Carter was creeping up from the cellar into the study. Megan heard them, too. But we just ignored it, assuming that it was no more than their usual midnight activities. Then came the thuds and the flickering lights while we were discussing the retention pool before the tea started yesterday afternoon. I thought that it was a little odd, because I mistakenly connected it to Rosemarie and Percy. Now I understand that it was actually about poor Carter and the pool. And there were more noises and issues with the lights later on, but I can't recall exactly what we were saying or doing at each specific time. I do remember that the spirits didn't like our mention of' – she dropped her voice further – 'séances, especially ones related to Gina.'

'I agree with them on that,' Summer muttered, picking at one of the bronze nail heads on her chair.

Hope nodded.

'Instead of all the vague hints and signals that we have to decipher as though we're supernatural code breakers,' Summer continued in complaint, 'it would be nice if the spirits could be a little more precise and a little less ambiguous with their messages.'

'They would probably contend that their messages are perfectly clear, and it's our fault for not paying closer attention to them,' Hope replied. 'In any event, there's no question that they're continually paying attention to what's happening in and around the brownstone, which is why I suggest that we put Volume I, hopefully Volume II, and everything else of import in the attic with them for safekeeping.'

It was Summer's turn to raise an eyebrow. 'You want the spirits to guard the books?'

'I'm open to a different plan if you have one. But what other good option is there? It's not as though we can use a bank safety deposit box in this situation. If an emergency suddenly arises and we need to consult one of the books, we would have to wait until a weekday – but not a holiday – during standard business hours to access it.'

'The spirits aren't always so eager and willing for us to access the attic, either,' Summer reminded her.

'But that typically only lasts a short while,' she said. 'If there was a truly serious situation, I'm sure they wouldn't obstruct us and would want to help as much as they could. They always have in the past. And in the attic, the books are guaranteed to be protected from all earthly threats.'

'It's hard to argue with the last part,' Summer admitted. 'Fine, we'll let the spirits look after the books, assuming that we manage to regain possession of Volume II. Do you think that Carter took it, as well?'

Hope deliberated. 'He must have. No other scenario really makes sense. My guess is that Carter stole Volume II from the study first, although he may not have known at the time that the book was part of a set. After taking it, he crept back down into the cellar and out through the potato-coal chute. That was during the night. The next day, Carter did the same thing, taking Volume I instead, which is why he had that – but not the other book – hidden in his cloak when he died.'

Summer frowned and started to pick at the bronze nail head again. 'I understand that Carter could have come into the brown-stone undetected during the night, but wouldn't someone have noticed him during the day? Miranda and Paul saw him the previous morning along the side wall, albeit without recognizing him. And Megan saw him at the corner.'

'Carter might have still been trying to figure out how to get inside then. Maybe he wasn't entirely sure about the metal door and the potato-coal chute, and that's why he was lingering around the property and was spotted by everyone in the process. But once he had succeeded through the cellar the first time, it must have been a lot easier and faster for him the second go-around. He knew exactly what to do when and where. It probably all went so swiftly that unless somebody was looking at the exact moment he approached the door in the wall, he wouldn't have been noticed regardless of whether it was night or day.'

'He was lucky that none of us were in the study at that hour.'

'We were working in the boutique, as we always do. It would have been easy for him to check that with a quick glance through the front door or window.'

'It seems odd,' Summer mused, 'that Carter didn't take both of the books at the same time. Going into the study twice – even if he checked that we were in the boutique – only increased the likelihood that he would be caught.'

'I've been puzzling over that, too,' Hope said. 'It makes me wonder if the books weren't actually for Carter. He might have been stealing them for someone else, and either that person didn't know there were two books until after Carter came back with the one labelled Volume II, or the person didn't explain it clearly to Carter from the outset. Perhaps Carter didn't want to take the books at all. That could be another explanation for why he was pacing on the sidewalk when Megan saw him. He might have been debating with himself whether to go into the shop and tell us what somebody wanted him to do.'

'But who? And how would they get Carter to steal for them?'

Hope could only shake her head. 'As to who, it might be anyone. As to how, maybe Carter was bribed or promised something in exchange for the books. Or perhaps he was threatened that whatever affair he was having would be revealed. It's difficult to even venture a guess beyond that, because aside from the fact that Carter lived on Bent Mountain and was a member of a local book group, we have so little information about him.'

'Then we need to get more information about him!' Summer exclaimed. 'Right away, before the police start digging too much. The more they dig, the less we'll be able to find out ourselves. And if we don't find out something soon, then we won't have any reasonable chance of getting our book back—'

'Didn't you get your book back?'

Both Hope and Summer jumped at the unexpected voice, and they spun toward it. Detective Nate – in his customary work attire of tan slacks and a white button-down shirt – was standing just inside the hall at the entrance to the study. The lanterns cast him in a creamy ball of light. The sisters exchanged an apprehensive look. When had Nate arrived, and how much of their conversation had he heard?

He stepped into the doorway of the room. 'I was under the impression that your book had been returned to you last night. Dylan told me that he handed it to you personally at Morris's house.'

'Yes,' Summer confirmed. 'Dylan gave us the book you found in Carter's cloak.' She ended the sentence shrewdly, implicitly inquiring whether Nate was aware of a book that hadn't been found in Carter's cloak.

'Good. I'm glad to hear it,' he said. 'Dylan and I were in agreement that you would probably want the book back as soon as possible.' Nate smiled slightly. 'Before too many curious eyes asked too many curious questions.'

Hope and Summer exchanged another look, this one of considerable relief. Nate's smile didn't bother them. They were far too pleased by the rest of his response, which indicated that he hadn't been in the hall for long, and he had caught no more than a few words. He didn't know about the second book.

Summer's smile in return was warm, and she motioned toward the other armchairs. 'Won't you come in and take a seat, Nate?'

He didn't hesitate in accepting the offer. Hope restrained a laugh as he selected the chair that had the best view of Summer. With her peaches-and-cream complexion and wide, pouty mouth, Summer was always pretty, but in the glow of the lanterns, she had the delicate appearance of porcelain. Nate gazed at her admiringly.

'Have you received any news regarding the electricity?' Summer asked him. 'Did you happen to notice whether our neighbors had power when you came in?'

'The entire block is still out,' he answered. 'But the latest official update is that the electric company should have the problem resolved by mid-afternoon.'

Summer winked at her sister. 'Poor Miranda. That's probably not early enough to save the contents of her freezer.'

Hope chuckled.

'I hope you don't mind that I came into the brownstone uninvited,' Nate said. 'I was in the boutique, but you weren't there, obviously. So I followed the light until I found you back here.'

'Of course we don't mind. Isn't that right, Hope?' Summer didn't wait for her to reply. 'And we hope that you don't mind about the removal of the crime scene tape from the side lawn. It was Morris's doing. He got a bit anxious and overprotective. It was awfully sweet of him to worry about us so much, but we don't want you to have any trouble with the police chief because of it.'

'There's no trouble.' Nate gave a casual shrug. 'It's just tape.

I learned a long time ago not to argue with whatever my bosses decide.'

Summer's mood improved even more, and she leaned toward Nate attentively. He responded in kind. With the dim lighting, the room was taking on an intimate air. Hope decided that it was time for her departure.

'Sitting on the stepladder has worsened the crick in my neck from this morning,' she said, rising from the metal rung. 'I need to walk around to stretch my shoulders and back. I'll check on the boutique, in case anybody else has wandered in during our absence.'

Although Summer murmured a couple of sympathetic words regarding the crick, she made no attempt to stop her sister. Neither did Nate. They were too engaged in each other. As Hope walked toward the doorway, she passed by the barrister desk and picked up the book from the blotter. She didn't plan on bringing it to the attic immediately, but she had no intention of leaving it behind, either. They were already missing one book. She wasn't going to take the chance that Volume I would disappear a second time.

Exiting the study, Hope quietly pulled the door closed behind her. She instantly wished that she had taken one of the lanterns, because the hall was a murky tunnel. She moved with slow steps and a cautious hand on the wall until the light from the windows in the foyer illuminated her way. The boutique was her first stop, and she promptly locked the front door to prevent any additional surprise visitors, welcome or unwelcome. Then Hope – with a candle to supplement the windows – went upstairs. After tucking the book between the spare pillows in the linen closet, she headed to the shower. The water was only lukewarm, but it still felt good, and the crick in her neck eased.

When she emerged from the bathroom, she found Summer sitting with both lanterns on the edge of the stairs, waiting for her.

'What's the verdict?' Hope asked, already knowing that the answer was a favorable one from the happy blush in her sister's cheeks.

'Nate and I have a date for Saturday night.'

'Brilliant.'

'I tried to find out about the case,' Summer went on. 'Especially about Carter, because we need more information on him. But it was difficult. Nate is so tight-lipped when it comes to his work.'

Hope smiled. 'Am I correct in assuming that you found a way to loosen the dear detective's lips?'

Summer's nose twitched. 'I mentioned to him that if the weather is good on Saturday evening, we should go for a drive to watch the stars and the fireflies.'

The smile grew. 'Stars and fireflies. Very romantic.'

The nose twitched again. 'I suggested that the mountains would be the best place, because it's much darker up there than in the city.'

'Much darker,' Hope concurred.

'I'm not sure exactly how the subject came up, but we agreed that Bent Mountain has particularly nice views.'

Hope's smile became a grin.

'And then,' Summer said, her nose twitching once more, 'I got Carter Dalton's home address.'

EIGHTEEN

B ent Mountain was indeed bent. The road twisted and curled, up sharp inclines and around winding curves. It snaked through dense forest and emerged abruptly at the tip of a steep precipice, after which a hairpin turn brought it back to the forest. The road climbed ever higher, spiraling upward and shrinking in width until it became no more than a narrow single lane with a sheer rock face on one side and the vertical drop off a cliff on the other.

'What do we do if a vehicle approaches?' Summer asked.

'Pray that it doesn't,' Hope replied, 'because there's no room for us – or them – to pull over and let the other pass.'

Summer gave a little whimper. 'I'm really glad that you're the one driving, because I couldn't do it.'

Hope glanced at her in surprise. Summer was normally a confident and competent driver. She found her sister a spring-apple shade of green.

'All the twists and turns are getting to you, eh?'

Summer nodded. 'The leftovers from the snack platters that I ate before we left the brownstone aren't sitting well.'

'Be grateful that you only had some crackers with a half of a pear and nothing more daring.'

She nodded again and added another whimper.

'I'd stop so that your equilibrium can readjust itself,' Hope said, 'but there's nowhere to go except forward right now. We passed a dirt driveway – at least I think it was a driveway – a short while ago. The next one that I see, I'll pull in and give you a rest.'

'No, it would be better if you kept going. There's no sense in stopping and starting. It'll only help for a minute, and then the motion sickness will kick in again. Let's just get to Carter's house. I'll have a long break there.' There was a brief pause, and then Summer added, 'I can promise you one thing.'

'And that is?'

'I will *not* under any circumstances be coming to Bent Mountain for my date with Nate on Saturday evening.'

Hope laughed. 'The queasiness would probably interfere with the enjoyment of the stars and the fireflies.'

At that moment, they reached a particularly tight set of bends in the road.

'They sure picked an appropriate name for this place,' Summer muttered, clutching her stomach with both hands.

'I was thinking about that myself. Or whether there was at one time a family named Bent who owned the land up here.'

'That could be, too. I always assumed that Poor Mountain was based on a family surname, but then I read that there used to be a poorhouse on the mountain many years ago. Hopefully it was located at the base rather than the tip, because forcing the ill and the indigent to climb to the top of the mountain for food and shelter is really taking it a step too far, no pun intended.'

Hope slammed on the brakes.

'Oh why,' Summer moaned, clutching her stomach even harder. 'Why did you have to stop so suddenly?'

'Because of that.' Hope pointed through the open window.

On their left side was a gravel driveway with a tarnished aluminum mailbox set just off the road. Both the mailbox and the equally tarnished metal post on which it sat had numerous dents and scratches, no doubt from vehicle collisions in the darkness of the night. Reflective silver lettering had been attached to the door of the mailbox. The last letter was missing and several others were beginning to peel off, but they were still legible enough for Hope and Summer: *C Dalto*.

'Carter Dalton!' Summer exclaimed.

'We were lucky to spot it,' Hope said, 'because the navigation system is currently showing only wilderness and no homesites around us. The address you coaxed out of Nate got us to the correct main road, but up on some of these mountains, it's nearly impossible to find an exact house number if you haven't been to the place before and aren't already familiar with its location.'

'Good,' Summer declared in a tone of triumph. 'Then there's a chance that we're here before anybody else.'

Hope turned into the driveway and started to travel down it

slowly. Going fast – or even at a moderate speed – wasn't an option. The driveway was only marginally wider than the car, and its gravel hadn't been replenished in a long time. It was a minefield of sunken holes and uneven ruts and heavily eroded gullies, many of which were concealed by a thick layer of fallen leaves and other vegetative debris.

As they bumped along, Summer gulped. 'This is almost as bad as the climb up the mountain.'

'It can't be much farther,' Hope told her, trying to sound optimistic, although in actuality, she had no idea what the distance might be. 'The house will appear at any second.'

'I don't care how spectacular anyone's house is,' Summer remarked. 'No view could possibly be so magnificent as to justify suffering through this drive twice every day, first out and then back in. And we're doing it in perfect weather right now. Can you imagine what it would be like in a downpour or with snow and ice covering the road?'

'It wouldn't be fun,' Hope agreed. 'But I'm starting to wonder whether there will be any view at all.'

'What do you mean?'

'Well, take a look around us. It's almost entirely pine. Old-growth eastern white pine, to be specific. They're mature trees and probably at least a hundred years old, maybe substantially more. They wouldn't survive for that long with the wind and the storms on the exposed side of a mountain. I'm not entirely sure, because all the curves and switchbacks have muddled my sense of direction, but I think that we're in the interior of the woods rather than along the edge of them.'

Summer leaned forward in her seat for a better look through the windshield. 'You're right. I don't see an end to the pine stands in any direction. There's blue sky above us but no blue sky ahead of us or to either side. Although I believe' – she squinted slightly – 'that there might be a clearing coming up . . .'

Her eyes hadn't deceived her. After another few rocky jolts along the driveway, followed by one large hole that was deep enough to potentially break either an axle or a leg depending on which had the ill-fortune to fall into it, the pines parted to reveal a modest clearing. The clearing was divided into three unequal parts. The smallest area – on the left – was occupied by a fenced vegetable garden. The intermediate-sized area – on the right – consisted of a wildflower meadow filled with towering goldenrod in stunning full bloom. And the largest area in the middle held a chic two-story log cabin that had more skylights than roof and a wrap-around porch on both the ground and the upper floor.

'Wow!' was the sisters' joint reaction.

Hope pulled the car on to the thin border of wilted grass and clover that lay at the front of the cabin, and for a minute, neither she nor Summer spoke, too surprised – and impressed – by what they saw.

'It's lovely. And it's designed to fit so beautifully into the surrounding forest,' Summer said. 'I didn't think that Carter lived in a one-room hut with a pit privy behind it, but I also didn't expect this. Consider how long it must have taken and what it must have cost to bring all that sawn timber up here.'

'Consider also how isolated it is,' Hope added. 'Either you really want to live in the midst of nature, or—'

'Or you really want to get away from the rest of the world,' Summer finished for her.

After sitting for another minute in silent admiration of the situation of the cabin, they climbed out of the car, closing the doors softly behind them, as though any sharp noise between the intermittent birdsong and the light hum of the wind through the upper pine branches would irreparably damage the peace of the place.

'Do we assume that it's all right to take a look around?' Summer asked, with a touch of uneasiness.

Hope shared her sister's hesitancy. There hadn't been a gate blocking the entrance to the driveway or any visible *No Trespassing* signs along the way, but it was nonetheless wise to be cautious before wandering about rural North Carolina. Plenty of people in the mountains were armed – some quite heavily – and many did not take kindly to seeing strangers step on to their property, even harmless strangers with innocent intentions.

'There isn't a vehicle,' Hope observed. 'And nobody has appeared at the front door or on the porches—'

'With either a warm welcome or a double-barreled shotgun aimed at us,' Summer interjected.

'Happily not, with regard to the latter. If there was a person in the cabin, they would have surely heard the car and come outside by now to find out who we are and what we want. It would be impossible to live up here for even a little while and not become attuned to which sounds are natural and which are man-made.'

Summer nodded. 'So we're safe and alone. Probably.'

'Probably,' Hope concurred. 'But we should keep an eye out just in case. Somebody could be in the woods or have driven away on an errand and return at any time. They might not be thrilled to discover us here.'

'Then we won't dawdle. Better to learn what we can and make a clean exit. Plus, the police will show up eventually. I'm not eager to have Nate discover us here, either. He'll think that we're sniffing around.'

'We are sniffing around.'

'Yes, except Nate doesn't need to know that.'

Hope smiled. 'Because it might interfere with the romantic effect of the stars and the fireflies?'

'Precisely. Speaking of insects, before we go to the cabin, let's take a quick peek at that wildflower meadow to the right. I can see a million bumblebees working busily on the goldenrod. There could be some other interesting native plants in the patch. As you know, I'm always on the hunt for a rare or unusual variety.'

Before they had taken even half a dozen steps in the direction of the meadow, Summer was already identifying and critiquing species.

'In another week or two, those blue asters will open. And over there is a healthy clump of mountain mint. That butterfly weed is brown and has gone dormant now, but it appears to have had a lot of nice seed heads earlier in the season. This area must have had some heavy rain recently, because the sage is flopping. It doesn't have enough tall neighbors for proper support. I wish that the drive up here wasn't such a nightmare, because I would love to see those chrysanthemums when they explode in color. If you look over in that corner' – Summer pointed for Hope's benefit – 'the first buds are just beginning to—'

She broke off so abruptly that Hope glanced around hurriedly, thinking that her sister had spotted somebody approaching them. But there was no one in sight.

Summer started to speak again slowly and once more directed Hope's attention to the chrysanthemums in the corner. 'That apricot cultivar with the red-tipped petals was only introduced to the public a year or two ago, and it certainly isn't native to the region. Chrysanthemums aren't native to North America at all.'

Hope shook her head, not understanding why that had startled Summer to such a degree.

'Which means,' she explained, 'that the specimen was planted here recently and selected purposefully even though it won't survive long-term.'

Hope shook her head again, still not understanding the import.

'And next to it are more chrysanthemums,' Summer continued. 'Although attractive, they're not horticulturally noteworthy. They're readily available for purchase everywhere. Except take a look at the buds. A few have opened on the lower sunny side. Do you see the color?'

'They're white.'

Summer responded with a nod. 'To the average person standing in the nursery with a hundred different pots to choose from, they're simply pretty white flowers. But in this place, with an extremely unusual chrysanthemum next to them, and all of these other plants – flopping sage aside – that I now realize have been sited and managed with great care, it's clear that they aren't simply pretty white flowers. They have deliberate meaning. White chrysanthemums are a flower of grief and lamentation. In some East Asian and European countries, they're used at funerals and on graves.'

Hope looked at the white chrysanthemums, and the apricot chrysanthemums with the red-tipped petals, and the blooming goldenrod and the nearly blooming asters, and all at once, she understood. 'It isn't a wildflower meadow. It's a memorial garden.'

'Exactly.'

As she and Summer gazed contemplatively at the garden, Hope noticed a glint next to the flopping sage. The sunlight was evidently reflecting off something, but there were too many riotous stems and leaves blocking her view. Stepping forward, she lifted the plants gently out of the way, and a cloud of tiny dappled butterflies rose around her. They had apparently been feasting on the nectar in the sage's azure flowers. There was another glint, and this time, Hope saw where it came from.

Two oval stones rested flat on the ground with their curved edges touching. Both were polished quartzite and approximately two feet at their widest point. One was an ivory shade and slightly larger. The other was rose colored and slightly smaller. Each was inscribed with a name. The ivory read: *Kay Douglass Dalton.* The rose-colored read: *Bonnie Jean Dalton.* Nothing else was written on them. There were no dates, or religious symbols, or poignant sayings. They were stones of remembrance, not tombstones. Based on their spacing and location, it was clear that graves did not lie beneath them.

Summer – who hadn't stepped into the garden with Hope – asked, 'Did you discover something interesting?'

'Yes. We now know why the sage is flopping and doesn't have enough tall neighbors for proper support.'

'We do? Why?'

'Because the neighbors are short.' Hope lifted the sage further and motioned toward the ground.

Summer moved closer, and when she saw the stones, she gave a little cry. 'Oh!'

The sisters stood together, enveloped in a mass of dainty butterflies and fuzzy black-and-yellow bumblebees.

'I don't think,' Summer said after a long moment, 'that anything Austin told us was true.'

Hope looked at her questioningly.

'I don't think,' she went on, 'that Jill was having an affair with Carter. I don't think that Gina or Miranda was having an affair with Carter, either. I don't think that Carter was having an affair with anyone. I think that Carter was in mourning.'

'You're right,' a voice confirmed.

With a shared gasp, Hope and Summer whirled around in astonishment. There had been no approaching footsteps, or a shadow drawing near from either side, or even the slightest hint of a person being in the clearing with them. But a woman was now standing one short step away, next to the clump of mountain mint.

'You look so sad about Kay and Bonnie Jean,' the woman said. 'But there's no reason for it. Nor should you be sad about Carter. They're not lost or separated any more. They're all together now. It's as it should be.'

NINETEEN

'Peapod?'

'Um, yes, thank you.' Hope took a bulging, freshly picked peapod from the woven willow basket that the woman held toward her.

The woman offered the basket to Summer next, but Summer just stared at it, having yet to recover from the shock of her appearing without any sort of warning behind them in the clearing.

'The peas have been excellent this year,' the woman told them. 'This is the second crop, and it's even better than the first, which was quite good. Typically, it's somewhat of a gamble whether the second sowing will mature before the autumn frost hits at this elevation, but the conditions have been ideal this month. Warm, but not blistering hot. Rain, but not so much as to keep the ground soggy. And lots of sun, although the last couple of days were a bit too gray and drab for my liking.'

'We didn't care for them, either,' Hope agreed politely. She didn't add that her and Summer's dislike of the last forty-eight hours was only slightly based on the gloomy weather. The majority was due to Carter drowning in the retention pool on their side lawn.

'I can see that you're debating whether to shell them,' the woman said to Hope. 'But shelling isn't necessary. They're snap peas, not sweet peas. The entire pod – even with the biggest, roundest peas inside – is edible.' And to prove the point, she promptly popped a trio of peapods into her mouth and crunched down on them with vigor.

Hope followed suit with her single pod. It was crisp and tender and tasted exactly like a peapod straight from the vine ought to. 'My compliments. That really is an excellent crop you have.'

The woman smiled with pleasure. 'Take another. Take a whole handful! You can bring an entire bag of them home with you. There's no shortage. The plants are bearing more than I could ever possibly eat myself.'

In response, Hope selected a modest number from the willow basket. They were genuinely good, but she didn't want to appear greedy, and it was a very odd situation. She was standing in the middle of a memorial garden talking to a woman who she didn't know while munching on her peapods, which presumably came from the fenced vegetable garden on the other side of Carter's log cabin.

Again, the woman offered the basket to Summer. 'I could see that *she*' – she indicated Hope – 'wasn't sure about the shelling. And I can see that *you* need to eat something to soothe your stomach. You're not as green as these peas, but you've definitely got a funny tint around the gills. I would guess that you're prone to motion sickness. Am I correct?'

'You're correct,' Summer admitted with some hesitation.

The woman nodded sympathetically. 'When I first moved to the mountain, it took me almost a year to get used to it. I was woozy and nauseous whenever I drove up or down, regardless of how short or far I went.'

Summer frowned at her. 'You lived here voluntarily for an entire year even though you were sick every time you got into a vehicle? Why on earth would you do that?'

'For the peas,' she answered. 'You can't get peas – or for that matter, most of the other veggies I grow – like this in the city, even at the farmers' market.'

There was a degree of truth to it, which the sisters couldn't dispute. The peas in the brownstone's little garden were never especially plentiful or flavorsome. And unless you were lucky to develop a relationship with a particular vendor, the produce at the farmers' market could be somewhat hit-or-miss. Summer's frown remained, however.

The woman nodded once more. 'I know it's hard to understand, but there's something special about this place. You can't quite put your finger on it. At first you think it's just like any other spot in the world, and then after a while you realize it's different. The air smells sweeter. The breeze feels silkier on your skin. Nature all around you is happier. And that makes you happier.'

It was impossible to argue with being happy.

'Although,' the woman continued after a moment in a more wistful tone, 'happiness can be fleeting.' She looked down at the remembrance stones that Hope had discovered next to the flopping sage, and she sighed. 'There used to be so much happiness here, and in an instant, it was all gone.'

'My condolences,' Hope said. She wasn't sure if it was the right thing to say, because she still didn't know who the woman was or what her relationship to those named on the stones might be, but she felt that something was required under the circumstances.

The woman must have noticed the uncertainty in Hope's tone, because she explained, 'We weren't family. We were neighbors. My house is only a short distance beyond the pines over there.' She pointed in the opposite corner of the clearing from where they were standing, and then she suddenly began to sway as if a strong gust had caught her unawares, even though there was no more than a hint of wind around them.

Hope moved toward her quickly, alarmed that she might fall over. 'Are you all right?' she asked.

Drawing a deep breath, the woman held it in concentration for several long seconds until she grew visibly steadier and her feet firmed beneath her. 'It's kind of you to be concerned, but I'm fine now. It happens to me on occasion. Along with the sweeter air and the silkier breeze, the sun is also stronger at this elevation. It's certainly beneficial for the peas, but it isn't as beneficial for me. I may have conquered the motion sickness, but the vertigo will unfortunately remain with me until the end of my days.'

The woman took another long breath, and then she gave a little laugh. 'It usually passes quickly enough, as it did just then. But there was one sweltering day this past July when Carter found me in the middle of the vegetable garden spinning like a top. I tumbled straight on to my face, splat in the patty pan squash.' She laughed harder and pulled the sun-bleached straw hat that she was wearing lower on her head. 'The hat helps somewhat, but a comfortable seat in the shade would be better. Will you join me?'

Waving for them to follow, she turned and headed toward the log cabin. Hope and Summer didn't need to deliberate, and they immediately hurried after her. They no longer needed to worry about someone appearing at the front door or on the porches with a double-barreled shotgun aimed at them. They were now in the company of a neighbor who had apparently been close enough to the Dalton family to tend the property's vegetable garden.

The woman climbed the short set of stairs to the cabin's lower wrap-around porch, on which stood a long row of woven willow rocking chairs that matched the basket containing the peapods. Depositing the basket on the first chair in the line, the woman took a seat on the second chair. She pulled off her straw hat and tossed it on top of the basket, after which she fluffed her pepper-and-salt hair, although it made little difference with her pixie cut. She smiled at the sisters warmly and introduced herself.

'I'm Harriet. Harriet Lipscomb.'

When Hope and Summer introduced themselves in turn, there was no change in Harriet's expression. Their names didn't appear to mean anything to her, which Hope took as a sign that however Harriet had learned of Carter's death, she had not been informed that it took place on the Baileys' side lawn.

As though reading the direction of Hope's thoughts, Harriet asked, 'How were you acquainted with the Daltons?'

There was an awkward silence. In an effort to think through an appropriate reply, Hope took her time moving a chair so that it partly faced Harriet's. She didn't know how forthright she should be with her. After all, their goal was to gather information about Carter, not to supply it, and they didn't know if a lack of a personal relationship with the Daltons would alter Harriet's friendliness toward them. When Hope glanced at her sister – who also delayed by adjusting a chair – Summer provided no more than a slight shake of her head, indicating that she wasn't sure of the best course, either.

'We didn't know the family,' Hope confessed at last.

'You didn't?' Harriet blinked at her. 'But you' – she motioned toward Summer – 'said by the flowers that you thought Carter was in mourning. You must have known him to some extent to be aware of that.'

Summer shifted uncomfortably in her seat. 'Our contact with Carter was only very recent.'

Hope shifted uncomfortably, too. Although it was technically the truth, it was somewhat misleading.

Harriet blinked again, but she didn't appear especially troubled by their admission. 'I also heard you say that you didn't think Carter was having an affair. You were right about that, as well. Carter never would have done such a thing under any circumstance. Kay and Bonnie Jean were his entire world. It didn't matter in the least whether Kay was physically here or not. She had a permanent hold on Carter's heart. He wouldn't have looked at another woman with the remotest interest for even half a second. He was absolutely devoted to his wife – and his little girl.'

That answered one of Hope's questions, namely the relationship between the remembrance stones in the memorial garden. It did not, however, explain why Austin had falsely claimed that Jill was having an affair with Carter. Nor did it explain why Carter had supposedly been running after Gina, and constantly calling her, and skulking around her house at odd hours. It was possible that Miranda had fabricated or exaggerated the incidents, but that seemed unlikely to Hope. When Miranda had told Nate about Carter's behavior, she hadn't given the impression of being eager to spread lurid gossip. On the contrary, she had hesitated and lowered her voice and specifically said that she couldn't confirm whether or not there had ever been an actual romance between Gina and Carter.

'If I may ask and it isn't too painful for you to discuss,' Summer inquired tactfully, 'when did Kay and Bonnie Jean pass away?'

'It will be one year this October.' In response to the unspoken question, Harriet explained, 'Their car collided with a buck on the mountain. Sadly, that's not uncommon up here. The headlamps blind the deer while they're feeding at dawn or dusk, and they're so startled that they jump straight into you. Usually the vehicle bears the brunt of the damage, but in this case, Kay swerved hard to avoid the animal, and she hit the guard rail at full speed. The rail didn't hold. The subsequent investigation found that it had been weakened by a mudslide during the previous spring. The car went over the edge into a deep ravine. Kay and Bonnie Jean died on impact. Small mercies, at least.'

'Small mercies,' Hope agreed quietly.

'I miss Kay,' Harriet said, in a tone that showed she was

reminiscing more for herself than sharing information with the sisters. 'We had an instant connection. It was the kind of friendship where you meet someone, share one laugh with them, and know that you'll always get along well. Kay enjoyed gardening the same as I do, and when she learned that I have too much shade around my house for successful planting, she suggested that we enlarge her garden for the both of us. It worked wonderfully! Splitting the chores made them a good deal lighter and more enjoyable. And if one person traveled for a few days or was feeling under the weather, the other person could take care of whatever needed to be done in their absence. We continued like that for many years, until the accident. I was hesitant to carry on at first, afraid that it might seem disrespectful somehow, but Carter insisted that the garden be planted exactly as it had been previously. The psychologists would probably say that it was his way of keeping Kay alive. That's also why Carter planted the flowers on the other side of the cabin. Kay loved flowers, especially the natives that support the pollinators.'

Harriet turned toward the memorial garden and gazed at it reflectively. 'I don't know what will happen to the flowers now. I'll do my best to tend them, and the vegetable garden, until the end of the season. But next year? The land doesn't belong to me, of course. I have no idea who has a claim to it. The police asked me about possible kin when they telephoned yesterday evening. I had apparently been listed on some form from Kay and Bonnie Jean's deaths, and that was why I was notified of Carter's death. Otherwise, I wouldn't even know about it. I would have been weeding around the beets this morning and wondering why Carter didn't come home the night before. The police said that someone would drive up and speak with me in person today. When your car first pulled into the clearing, I thought that you might be them. But then you went to admire the goldenrod. In my experience, people in positions of authority don't usually take much interest in such pleasant things as goldenrod—'

Interrupting herself with a little start, Harriet turned back to the sisters abruptly. 'Are you kin of the Daltons? I realize that you said you didn't know the family and your contact with Carter was only very recent, but plenty of distant relatives are barely acquainted. Did you come because you'll inherit the property?'

She looked at them hopefully, no doubt because a new neighbor who admired the goldenrod and complimented her peapods was far better than many of the other potential alternatives.

Hope was sorry to disappoint her. 'No, we're not related to the Daltons. We came to the property because we wanted to pay our respects to Carter. As brief as our contact with him was, we were nonetheless saddened by his death.'

'Oh, but you shouldn't be sad. I told you that before. Carter and Kay and Bonnie Jean are a family again. They're finally at peace. Be glad for it.'

Harriet Lipscomb had an amazing way of making murder sound almost as though it was a good thing. But then it occurred to Hope that Harriet might not know it was murder. Considering that she was merely a neighbor and not the Dalton's next-of-kin or someone else with explicit legal standing to handle their affairs, the police may have simply informed her of Carter's passing without providing any additional details. Harriet didn't recognize the Bailey name, so she clearly hadn't been told the specifics as to the location of Carter's death. In the same vein, she probably also hadn't been told about the manner of his death. And Hope instantly decided that there was no reason that she should be told, at least not by her and Summer. It would serve no purpose other than to horrify Harriet, as it had everyone who had seen Carter's body lying entangled in the hoses in the pool.

'Be glad for it,' Harriet repeated. 'Kay and Bonnie Jean went quickly – and together. They didn't suffer, but Carter suffered terribly when they died. For days he wouldn't eat and couldn't sleep. It took weeks before he bathed and dressed himself properly. I don't think that he came out of the cabin at all for the first month after the accident. Then it was another month or two until he got into a car and drove somewhere. And this spring, he finally began to recover. He would never forget, of course, but he started to live again, bit by bit. He planted the garden for Kay. He had the stones inscribed for her and Bonnie Jean. He became a sponsor of an elephant orphanage in Tanzania, because elephants had been Bonnie Jean's favorite animal. Once in a while, Carter would smile. He even laughed in July when I fell into the squash. He knew that he wouldn't ever feel the same joy as before, but he tried to focus on the happy memories and create positive

habits, ones that he thought Kay would approve of. He participated in a book group. He volunteered at those river and stream
clean-ups where they collect the trash that's washed up on the
banks. He attended grief support meetings for those who have
lost loved ones. And that was when it went all wrong.'

Hope and Summer waited for her to continue, but she didn't.
Harriet sat stiffly in her willow rocker, her formerly cheerful
expression clouded.

'When exactly did it go wrong?' Summer asked her.

'At the grief support meetings. That's where Carter met that
wretched man.'

The sisters exchanged a glance. The mention of a wretched
man when things went all wrong for Carter was too coincidental
to ignore. Could the man have some connection to why Carter
stole the books from the brownstone's library, or how Carter
ended up dead in the retention pool?

'What man?' Summer prompted Harriet.

She pursed her lips. For a moment, it almost looked as though
she was about to spit on the ground as she spoke the man's name,
but she didn't. 'Austin,' Harriet said with contempt. 'Austin Berg.'

TWENTY

A hawk cried in the distance. A squirrel chattered from a nearby fence post. Hope and Summer looked at each other, wide-eyed.

'Austin Berg?' Summer said to Harriet. 'You're certain?'

'Do you know him?' she questioned in reply.

For the first time since they had met her, Harriet narrowed her gaze at the sisters warily, as though, if they knew Austin, then they by association might be as wretched as he was.

'We're only slightly acquainted with him,' Summer answered quickly.

'Yesterday was our first encounter with him,' Hope further clarified. 'And we don't like him.'

'We *really* don't like him,' Summer added with emphasis.

Harriet's gaze relaxed. Her body, however, remained stiff in her chair. 'I don't like him, either. He's deceitful and disreputable. That wife of his is just as bad.'

The sisters looked at each other again.

'Jill?' Hope asked Harriet.

'Yes. Did you have the misfortune of encountering her yesterday, too?'

As Hope nodded in the affirmative, she thought back to the palm reading from the previous morning. Although Jill's reading had been reasonably simple and straightforward, it hadn't felt entirely natural. Usually people went to great lengths to conceal their extramarital activities, not draw attention to them. But Jill had belabored the subject, even gasping dramatically when the lights in the shop had flickered and announcing that it was a message intended for her. At the time, Hope had been more amused than troubled. But now that she knew for certain there had been no affair between Jill and Carter – and Harriet described Jill as being as deceitful and disreputable as Austin – she was beginning to wonder if something had been wrong with the palm reading, after all.

Maybe it wasn't so simple and straightforward as it had originally appeared.

'Those Bergs are a nasty, grasping pair,' Harriet said.
'Downright evil, my mother – if she were still with us – would
have called them. Bless my mother's heart, she could always
tell when someone was up to no good. And the Bergs were
certainly up to no good when it came to Carter. I had my doubts
about them from the very beginning. They claimed to be
attending the grief support meetings because they had lost a
child. But as soon as I looked at them, I knew that it was a lie.
They visited the cabin while I was working in the garden, and
I saw it in their eyes. Anyone who has truly lost a child has a
deep well of sadness inside that can't ever be filled. But the
Bergs had nothing. There was no genuine sorrow beneath their
fake tears and phony sobs. Jill and Austin hadn't lost anything
but their own souls.'

They were strong words, and Hope and Summer listened
intently.

'It came as no great shock to me,' Harriet continued, 'that the
Bergs' make-believe child was a daughter who happened to be
almost exactly the same age as Bonnie Jean. They said her name
was Betsy Alice. At the outset, Jill and Austin pretended to mourn
and commiserate with Carter regarding their mutual bereavement,
alternately weeping over the tragedy and resolving to come to
terms with it. And then one day, the pair drove into the clearing
and declared that a miracle had occurred. They had seen their
beloved Besty Alice once more!'

Summer drew a sharp breath. 'Oh no. A séance?'

Hope turned to her sister in surprise.

'Yes, it was a séance,' Harriet confirmed, also appearing
surprised. 'How did you know?' When Summer didn't immediately answer, she said, 'Did the Bergs try to pull the same trick
with someone close to you? Is that how you encountered them?'

A full explanation of their dealings with Jill and Austin was
far too long and complicated, and any explanation of their exten-
sive experience with séances was out of the question, so Hope
gave an ambiguous reply, letting Harriet interpret it according to
her wishes. 'We've heard stories.'

Harriet inclined her head. 'The Bergs are consummate storytellers, and word is bound to spread over time, especially with something like this. They told Carter that at the first séance they attended, there was a puff of air and a hazy shadow. At the next séance, a faint outline of a person appeared. At the third séance, the outline was possibly of a young girl. At the fourth séance, the figure bore some resemblance to Betsy Alice. And finally, at the fifth séance, Betsy Alice was definitively standing before her parents.'

Summer sighed. 'Carter desperately wanted to believe them, didn't he?'

'That's exactly right!' Harriet exclaimed. 'He was *desperate* to believe them. Carter was an intelligent, rational man. He knew that the hands of time couldn't be turned backwards and the accident couldn't be undone. And yet—'

'And yet,' Summer finished for her, 'he clung to the hope that somehow he might be able to see Kay and Bonnie Jean again.'

Harriet nodded vigorously. 'The wretched Bergs preyed on that hope. When their initial accounts of the séances didn't persuade Carter to participate, their supposed interactions with Betsy Alice became more intimate. At one, she smiled at her parents. At another, she tried to hold their hands. She almost spoke on several occasions, coming quite close to uttering something that sounded like *Mommy* and *Daddy*.'

Summer rolled her eyes.

'That was my reaction, too,' Harriet said, nodding some more. 'The whole thing was obviously one big trick. And it was also obviously not a new trick for the Bergs. They were much too smooth and practiced. They had clearly used the scheme before, possibly many times. Every explanation, every justification, every argument in their favor was perfectly rehearsed. It was as though they knew in advance how I would attempt to reason with Carter, and they had already pre-empted it. I disputed, debated, cajoled and pleaded with him. But none of it worked. No matter what I said, no matter in what way I tried to convince him that it was a lie and a scam, he didn't listen to me.'

'Because he didn't want to listen to you,' Summer replied.

Harriet threw up her hands in frustration. 'What could I have done! How could I have stopped him?'

'You couldn't have stopped him,' Hope told her gently. 'There was nothing more that you could do. I'm sure that Carter had his doubts – particularly since he wasn't persuaded by the initial stories of Betsy Alice – but in the end, it was simply too easy for him to push his misgivings aside. You said that Kay and Bonnie Jean were his entire world. They had a permanent hold on his heart, and he was absolutely devoted to them. It's highly unlikely that someone with such strong emotions would remain unwaveringly sensible and not have a moment when he weakened and figured that anything was worth a try.'

'Did Carter try a séance?' Summer asked Harriet.

'Yes. It wasn't successful, naturally. I wasn't there, because I refused to participate in such a disgraceful sham. But Carter said that nothing happened. Nothing at all.'

'Did Jill and Austin encourage him give it another try?'

'Of course! They reminded him that they hadn't been successful the first time, either. It had taken many, many séances for them to have results with Betsy Alice.'

'And these many, many séances all required a cash payment, I presume?' Summer said.

'Of course!' Harriet exclaimed again. 'The Bergs claimed that the cost was negligible and irrelevant; they barely even thought of it. They told Carter that no price could possibly be placed on having contact with their precious Betsy Alice.'

Summer gave a derisive snort.

'If I hadn't been so furious at them, I would have laughed in their face when they said that.' Harriet stomped an angry foot on the porch. 'It's practically blasphemous. A person should be allowed to mourn in peace, and the dead should be allowed to rest in peace. Fabricating a deceased daughter who returns from the grave to cheat a grieving man out of his money is appalling.'

'There isn't much worse than that,' Hope agreed.

'So Carter paid for additional séances?' Summer inquired. 'Did any of them purport to work in any way?'

'No.' It was Harriet's turn to roll her eyes. 'There was constantly some sort of an excuse as to why the séances didn't function as advertised. The temperature of the room wasn't suitable that day. Carter wasn't relaxing his body and opening his mind sufficiently. The moon was too full or not full enough. No refunds were given for the failed attempts, of course. But each time, there was the promise that the next time would surely be successful. Except it wasn't, either. And the next time always cost more.'

Harriet exhaled wearily before continuing, 'I don't know how much Carter paid for it all. But it must have been a very large sum, because at one point, he let slip that he was talking to the bank about taking out another mortgage on the cabin. Carter wasn't some plush multi-millionaire with a private jet and a fleet of yachts. He needed his money to eat and live! And even setting the obscene amount of money aside, the way in which the Bergs went about stealing it from him is unconscionable. To attend grief support meetings to find and target your victim? It's reprehensibly cruel!'

Hope and Summer had no response, because the truth of Harriet's statement spoke for itself.

'As though a person could wave a magic wand or snap their fingers and like a pack of obedient hounds, the spirits would wondrously appear from the Great Beyond. Ghastly.' Harriet shuddered. 'Absolutely ghastly. And if you consider—'

'Who waved the wand or snapped their fingers?' Summer interjected suddenly.

Harriet was startled by the interruption. 'Huh?'

'I was so involved in what you were telling us about Jill and Austin,' Summer said, 'and I was so offended on Carter's behalf that I didn't think about the actual séance. Who was the medium?'

'The medium?' Harriet scoffed. 'That isn't the word to describe her. *Swindler* is more accurate. The swindler owns that enormous house on the side of the mountain. She's another deceitful and disreputable creature. She has the most absurd sign at the entrance to her property. Some of the neighbors have been trying to get her to remove it, but they haven't been successful so far. She calls herself *Madam Gina*. Isn't that ridiculous? It sounds as though she's running a brothel.'

Despite the gravity of the situation, Hope almost smiled. That was exactly the same view Summer had of *Madam Gina*.

There was a bitter laugh from Summer. 'We should have known, Hope. We should have realized that Gina was involved in this dirty business.'

'Have you met Gina?' Harriet asked curiously.

'Briefly,' Summer replied. 'With her fancy shopping bags, and her designer clothing, and her pricey jewelry.'

'Every time I've seen her, she's been expensively dressed,' Harriet concurred. 'Which is another thing that bothers me! She's obviously wealthy, but she's still cheating people like Carter. I guess the rich are never rich enough in their minds. If Gina can swindle more, then she'll swindle more.'

Summer looked at her sister. 'I told you that Gina is making money from her séances. I told you that she's an avaricious charlatan who pretends to talk to the dead for money. But you didn't believe me. You thought that she might have gotten her wealth through honest means and that she might be just a harmless woman who was having some silly fun. Well, there is nothing at all honest or harmless about Gina Zaffer. In fact, she's even worse than I imagined. I assumed that she was finding her quarries through the local obituaries. It never occurred to me that she'd stoop so low as to use shills like the Bergs to lure people in.'

'On the bright side,' Hope said, 'at least now we know how Gina and Austin are acquainted and the reason they wanted to keep it hidden.'

Summer nodded. 'They were afraid that their scam would be exposed. It's difficult to be the secret accomplice to a con artist if everybody is already aware that the two of you are bosom buddies.'

Hope was thoughtful. 'But why did Austin burst into the boutique and put on that act about the supposed affair? What was the point of it? And while we're on the subject of putting on acts, why did Jill come in for the palm reading, which she was clearly also trying to connect with the supposed affair?'

'Palm reading?' Harriet echoed in surprise. 'You do palm readings?'

There was a slight pause before Hope answered. She wished that she had been more careful in what she said. She didn't want Harriet to equate her palm readings with Gina's séances.

'Summer and I own a little shop in the historic district,' Hope explained. 'We sell crystals and candles and the like. Summer also works with teas and tinctures. I do a bit of palm reading.' She deliberately didn't mention the Tarot, which was journeying even further into the realm of mysticism.

Harriet pondered for a moment, and then she smiled. 'Now it makes sense. You're the competition.'

'The competition?' Hope shook her head. 'I don't understand.'

'One afternoon a few days ago,' Harriet said, 'Carter returned from the city. He may have been meeting with his book group, although I'm not certain. He was in an unusually good mood, almost happy. He said that by chance he had come across a shop in the historic district where the people might be knowledgeable about séances. When I asked him what kind of shop it was, he told me that it was a possible competitor to Gina, and that meant the people there might give him truthful information.'

Neither sister spoke.

'Don't you see?' Harriet went on excitedly. 'He was talking about your shop. You're the competitor!'

Summer turned to Hope. 'Carter must have noticed the boutique when he was visiting Miranda.'

'That's why he was pacing on the sidewalk in front of the window when Megan saw him. He wanted to come in and talk to us about Gina and the séances.'

'But it still doesn't explain all the nonsense with Austin and Jill about the supposed affair.'

'Except maybe it does,' Hope responded contemplatively. 'Maybe Carter told Gina that he had learned about the boutique, and he used it as a threat or an ultimatum with her. If she didn't provide him with a more successful séance, then he would go to us. Gina wouldn't have liked that. It would have also made her nervous. She already knew how fond Rosemarie is of us. Gina wouldn't have wanted Carter to defect to our camp. Having too many defectors is bad for business.'

'So you think Gina sent Jill to investigate or keep an eye on us?'

'More likely she was sent in an attempt to discredit us. The plan was probably for Jill to tell Carter after the palm reading that I said – falsely, of course – they were having an affair. It would have certainly upset him and possibly kept him from ever trusting us. Maybe Gina thought that it would work on a larger scale, too, and that was the reason behind Austin's public tirade. His appearance in the boutique was conveniently timed for maximum exposure during the Wednesday afternoon tea.

Gina could have been hoping to turn some of our clients and customers into her clients and customers by making us look bad in front of them, hence Austin's repeated references to *bloody witch* and *homewrecker*, which aren't words that generally inspire confidence.'

'Austin is the bloody one,' Summer muttered. 'But I can understand why Carter fell victim to him and Jill. The Bergs played their parts to perfection. I really believed that Austin was enraged about the supposed affair. And I also believed that Jill was spooked and awestruck by the flickering lights during the palm reading.'

'Gina probably uses fake flickering lights during her séances, and Jill has had plenty of opportunities to act spooked and awestruck at the appropriate moments. Don't forget, her bank account depends on a good performance—' Hope broke off abruptly. She turned to Harriet. 'How low was Carter's bank account?'

'Are you asking for an exact dollar amount?' Harriet frowned at her. 'I don't have any idea about that.'

'No, I'm interested in whether Carter's finances had become so strained of late that instead of paying for a future séance with cash, he might have proposed a different form of compensation.'

Harriet's frown deepened. 'I highly doubt that experienced fraudsters like Gina and the Bergs would accept a check or credit card for their alleged services, leaving behind a trail of receipts for the police and the taxing authorities to follow.'

'I don't mean money at all,' Hope said. 'I mean a trade.'

Summer – who had been slouched in her chair – sat bolt upright. 'You mean the books!'

'Precisely. We know from Miranda that Carter was running after Gina, and constantly calling her, and skulking around her house at odd hours. You suggested that he was stalking her, and you were right. Except it wasn't a romantic obsession; it was a spiritual one. It sounds to me as though Carter was desperate for another séance. And if he didn't possess sufficient money to purchase one, he might have tried to use us as an alternate type of payment. Either by threatening Gina that he would talk to us, or—'

'Or by offering our books to her in exchange,' Summer concluded. She spun in her seat toward Harriet. 'Did Carter bring home an old book in the last day or two?'

The sisters looked at Harriet in anticipation.

She frowned some more. 'An old book?'

'Tattered leather cover,' Summer described. 'Bare spine. Yellowed pages. Overall decrepit appearance, with a noticeable mildew smell.'

'Well, I'm not sure of the specific day,' Harriet began slowly. 'It was earlier this week. I picked a colossal bowl of cherry tomatoes in the garden. I remember that Carter was sitting on the porch with a worn book in his lap . . .'

Hope and Summer held their breath.

'But it didn't have a leather cover,' Harriet told them. 'It was a dog-eared paperback. A travelogue on the headwaters of the Amazon River, I believe.'

They exhaled with disappointment.

Summer stood up briskly, causing the willow rocker to tip over behind her. 'Carter must have given the book to Gina, and that leaves us with only one course of action.'

'Which is?' Hope asked.

'Go to her house and get it back from her.'

TWENTY-ONE

After Hope and Summer had solemnly promised that they would return to the cabin before the end of the month to choose a pumpkin from the garden, Harriet sent them on their way with a large bag of peapods, a slightly smaller bag of cherry tomatoes, and detailed directions on the least winding route to Gina's house. The drive down Bent Mountain was only marginally kinder to Summer's stomach than the ascent had been, but she suffered less, primarily because instead of paying attention to her motion sickness, she was focused on devising a plan of attack against Gina.

'As I see it,' Summer said, 'we have two options. The first is to dance around the subject of the book with her and see if we get lucky somehow. The second is to dive straight in and demand that she give us back our property.'

Hope deliberated. 'Both methods are problematic. Gina is extremely crafty, so dancing around anything with her will be difficult. But a direct approach might not be wise, either. At this point, Gina can't be sure how much information we have. She can only speculate as to what we've learned about Carter, or uncovered regarding Jill and Austin, or whether we've even discovered the theft of the books. Setting aside Gram and Morris, no one other than the police and Dylan is aware that Volume I was found in Carter's cloak and safely returned to us. It might work to our advantage if we conceal from Gina the exact details of what we know, especially if she is currently searching for Volume I.'

Summer nodded. 'Gina will be forced to watch her step if we keep her guessing and off balance.'

'But at the same time,' Hope replied, 'we don't want to push her too far off balance. Don't forget, somebody killed Carter. We aren't any closer to figuring out who that person is. Considering that nearly everyone we deal with could be the murderer, we have to tread carefully.'

'And stay away from retention pools,' Summer added dryly.
Hope raised an eyebrow at her sister. 'That isn't funny.'

'It isn't funny,' she agreed apologetically. 'I would ordinarily
say that the most obvious motive for killing Carter was fear. Gina
or the Bergs were afraid that he would disclose their fraudulent
activities. But in this case, Carter was a source of money for
them. People don't usually slaughter a goose that lays eggs.'

'Unless the goose had dried up and the only remaining eggs
were our books. Once Gina had those – or at least one of the
books – Carter was nothing but a potential liability to her and
the Bergs.'

'But isn't it an even greater risk for them to kill Carter?'
Summer responded. 'Based on how wealthy Gina is and how
proficient Jill and Austin are at fooling people, they've clearly
pulled this or a similar scam many times before. Harriet thought
so, too. If they murdered every person who they had conned out
of money with a séance, there would probably be an entire
graveyard full of bodies.'

Hope grimaced. 'What a gruesome picture. But you're right.
They wouldn't kill everyone they had tricked. So if they're responsible for Carter's death, then he must have been different from
the other victims of their schemes in some way. It's possible that
Carter turned out to be a greater threat than they previously
believed. Or perhaps the books altered the equation.'

'The more I think about it,' Summer mused, 'the more I think
that something must have gone unexpectedly wrong yesterday
afternoon. I'm obviously not an expert on the preferred modes
of murder, but I highly doubt that anyone would construct a plan
to drown Carter with giant rubber hoses in dirty drainage water
that had been pumped out of the Larsons' cellar. It's much too
unreliable, and it might take too long, and too many people could
wander by the side lawn while it's occurring. So the murderer
in all likelihood acted impulsively, in the heat of the moment.'

'Maybe Carter and his killer agreed to a meeting to hand over
the second book, and they got into an argument during it. Carter
may have wanted to renegotiate the deal. Perhaps he realized
that once he had given up both books, he would no longer be a
valuable goose, and he was concerned about surrendering his
leverage too easily.'

'He might have also been asked to surrender his leverage to a different person,' Summer suggested.

'What do you mean?'

'Well, what if Carter had arranged to give the book to Gina, but Austin showed up to collect it instead? Or Jill? With three people, several combinations are possible. Carter could have gotten nervous and tried to back out of the deal with the new person, especially if he was growing increasingly inclined to talk to us. And the new person could have become nervous in turn, worried that the others would find out about the substitution. After that, the whole thing went off track, and Carter ended up dead.'

'If that's indeed what happened,' Hope said, 'then the murderer could be any of the three.'

'Any of the three,' Summer confirmed. 'They all had the opportunity to do it. Gina disappeared from the boutique sometime between Austin's arrival and the power going out, so she had the opportunity. Austin came into the boutique wet – either from sweat or water out of the retention pool – and breathing heavily, so he had the opportunity. And we only saw Jill in the morning during the palm reading, so she presumably also had the opportunity.'

Following Harriet's directions, Hope turned down an unnamed side road that was marked by a crimson stripe of paint on a decaying tree stump.

'And two of the three,' Summer continued, 'probably don't know who the murderer is, either. There's a good chance that they're guessing the same way we are right now, only much more anxiously.'

'Jill and Austin, too?' Hope questioned. 'Don't you think that they would tell each other if one of them had killed Carter?'

'No, I don't. On the contrary, I would wager that in the case of the Bergs, their cons come well before their marriage vows. With Jill and Austin – and most certainly Gina – there is no honor among thieves.'

Hope smiled. 'Are you saying that because of Nate's remark when Dylan translated the title page of Volume I for him?'

Summer gave an indignant little sniff. 'Both Nate and Dylan should be more respectful of crows.'

The smile grew. 'If you happen to see any crows during your date on Saturday, you can tell Nate that. It might, however, detract from the ambiance of the stars and the fireflies.'

There was another sniff from Summer. She started to respond but cut herself off with a chortle. 'Oh, she's definitely anxious.'

'Who is?'

'Gina. We're here.'

Hope slowed the car. She had been so focused on following the curves of the narrow road and making sure that they didn't careen off the edge into a ditch, she hadn't noticed that the road terminated a short distance ahead of them in a cul-de-sac. A solitary driveway lay at the far end of the cul-de-sac. Unlike Carter's open driveway, this one was blocked by a large, black steel security gate. A matching black steel fence stretched along both sides. It wasn't clear if the fence enclosed the entire property, but there was no visible end to it. There was also no visible mailbox or any indication of the owner's name or house number.

'How can we be sure that it's Gina's?' Hope said.

'I'm sure. You followed Harriet's directions faithfully. She said that it was a lone house on a dead end with a gate, just like this. And that' – Summer pointed toward a pair of tall posts standing at one corner of the gate – 'was where the sign Harriet told us about used to be. It was obviously torn down in a great hurry. You can still see the ripped corners left on the posts. Gina – or *Madam Gina*, I should say – must be awfully anxious about something if she's suddenly taken the sign away now, even though she wasn't willing to remove it before when the neighbors complained.'

Hope nodded. 'If only we knew what exactly Gina is anxious about.'

Summer chortled again. 'Yes, there are so many possibilities. Being in possession of stolen goods, fraud, murder . . .'

Driving slowly around the cul-de-sac, Hope peered through the thin gaps in the fence. 'I don't see the house. Do you?'

'Not even a glimpse. It makes me question the supposedly wonderful view that it has. Maybe Gina's house will turn out to be the same as Carter's cabin, and there will be no view at all.'

'That seems odd. I remember Miranda specifically saying that the house was on the edge of the mountain, overlooking the valley. I had assumed that meant it would be up high. But we've gone nearly the whole way down.'

'Harriet described it as being on the side of the mountain. Are we on the side?'

'Honestly, I have no idea.' Hope stopped the car short of the driveway and glanced in the rearview mirror. 'Speaking of Miranda, I think that she might be behind us.'

'Really?' Summer twisted in her seat for a better look. 'You're right. That is Miranda – or at least it's her car.'

The approaching car halted for a moment as though the occupants were as astonished to see another vehicle on the road as Hope and Summer were. Then it continued forward, pulling up beside the sisters.

'Miranda is driving,' Hope observed. 'There's no sign of Paul.'

'Why is she visiting Gina?'

'Your guess is as good as mine. To discuss the next selection for their book group? To plan another get-together? To admire a purportedly spectacular house where the cellar isn't leaking and the electricity remains on?'

'It's rotten timing for us,' Summer complained.

'Maybe not,' Hope replied.

Summer looked at her in surprise.

'The gate is impossible for us to climb, and we can't drive around the fence. If Gina is as anxious as we think she may be, then there's a high probability that she won't allow us on the property. But Miranda may have more success.'

'Clever,' Summer complimented her, and she turned toward the gate. 'Do you see a camera?'

'No, but there must be one, possibly several of them. If we're lucky, their range is poor. Let's linger toward the rear while Miranda goes ahead of us.' Hope reached for the handle of the door. 'She's getting out, so we'd better follow suit.'

Smiles and greetings were exchanged as the sisters and Miranda exited their respective vehicles.

'What a funny coincidence to find you here,' Miranda exclaimed. Her voice was extra squeaky, but her tone was as friendly as always.

'Hope and I were just saying the same thing,' Summer responded, ending the sentence on a questioning note.

Miranda must have caught the subtle hint, because she held up a slim tote bag. 'I promised Gina that I would share some cookbooks with her, and I've been tardy about it. After all that has happened at the brownstone' – her smile faded, and she sighed wearily – 'I needed to get away for a little while. I've been running errands most of the day, trying to keep busy and distract myself.'

'We've been running errands, too,' Summer told her. 'We don't even know if the electricity has been restored.'

'I don't know, either. I tried calling Paul a few minutes ago to check if there had been an update, but I couldn't reach him. The reception is terribly spotty on the mountain. In some locations, it's fine. In other locations, it's impossible to get a connection. I also tried calling Gina. I wanted to advise her that I was planning on stopping by. But I didn't have any better success with her. Is she expecting you?'

Summer shook her head.

Miranda's brow furrowed. 'Then she might not be home. She usually keeps the gate open when she's here.'

There was a pause. Hope and Summer exchanged a glance. They needed Miranda to approach the gate first.

'Is Gina an avid cook?' Hope asked, trying to spur Miranda on. 'I'm sure that she'll really appreciate receiving those books from you.'

'She was particularly interested in the one on crepes. She told me that she had recently purchased a specialized crepe pan, but the recipes that she had gotten from the internet weren't good.'

As she spoke, Miranda began to walk in the direction of the gate. Hope and Summer were quick to follow her.

'Gina and I have been talking about hosting a progressive dinner party,' Miranda continued, 'where we would go from one house to the next for different courses. Maybe you would be interested in participating?'

Turning so that Miranda couldn't see her, Summer pretended to silently choke. Hope struggled to restrain a laugh. Summer was right: Gina might very well try to poison them at such a dinner.

With a small cough, Hope replied politely, 'A progressive dinner party would be nice, Miranda, but isn't the distance between the houses somewhat prohibitive?'

'Not necessarily. We could do the hot foods in the city and then conclude with the dessert up here. Or we could start up here with cocktails and appetizers and then move down to the city for . . .'

The sentence was left unfinished as the unmistakable sound of car engines came from behind them. They collectively turned toward the road and found two vehicles approaching the cul-de-sac. The first car was unidentified. The second was a marked police car.

'Gracious,' Miranda said with concern. 'I hope that Gina is all right and nothing bad has happened to her.'

The sisters looked at each other gravely.

'The Bergs?' Summer whispered.

Hope had no answer. If Jill or Austin had killed Carter, would they go after Gina next?

Summer's expression lightened. 'Maybe the police have come to arrest Gina.'

This time she apparently didn't speak quietly enough, because Miranda blinked at her, startled.

'Arrest Gina?' Miranda echoed. 'Why would the police do that?'

Not prepared for the lengthy explanation that was required, Summer faltered. 'Oh, well, I—'

She was saved from having to struggle further by the arrival of the two cars. They pulled into the driveway, the marked police car behind the other. The first car stopped directly next to Hope and Summer. Its glass was so darkly tinted that they couldn't see the interior. The window on the driver's side lowered.

'Nate!' Summer exclaimed.

Miranda hurried toward him. 'Are you going to arrest Gina?'

Nate didn't immediately respond. He looked from Summer to Hope to Miranda. He didn't smile or greet any of them by name. A man sitting in the front passenger seat next to him said something that Hope couldn't hear. Nate replied with a slight nod. A moment later, the black steel gate started to open slowly. Both Hope and Summer took a step backwards in surprise.

Nate looked at them again. 'I don't know what you're doing here,' he began, his voice stern.

Although he gave the impression of speaking to the three as

a group, Hope could tell by the focus of Nate's gaze that his words were intended more for Summer and her than for Miranda.

'But you need to leave,' he continued. 'Go home.'

'Are you going to arrest Gina?' Miranda asked a second time.

'Gina Zaffer is being interviewed as a witness,' Nate said in a formal tone.

'Then she's all right? Nothing bad has happened to her?' Miranda breathed a sigh of relief. 'I've been so worried about everyone and everything since yesterday. I can't stop fretting.'

'We're all fretting,' Summer commiserated.

There was no sign of sympathy from Nate. Instead, he repeated even more sternly, 'You need to leave. Go home.'

Summer frowned.

'Gina is a witness?' Miranda pursued. 'Is it in connection to Carter?'

'Yes.' Nate hesitated, as though debating how much to say. 'Gina informed us that she held a séance . . .'

The man in the passenger seat snickered. Although it was barely perceptible, Hope saw Nate wince. She understood his reaction, because she winced, too.

Miranda's jaw sagged. 'Gina held a séance?'

'A séance,' Nate confirmed grimly, 'during which Carter Dalton is claimed to have appeared and is claimed to have identified his killer.'

There was another snicker from the man next to him.

Miranda's jaw sagged lower. 'But that can't be correct. How can that possibly be correct?'

No one answered her. The gate finished opening with a loud clang.

'Leave,' Nate instructed them one final time. 'Go home *now*.' And as his car began to pull forward through the gate and up the driveway, he glanced quickly back at the sisters and mouthed, 'Gina said it was you.'

TWENTY-TWO

'The bloody witch,' Summer spat, simultaneously tossing a moldy half of a lemon into the trash bag. 'The bloody, bloody witch.'

'Our ancestors will not thank you for saying that,' Hope – who was examining the contents of their refrigerator and handing the discards to her sister – reminded her.

'Our ancestors never would have held a fake séance to accuse an innocent person of murder,' Summer rejoined.

'But are we certain that's what Nate meant? Gina identified us – ostensibly through Carter – as his killer?'

'Of course that's what Nate meant! There is no other interpretation. It's why Nate looked at us the way that he did yesterday in front of the gate. The way that he looked at *me*.' Summer groaned. 'He despises me now.'

Hope suppressed a sigh and studied a wilting head of lettuce. Summer had been alternating between fuming about Gina and lamenting over Nate ever since they had climbed back into their car on the cul-de-sac and returned to the brownstone the previous afternoon. Although she had been too tired to continue for long in the evening, Summer had recharged the grievance battery overnight and started afresh in the morning.

'It must have been awful for Nate when they reached Gina's house and she gave them a detailed account of the supposed séance and the alleged apparition of Carter,' Summer said. 'Can you imagine how Nate's colleagues must have reacted to her story? Their smirks and sarcastic comments?'

'We've dealt with skeptics and cynics all of our lives,' Hope replied, deciding that the lettuce remained edible for another day or two. 'Gina Zaffer's fabrications are precisely what make people cynical and skeptical. It isn't new for us. And it isn't entirely new for Nate, either. He winced only slightly when his colleague in the car snickered at the mention of the séance. In my opinion, Nate handled the situation shrewdly. He didn't identify us by name in the driveway or distinguish us from Miranda in any manner. We were simply three women who happened to be visiting Gina and told by the police – firmly but politely – to leave the property while they interviewed her. Nate warned us about the séance so that we could be on our guard, which is a clear indication that he doesn't despise you in the least. On the contrary, he wants to protect you.'

'I never thought of it that way.' Summer's cheeks flushed.

'While you're thinking of it and looking pleased about Nate's protective instinct, smell this mayonnaise and tell me if it should stay.'

Summer put her nose to the container of mayonnaise and promptly added it to the trash bag. 'If we have to throw away this much rotten produce and spoiled condiments from our refrigerator after being without power for a day, then Miranda must have lost everything in her freezer. She's probably very unhappy.'

'Yes, but with the electricity back on, she can begin to restock her shelves, and that will distract her from what she heard yesterday about the séance. She was somewhat rattled by it, which is understandable. It's one thing to have seen a sign on a post for *Madam Gina*; it's quite another to learn that Gina is purportedly communicating with the ghost of a man who drowned in the water pumped out of your cellar.'

Summer nodded in agreement. 'Maybe we shouldn't have left Miranda alone outside the gate.'

'I asked her three times if she wanted to drive back to the city with us in convoy, but she said that she was going to try to call Paul again and then continue running her errands. We couldn't drag her into the car and force her to return home just because she looked a little flustered.'

'We should go next door and check on her later.'

'Do you really think that's necessary?' Hope passed on a pair of shriveled apples. 'Miranda was disconcerted by the séance, but she wasn't horrorstruck by it. Plus, she has Paul for support.'

'But it's a good excuse to talk to her,' Summer said. 'If we sympathize over her freezer and feign interest as to when Gina will receive the crepe cookbook from her, then we can find out how long Miranda remained on the driveway after we departed and whether she heard or saw anything of interest during that time.'

Hope smiled. 'You're even shrewder than Nate.'

Summer did not return the smile. 'My goal is to prevent us from being arrested for Carter's murder. Gina has apparently decided that we're the prime enemy. If she's willing to draw attention to herself and her fraudulent séances by contacting the police, then she must be extremely concerned about us.'

'That's true. She would only take such a risk if she viewed us as an even greater potential risk.'

'Which means that Gina is the murderer, doesn't it? She's afraid that we'll accuse her, so she's accusing us first. Could there be another explanation?'

Holding a jar of spaghetti sauce that had a variety of green and brown spots growing along its rim, Hope considered for a moment. 'Perhaps Gina is attempting to extort us to gain possession of the other book.'

Summer shook her head. 'As you said yesterday, aside from the police and Dylan, no one is aware that Volume I was found in Carter's cloak and safely returned to us.'

Hope considered some more. 'We could be wrong.'

'In what way?'

'Maybe Gina isn't concerned about us at all. Maybe she's actually concerned about the Bergs, and she thinks that pointing the finger at us will protect her from them somehow.'

'Then that would mean Jill or Austin is the murderer.'

'Either way' – Hope threw the spaghetti sauce into the trash bag and closed the nearly empty refrigerator – 'it doesn't give us any more useful information than we had before. We already knew that one of the three was responsible for Carter's death. And it also doesn't bring us any closer to getting Volume II back from Gina.'

Summer knotted the top of the trash bag. 'I have no idea how we'll retrieve the book now. We can't go to Gina's house and knock on the gate after what she told the police. She could make all sorts of additional accusations against us for trespassing and threatening her and the like.'

'Miranda's crepe cookbook isn't enough of a subterfuge to help with that.'

'I wish that we – and Miranda – had been at the gate a little earlier yesterday. Then we might have managed to get into the house before the police arrived.'

'Possibly.' Hope walked to the door that led outside from the kitchen and opened it for her sister. 'But it's just as possible that we would have ended up in worse trouble depending on how the situation with Gina and our book unfolded.'

'I suppose so.' Summer carried the trash bag through the open doorway. 'I suppose that we—' She stopped with a sudden cry.

'What is it?' Hope asked, hurrying after her. 'What—' She broke off with equal abruptness.

Three short steps descended from the kitchen to the outdoor garbage can and the back corner of the brownstone. Rosemarie Potter was sitting on the middle step.

'I'm sorry if I startled you,' Rosemarie apologized.

Although Hope wanted to respond, she was too astonished. Rosemarie always visited them using the front entrance of the boutique, and her arrival frequently involved a voluble kerfuffle; she never turned up quietly and unannounced outside their kitchen door. But that didn't surprise Hope nearly as much as Rosemarie's choice of apparel. Even during the chill of winter, Rosemarie had a penchant for billowy, flowered dresses in vivid colors. Today, however, she wore a black taffeta evening gown with elbow-length, black satin gloves. Her scarlet hair was gathered in a big pouf on the top of her head. Based on her appearance, Rosemarie could have been waiting for a limousine to convey her to the opera. Except she was perched on the edge of a dusty concrete step beside the sisters' recycling bin.

Summer gurgled a few disconnected words. 'Why . . . How . . .?'

'I don't like him,' Rosemarie announced. 'I don't like him at all.'

Hope cleared her throat and found her voice. 'Who?'

'Him.' Rosemarie pointed straight ahead.

The back corner of their brownstone was almost directly opposite from the back corner of the Larsons' brownstone, and both households put their garbage cans in the same respective location for easy access to the alley on trash collection day. Although the distance was more than sufficient to keep everybody's conversations private, the view from one property to the other was unobstructed. Paul was presently standing at his garbage can, arranging a mound of bags to squeeze in as many as possible. It was not difficult to guess that the bags were filled with the former contents of the freezer.

'That hair of his.' Rosemarie pointed some more. 'It's too bright.'

With effort, Hope swallowed a laugh. Paul's orange shock of hair was indeed bright, but he had the excuse of it being natural. Rosemarie couldn't make the same claim for her blazing red-dyed tresses.

'And he's not environmentally conscious,' Rosemarie continued. 'If you had seen all of the things that he's thrown away.'

'It's spoiled food from the power outage,' Summer told her. 'The same as us.' She motioned toward the bag that she was holding. 'The city is working on setting up a composting program, but there have been some hiccups with the implementation.'

Rosemarie shook her head. 'It's much more than food. I've been watching him for the last half an hour. There were cardboard boxes, and a doormat, and what looked like a set of old towels, and . . .'

As Rosemarie proceeded with a comprehensive list of Paul's refuse, Summer deposited their refuse in the garbage can with a deliberately loud thud. When that didn't stop Rosemarie, Summer interrupted her.

'The Larsons' cellar was flooded, Rosemarie. It's only logical that they would have extra items to dispose of.'

Rosemarie frowned. She seemed to want to carry on with her condemnations of Paul, but she couldn't think of a way to do so. Hope understood why. Rosemarie was rarely so critical of anyone. Her natural instinct was to like and trust everybody, oftentimes far too much and far too quickly for her own good. In this instance, however, Paul had committed a cardinal sin: he had called her darling Percy a nuisance and a menace. He had also threatened to contact Animal Control to potentially take possession of the pug. Others might have expressed their anger toward Paul more forcefully and directly, but being a kind and gentle soul, Rosemarie's wrath was limited to the belated censure – to Hope and Summer – of his hair and trash.

Reminded of Percy, Hope looked around the steps, but the pug was nowhere to be seen. 'Where is Percy?' she asked Rosemarie. 'If you didn't bring him with you because you were worried about Paul, there's no need for you to be anxious. Paul was stressed about his cellar and all of the associated costs, so he got a little short-tempered the other day. He would never actually contact Animal Control.'

After frowning for a moment longer in Paul's direction, Rosemarie's expression softened, as though she had made the decision to forgive and forget all past transgressions. Then she said, 'Percy is with the dog-sitter for the evening. I promised that I would call him once an hour, so he can hear the sound of my voice. Percy's fond of the sitter, but I don't want him to think that I've abandoned him.'

Hope smiled. 'Percy is lucky to have you, Rosemarie.'

'I'm lucky to have him,' she responded earnestly. 'Although sometimes his fur can get a bit troublesome.' She brushed at the taffeta cascading across her lap. 'I spent most of the morning picking it clean. Black may be good at hiding a stain or spot, but it shows every tiny piece of lint and hair.'

'You look very nice in your gown,' Hope complimented her.

'Very nice,' Summer concurred. 'You must have a big date this evening.' She checked her watch. 'But isn't it a little early, even for a Friday?'

The question appeared to momentarily confuse Rosemarie. 'I didn't want to take the chance of being late.'

'But you should have gone inside instead of sitting out here on the steps and potentially getting your gown dirty,' Hope said.

'The boutique door was locked,' Rosemarie explained, 'so I came around this way to wait for you.'

'The boutique door was locked?' Hope asked.

'I locked it when we went into the kitchen to clean out the refrigerator,' Summer said. 'Too many people have been wandering in recently and helping themselves to things that don't belong to them, if you understand my meaning.'

Hope nodded. 'You're right. We need to be more careful.'

Summer nodded back at her. 'Even though the police tape was removed expeditiously, I have no doubt that some news of what happened on the side lawn still managed to spread, and a camper

van full of conspiracy theorists could show up in front of the
brownstone at any time. We don't want them to wander in uninvited, either.'

A crease formed in Rosemarie's brow. 'A camper van full of
conspiracy theorists? Why would they come here?'

Hope promptly switched the subject. 'Next time, Rosemarie,
simply knock on a door or give us a shout through a window,
and we'll open up right away. Now let's go inside and sit down
on some clean and comfortable chairs. Then you can tell us all
about your exciting plans for the evening.'

The crease deepened. 'But you know about the plans.'

'We do?' Hope said, helping Rosemarie to rise from the step
and straighten her gown. 'Did you tell us previously?'

Similar to when Summer had commented on the early hour
of the date, the question appeared to momentarily confuse
Rosemarie. 'I was told that you were told.'

Now Summer also looked confused. 'Huh?'

There was a pause, as though Rosemarie wasn't sure how to
answer. Then she said, 'I don't want to be one of those pushy
people who herds others along, but shouldn't you be getting
ready yourselves?'

'Getting ready for what?' Summer responded with a touch of
annoyance. 'My date isn't until tomorrow, assuming that Nate is
still interested.'

'Of course he's still interested,' Hope said. 'It wouldn't matter
to him that—'

Without warning, her sentence was concluded by Dylan.

'It wouldn't matter to him that a ghost has accused you of
being a murderess.' Dylan chuckled. 'It might even make you
more desirable in Nate's eyes. He is a detective, after all.'

Dylan's unanticipated arrival surprised Hope. But when she
turned to look at him standing at the base of the steps, she was
so taken aback that she had to hold on to the kitchen door to
steady herself. Dylan was wearing an immaculately tailored suit
in a shade of smoky blue that changed subtly to gray and then
almost to black depending on how the light hit him. His shirt
was unbuttoned at the collar; he wore no tie. His shoes were
perfectly polished. His sandy hair curled casually and yet fell
flawlessly into place.

'Mercy me,' Rosemarie exhaled, gaping at him.

Dylan smiled. It was a smile of confidence. He knew that he was well dressed and looked good.

'I don't think,' Rosemarie crooned, 'that I've ever seen such a handsome man in all of my life.'

The smile grew. 'I'm glad that I meet with your approval. I certainly don't want to disappoint my date.'

Summer choked. 'Your date?'

'Allow me to add,' Dylan continued suavely to Rosemarie, 'that you are quite stunning yourself. Too many women fall back on a black dress out of safety. For you, however, it's an excellent choice.'

Every visible inch of Rosemarie's skin turned salmon pink, and she giggled with delight.

'As for you two . . .' Dylan turned a disapproving eye toward Hope and Summer.

'Not that it's any of your business,' Summer snapped in defense, 'but we just finished cleaning out the refrigerator.'

'That explains the mustard and pickle juice stains,' he said.

Summer examined her clothing. 'There isn't any mustard or pickle juice!'

Dylan shook his head at her in amusement. 'It's no wonder that Gina thinks she can get away with all of her stunts. You – and so many others – believe things far too easily.'

'I've never believed a single word that has come out of Gina's lying—'

Hope interrupted her sister with a sharp cough.

'Shouldn't we believe Gina?' Rosemarie asked innocently.

'You can judge for yourself tonight,' Dylan replied. 'When we're at her house.'

Hope stared at him, stunned. Dylan and Rosemarie – in evening wear – were going to Gina's house?

Dylan laughed at her expression. 'Don't be jealous. Rosemarie may be my date, but we'll all be there together. Nate has arranged everything.'

'What has Nate arranged?' Summer demanded.

'Gina's next séance.'

TWENTY-THREE

Hope was rendered speechless. Nate had arranged for Gina to have another séance? She must have heard Dylan wrong. She looked at her sister to see if she had understood him any better, but Summer appeared to be equally at a loss.

Dylan tapped his elegant wristwatch. 'Time is ticking by, and at the rate we're moving, we'll be unfashionably tardy. As I was arriving, your neighbors were in the process of departing, which means that we'll be behind them by a considerable distance.'

The neighbors? They had departed? Hope turned to the back corner of the Larsons' brownstone where Paul had been standing a short while earlier. He was no longer there, nor was he visible anywhere else on his property. His garbage can was closed, with all of the trash bags tucked neatly inside. She tried to recall what Paul had been wearing, but she hadn't taken notice of his clothing.

'I made sure to come here early,' Rosemarie informed Dylan proudly. 'I told Hope and Summer that I didn't want to take the chance of being late.'

'And they apparently didn't listen to you,' he replied, 'because they're still standing on the steps gawking at us instead of going inside and getting properly attired, so that we can start our drive up the mountain.'

Summer made a spluttering noise.

'Let me get this straight.' Hope spoke slowly. 'You're dressed up to go to Gina's house – for a séance – which was arranged by Nate?'

Dylan inclined his head.

'The Larsons are going there, too?' she continued.

He inclined his head again.

'And you're expecting us to go also?'

'Indubitably,' he said.

Summer's spluttering noise repeated itself, followed by a host of spluttering words. 'Have you lost your mind? Hope and I are *not* under any circumstances going to Gina's house for a séance!'

Dylan's gaze narrowed. 'You're going.'

'No, we're not—'

'Yes, you are,' he cut her off brusquely. 'This is your best option. Nate thinks so. I think so. And if you can control your temper and consider what's at stake, you'll think so, too—'

Interrupting him, Hope turned to Rosemarie. 'The reception on Bent Mountain is spotty. If you want to call the dog-sitter and check on Percy, now would probably be a good time. Why don't you go into the kitchen? That way Percy will be able to hear your voice without being distracted by our background chatter.'

'Oh, that's a great idea. I didn't know about the spotty reception. I'm so glad that you mentioned it. I'll call right away . . .' Rosemarie hurried into the kitchen.

'Smart,' Dylan complimented Hope, as they in turn moved further from the open doorway. 'The less that Rosemarie hears, the better. She's much too naive when it comes to Gina.'

Hope nodded. 'And if she gets excited, she may inadvertently repeat something to Gina that we don't want repeated.'

Summer folded her arms across her chest. 'It doesn't matter what Rosemarie hears or repeats to Gina, because we won't be at the séance.'

'Don't be a fool,' Dylan rejoined. 'You've already been accused of murder once without being there to defend yourself. Nate did an outstanding job of muddying the waters as to that alleged séance, and you should be grateful to him for it. He pointed out to Gina that there were no witnesses to corroborate her claims, and she said that she would hold another séance, with everyone present this time.'

'Everyone?' Hope inquired.

'Everyone who had any connection with Carter on the day that he died. That was Nate's stipulation for his attendance, and Gina agreed to it.'

'Including the Bergs?'

'Including the Bergs,' Dylan confirmed. 'According to Gina,

a séance is most likely to be successful when all of the partici-
pants are in pairs. Thus, we have the Bergs, the Larsons, the
Bailey sisters, and my date with Rosemarie.' He smiled at Hope.
'I told you that you didn't need to be jealous.'

'I'm not jealous,' she replied. 'You're free to gallivant around
town and charm whomever you like.'

Dylan's smile became rakish. 'So you think that I'm charming?'

To Hope's annoyance, her cheeks warmed. To her further
annoyance, she found herself rather relieved at Dylan's explanation of the circumstances surrounding the séance. Although she
had never thought that he and Rosemarie were going on a true
date, she had – if she was entirely honest – felt an uncomfortable
twinge when confronted by the possibility that Dylan had glam-
orous plans for the evening.

'Having everyone in pairs doesn't help a séance,' Summer
disputed. She turned to her sister. 'How would having everyone
in pairs help a séance?'

Eager to focus on something other than Dylan's charm and
rakish smile, Hope gave the subject her full attention. 'It wouldn't
help at all. An even – or odd – number of participants doesn't
make a séance any more likely to succeed or fail.'

'But why would Gina spout such rubbish?' Summer said.

'She might have been trying to sound knowledgeable to Nate.
Or,' Hope added thoughtfully, 'perhaps she wants to be sure that
a particular person attends the séance. Austin *and* Jill, for
example.'

Summer nodded. 'If that's the case, then it's crafty rubbish.'

'Another piece of rubbish from Gina,' Dylan said, 'is that a
séance should always be held at dusk.'

There was a slight pause.

'That isn't rubbish,' Hope told him.

He raised an eyebrow at her.

'Dusk isn't strictly necessary,' she explained, somewhat reluctantly. 'A skilled medium can ply her talents effectively at any
hour of the day. But the veil between the worlds grows thinner
as the sun falls below the horizon, and the spirits tend to become
more communicative then. So sunset is good, twilight is better,
and dusk is arguably ideal for a séance.'

The eyebrow remained raised, but Dylan didn't say a word.

'I wonder how Gina would know about that?' Summer mused.

'If she's swindled as many people with her séances as we think that she has,' Hope replied, 'then she's bound to have picked up some proper terminology and genuine information along the way.'

'That's probably why she likes stealing books on the occult, so she can make her scams sound more authentic.' Summer gave a bitter laugh. 'Although next time she should take a book that she can actually read and doesn't require a translator.'

Dylan was quick to understand the reference. 'Does that mean there is a Volume II? And Gina has it?'

Hope's initial instinct was to refute and deny everything, but then she realized that there was no good reason to do so. On the contrary, since Dylan already knew about the first book, he could help in their search for the second book. The more eyes that looked for the book, the more likely they were to find it.

Instead of responding to Dylan, Hope turned to her sister. 'We have to go to the séance. It's the only way for us to get into Gina's house and retrieve our book from her.'

Summer's mouth opened in protest, but after a moment of reflection, she grudgingly agreed. 'We'll go to the séance.'

Half an hour later, they were headed out of the city and toward Bent Mountain. It would have been even faster if Hope and Summer hadn't changed their clothing. Although they had been fully content to remain in their refrigerator-cleaning jeans, both Dylan and Rosemarie had objected, albeit for different reasons. Dylan's argument had been the persuasive one. If they wanted Gina to believe that they were participating in the séance and therefore be invited into her house, they needed to dress accordingly. Rosemarie's argument had been more decorative. After concluding her cooing phone call with Percy, Rosemarie was in a jubilant state, anticipating a splendid evening ahead, and she was convinced that Hope and Summer would be in a similarly buoyant mood if they were wearing pretty things. Neither sister was willing to go to the extent that Rosemarie had, with a formal gown and gloves, especially on such short notice and with the knowledge that the séance was a sham. After some debate, they had settled on a middle ground: Summer in a flattering burgundy jumpsuit, and Hope in a three-quarter sleeve sweater dress in cobalt blue.

As Dylan's date, Rosemarie was given the honor of sitting in the front passenger seat next to him. Dylan had elected himself as their driver, and he quickly proved up to the task. He handled the twisting mountain roads so smoothly and skillfully that he compensated for some of their delay in leaving the brownstone. Gina's house was at a much lower elevation than Carter's cabin, so they arrived at their destination before Summer's stomach experienced too many ill effects from motion sickness.

The black steel security gate at the end of the cul-de-sac stood open. As Dylan pulled through it, Hope shifted in her seat with a sense of uneasiness. What if they were making a terrible mistake? What if their calculations turned out to be wrong, and instead of helping them to regain possession of their book, attending the séance brought them further trouble? This time an accusation of murder would include a large number of witnesses – including the police, namely Nate. Hope caught a glimpse of Dylan's expression in the rearview mirror, and its gravity brought her no comfort.

'Isn't it a beautiful approach?' Rosemarie gushed, as they traveled along the driveway. 'Gina must have a team of gardeners to keep all of those hedges so neatly sculpted. Wait until you see her fabulous house. It's just over the next rise. We're lucky that it's a clear sky. We could have a glorious sunset in a little while.'

There was some tetchy muttering from Summer. Given the circumstances, she wasn't interested in the neatly sculpted hedges or the prospect of a glorious sunset, and she was getting rather tired of everyone's euphoria toward Gina's wondrous house, particularly since the money for the house had in all probability come from the victims of Gina's schemes, including Carter. But Rosemarie wasn't distressed by Summer's remarks because, unlike Hope, she couldn't hear them over the continuation of her own enthusiastic commentary.

'When I was last here,' Rosemarie told them, 'we were in a big sitting room that has a whole wall of windows facing west. I hope that we're in there this evening, too. The colors will be gorgeous at the end of the day. The view over the valley is sublime . . .'

Summer started to mutter again, this time about the supposed view, but she was compelled to stop a moment later as they reached the top of the rise that Rosemarie had mentioned earlier, and Gina's house appeared before them. Harriet Lipscomb's description of the property was correct: it was an enormous house on the side of the mountain. And Miranda's description was also correct: it wasn't a house that anyone would easily forget. The house sat on the edge of a rugged crag that jutted out from the mountain like a thumb, except it was an extremely narrow thumb that gave the impression of possibly breaking off at any instant from a puff of wind or drop of rain. The house itself could have been a glossy photograph out of an architectural magazine. It was constructed of polished stone and gleaming glass, which reflected the late afternoon sun in a prism of colors.

Hope was so focused on studying the house, she didn't notice as they reached the end of the driveway. It wasn't until she heard Dylan's door open that she realized he had stopped the car and shut off the engine.

Summer pointed through her side window. 'That's the Larsons' car.'

'Nate's is on the far right,' Dylan observed.

'Gina's is by the garage,' Rosemarie added.

'I think the one across from us is Jill's,' Summer said. 'I recognize it from the other morning in front of the boutique when she came in for the palm reading.'

'So we're the last to arrive.' Dylan climbed out of the car and went around to open Rosemarie's door and help her to climb out, as well.

As Rosemarie thanked Dylan for his assistance and burbled about his gentlemanliness, Hope exited from the opposite side of the vehicle, with Summer following suit.

'Do we have a plan?' Hope asked.

'You mean other than crossing our fingers that Carter's purported ghost chooses someone new to blame for his murder?'

Before Hope was able to respond, Rosemarie came over to them, beaming with excitement.

'This is so thrilling!' she exclaimed.

The sisters did not echo the sentiment.

Rosemarie fussed with her gown and adjusted her gloves. 'I hope that I'm not overdressed.'

Hope smiled at her. 'No, you and Dylan outshine the rest of us. As soon as you walk into the house, everyone will admire you and not notice anybody else—' She broke off and turned to Summer. 'That's a possible plan. They go in first, and we hang back. It could give us an opportunity to nose around.'

Rosemarie shook her head, misunderstanding. 'But you don't need to hang back, out of sight. You both look lovely.'

Dylan shook his head, too, except he comprehended Hope's meaning. 'Hanging back won't work. Gina isn't going to let you nose anywhere.'

Again, Rosemarie misunderstood. 'Oh, Gina will be happy to give you a tour of the house!' And with dancing steps, she headed toward the front door.

As they followed her, Dylan walked beside Hope.

'You're a little liar,' he said in a low tone.

'I have no idea what you're talking about,' she replied.

He gave a quiet laugh and moved closer to her. 'Telling Rosemarie that she outshines you and that everyone will admire her but not notice you. You know perfectly well how untrue that it is and how striking you are in that dress.'

'Nonsense,' Hope scoffed, grateful that they weren't able to look directly at each other while walking, thereby keeping her blush undetected.

Dylan laughed again, and his fingers brushed against the back of her hand. 'Did you see the inn that we passed on the way up here? If it weren't for this farcical séance, we could go there for dinner . . .'

His touch was so distracting that Hope had to concentrate to put one foot in front of the other and not stumble in the process.

'And then get a room . . .' Dylan continued, his voice soft and tempting.

For an instant, everything disappeared around her. Gina's house and Bent Mountain; the séances and Carter's murder. The only thing that Hope thought of was having Dylan take her in his arms and to the inn. Then her sister brought her back to reality.

'Wait a minute,' Summer said.

Hope turned to her unsteadily. Summer had paused several paces behind them.

'If we're all in pairs for the séance,' Summer asked, 'who is Nate partnered with?'

This time Dylan's laugh wasn't muffled, because the answer was obvious. '*Madam Gina*, of course.'

TWENTY-FOUR

Together, Gina and Nate met them outside the front door of the house. Nate had added a navy sports jacket to his standard tan slacks and white button-down shirt. Likewise remaining loyal to her preferred solid and neutral tones, Gina wore a floor-length silk dress in an unusual shade of black that took on an almost purple sheen as the fabric shifted around her. It was certainly not the sort of black dress that Dylan could accuse Gina of falling back on out of safety. The silk had the delicacy of lingerie and flowed over her body, showing all of her contours. Around Gina's neck and both of her wrists were matching strands of black pearls that similarly adopted a purple hue as she moved.

'We were beginning to worry about what might be delaying you,' Nate said, stepping forward to greet them.

He smiled at each of them in turn – with his gaze lingering for an extra moment on Summer – then he took an additional step toward Dylan and shook his hand. Although from her angle, Hope couldn't see their full expressions, there was enough of a pause that she knew some look of import passed between the two men.

'I told Detective Nate that you couldn't have gotten lost, because you were already familiar with the location after coming here yesterday.' Gina purred the words, making them sound innocuous to everyone except Hope and Summer, who were informed that their visit to the gate on the previous afternoon had not gone unnoticed by her.

Rosemarie blinked at the sisters. 'You came here yesterday?'

Summer's reply was swift. 'We weren't at the house. We spoke with Miranda outside on the cul-de-sac.' She turned to Gina. 'Did you speak with Miranda yesterday also – after Hope and I left? Did she give you that book you were interested in?'

Gina's mouth twitched. To Hope, it appeared to be more a sign of uncertainty than agitation, as though she was trying to understand the purpose behind Summer's question. Hope was trying to understand it, too.

'Miranda was mistaken,' Gina said. 'I have no interest in the book.' Her mouth twitched again, but before Summer could comment further, she addressed Rosemarie. 'You look wonderful this evening. Let's walk to the back patio. That's where we are all assembled, and there's wine.'

With a wave of her hand indicating that the rest of the group should follow them, Gina ushered Rosemarie along a serpentine path of white pebbles that bordered the length of the house.

'She isn't taking us inside,' Summer whispered to her sister, as they trailed behind the others. 'We can't look for the book if we don't go inside.'

'Why did you ask her about the cookbook?' Hope whispered in return.

'When she made it clear that she knew about us being at the gate, I thought it was a good opportunity to see her reaction to the mention of a book. Did you notice how her lips twitched? Although we were technically talking about the cookbook, Gina realized that I was alluding to our book at the same time.'

'But haven't you now alerted her that we've come here for our book?'

'I'm sure that she had already guessed it. It's probably one of the reasons she decided to use the back patio. That way we're all together in a single, manageable space where she can monitor our movements.'

As the pebble path curved around the side of the house, Dylan stopped walking and waited for Hope and Summer to catch up. When they reached him, they stopped also, taking advantage of being momentarily out of view from everybody else.

'What book does Miranda have?' Dylan asked.

'A crepe cookbook,' Summer told him. 'It has no connection to our book, but . . .'

He nodded. 'You were testing Gina with it. She deliberated too long on her answer. She was definitely also thinking about your book.'

'That was my impression, too,' Summer agreed. 'Except how do we get our book if she keeps us outside?'

'She won't keep us outside if she actually intends on holding a séance,' Hope said. 'No one with the slightest knowledge of the spiritual world would take that risk, even a charlatan. The sun is close to setting. In another couple of minutes, everything on this mountain that was concealed in the shadows during daylight will start roaming about and be drawn straight to this spot if there's a séance.'

'Everything?' Dylan questioned. 'Everything like owls and whippoorwills?'

Summer rolled her eyes. 'Hope isn't referring to nocturnal birds. You have no clue what comes out of hiding after dark, do you?'

Hope responded before Dylan could. 'He's fortunate that he doesn't know, Summer. And we need to try to keep it that way. Not only for him, but also for Nate and Rosemarie and the Larsons. Which means that our immediate concern – more important even than retrieving our book – is to make sure that Gina doesn't attempt to hold a séance outside. But I don't think that she will. I think this is all a ruse.'

'Why do you say that?' Summer asked.

'Because of the wine. Gina told Rosemarie that there's wine on the patio. No serious séance ever includes alcohol – it muddles the connection to the other side – and again, even a charlatan with limited information would know that. More to the point, Gina would realize that we know it. She would also realize that we would be able to detect in an instant that her séance isn't real. So this must all be a ruse.'

'But what's the purpose of it?' Summer said. 'And do we confront Gina about it?'

'No,' Dylan answered without hesitation.

The sisters looked at him curiously.

'Confronting Gina may make you feel good temporarily, but it won't accomplish anything of substance,' he told them. 'It won't return your book to you, and it won't give Nate evidence to use against Carter's killer. Gina clearly has some plan in mind. Otherwise, she wouldn't have accused you of murder with the first alleged séance, or wanted to hold a second séance, or agreed so readily to Nate's stipulation that everyone be present at this one.'

Hope considered for a moment. 'If we don't confront her, then our only other option is to play along with her.'

'Exactly,' Dylan said. 'Pretend as though it's a real séance. See where she leads with it. You can always confront her later on if things start to go wrong.'

Summer frowned. 'I'm not using a Ouija board.'

'Definitely not,' Hope agreed. 'We'll draw the line at that.'

'And I'm not pretending that Gina and Nate are an actual pair.'

Dylan shook his head at her. 'You should trust Nate—'

'Gina is the one that I don't trust—' Summer interrupted him.

She was interrupted in turn by Rosemarie, who had come back from further up the pebble path.

'There you are!' Rosemarie exclaimed. 'Gina sent me to check on you. She was concerned that you might have twisted an ankle on the stones.'

'As if Gina cares about our ankles,' Summer muttered.

'We're all fine,' Hope assured Rosemarie, as she quickly tried to think of an excuse for their delay. 'We stopped to admire the view.'

Although they had been too involved in their discussion to take much heed of the surrounding scenery, the view was in fact impressive. Notwithstanding its modest elevation, the crag on which Gina's house was perched offered a full panorama over the valley. Tiny dots of light began to appear from the city below as the golden honey radiance of the sun faded along the horizon.

'It's marvelous, isn't it?' Admiring the view with them, Rosemarie sipped from a glass of red wine. 'I can't imagine a pleasanter evening. Gina has lit a fire in case it gets chilly or damp later.'

Dylan gave Hope a questioning look. Were they going to play along? She answered with a slight nod. He nodded in return and promptly moved next to Rosemarie.

'As nice as the view is,' he remarked smoothly, 'that glass of wine looks very nice, too. Will you show me where to get one?'

'Oh, yes.' With her free hand, Rosemarie took hold of Dylan's arm and turned with him up the path. 'Gina told me what type of wine it is, but the name was funny, so I don't remember it. It tastes good. I like fruity wines best . . .'

The remainder of the wine appraisal was lost to Hope as Rosemarie and Dylan proceeded toward the patio.

'How cliché,' Summer said dryly, 'to light a fire for a séance. My bet is that Gina will claim to see a face in the embers.'

Hope smiled. 'Then we'll pretend to see the face, too. Assuming, of course, that it isn't Carter accusing us of murder a second time.'

Imitating Rosemarie, Summer took hold of her sister's arm, and they followed the pair in the direction of the patio. 'For the record, I'm doubtful of this plan.'

'I don't have much confidence in it, either, but as Dylan said, we can always shift gears if things start to go wrong. Plus, Nate is here, which is reassuring.'

'But what about the Bergs—'

The question was left unfinished as the pebble path snaked around the rear of the house and emerged as a pebble patio. It was the only patio Hope had ever seen that wasn't flat, and she now better understood Gina's reference to them potentially twisting an ankle. Although the white pebbles were small and relatively uniform in dimension, they formed an uneven surface, which caused everything on the patio to be uneven. The metal chairs all tilted slightly. The large metal dining table sloped visibly to the left. A trio of jungle-sized ferns in metal planters leaned to the right. The area of the patio was approximately the same as Morris's, but in all other respects, there was no resemblance between the two. While Morris's patio was elegant and intimate, Gina's patio was cold and impersonal. The smile that Gina gave Hope and Summer as they approached was equally stony.

'Welcome to my home. May I offer you a glass of wine?'

Hope hesitated, recalling a troubling joke from Summer about Gina poisoning their food at Miranda's proposed progressive dinner party. Dylan solved the problem by handing a full glass to each sister and then taking a drink from his own.

'Cheers,' he said, in a tone that feigned merriment.

There was little actual merriment to be found. As Hope sampled the wine – which was so sweet and fruity that it could have been fortified grape juice – she surveyed the group. The only one who appeared to be in any sort of a good mood was Rosemarie, and even she had lost a considerable amount of her natural effusiveness. She stood next to Gina and Nate, chattering absently about the congenial outdoor temperature and the freshness of the mountain air. In contrast, Paul and Miranda Larson were silently seated in a pair of tilting metal chairs. Paul wore an ill-fitting worsted wool suit. His orange shock of hair had been combed into awkward submission. Miranda had on a red dress decorated with two vertical rows of gold-toned buttons. At her feet lay the tote bag containing the cookbooks that had been summarily rejected by Gina. Both of the Larsons held wine glasses, as did both of the Bergs. Jill and Austin were likewise seated in a pair of metal chairs without speaking. They were the most casually clad of the group. Jill had on a white tennis skirt with a pleated top. Austin wore a pair of seersucker pants and a striped golf shirt.

Leaning toward Hope, Summer said under her breath, 'You should tell Jill that you've had time to contemplate the markings on her palm, and they show that she'll be struck by lightning and then eaten by a bear.'

Hope had to bite her tongue not to laugh.

Although Summer's voice had been too quiet for the others to hear, Jill must have guessed from the direction of the sisters' gazes that the words were about her – and not of a flattering nature – because she wrinkled her nose and gave an indignant sniff.

'Don't act self-righteous with us,' Summer snapped at her. 'We know that you lied about the affair with Carter. We know that your husband's tirade in the boutique was make-believe. We know that—'

Hope elbowed Summer hard enough in her side to almost make her spill her wine, but it was necessary to stop her. She sounded as though she was about to mention Harriet Lipscomb next. Up to that point, they hadn't told anyone about their visit to Carter's cabin, and if they were going to play along with Gina and her séance, then they couldn't yet disclose everything that they had learned from Harriet.

There was a tense pause. Both Jill and Austin were visibly surprised by Summer's remarks, as were the rest of the group. Jill recovered before her husband.

'*I* never said that I'd had an affair with Carter.' She wrinkled her nose again, but this time there was no accompanying sniff. 'It was a misunderstanding.'

'A misunderstanding,' Austin concurred. 'There was some confusion between us. But no harm's been done, so you can forget about it the same as we have.'

'No harm?' Summer echoed irritably. 'You want us to forget that you pointed at Carter lying dead in the retention pool and announced that he—'

Hope was about to elbow her sister again, but Gina interrupted first.

'I'm glad that someone has broken the ice and mentioned Carter,' she said. 'It's always hard to broach the subject of those who have crossed over to the other side. But now that we've taken the first step, let's dive straight in. Why don't we all have a seat, so that we can begin the séance?'

Gina – with her wine glass – took the lead by walking toward the large metal dining table. The table was oval, and she placed herself at the chair on the narrow right end. Hope had no difficulty understanding her selection. Because the table sloped down to the left, Gina would be sitting slightly higher than everybody else.

'Detective Nate, if you would take the chair next to mine,' Gina suggested.

There was a little grumble from Summer.

'And Rosemarie,' Gina continued, 'if you would also sit next to me.'

Dylan pre-empted Gina's further seating arrangements by pulling out three chairs in a row on one of the long sides of the oval. 'Hope?' he said, indicating that she should sit in the middle chair. 'Summer?'

They agreed without discussion.

Also not waiting for Gina's direction, Paul pulled out a chair for himself and for Miranda across from the sisters and Dylan on the other long side of the oval. That left Jill and Austin opposite Gina on the narrow left end, sitting lower than the others.

Although Gina didn't appear to be entirely pleased with all of their positions, she didn't attempt to move anyone. She looked at the metal firepit that stood at an angle to the table, closest to her and Nate, furthest from Jill and Austin.

'I had assumed that the fire would have diminished some by

now,' she remarked, frowning. 'But the wood is burning unusually hot tonight.'

Hope and Summer exchanged a glance. As suspected, Gina had lit the fire as a séance prop. The problem for her was that the faces of spirits were typically alleged to be seen in dying embers, not roaring blazes. And the blaze in the firepit seemed to be strengthening rather than weakening. Its flames reflected off the metal table and chairs with an eerie red glow. The patio had no lighting and, as dusk descended upon them, the fire offered the only illumination for the group.

Gina turned her attention back to her guests. 'If you have all settled yourselves comfortably . . .'

There was some shifting in seats.

'And finished your wine . . .'

Glasses were drained and set aside.

'I would ask for everyone to put their hands on the table, palms turned up, open and relaxed.'

They all complied, except for Paul.

In response to their questioning looks, Paul said wryly, 'If God had intended for us to speak with the dead, he wouldn't have made them dead.'

Hope and Summer exchanged another glance. Paul had risen in their esteem. He apparently didn't believe in Gina's parlor – or, more accurately in this instance, patio – tricks any more than they did.

'This will not work if there are doubters among us,' Gina replied with a touch of haughtiness.

'Please, Paul,' Miranda squeaked beseechingly.

Nate cleared his throat, as though also encouraging Paul to participate.

'Oh, all right.' With a desultory thump, Paul deposited his hands on the table to join the others.

Gina thanked him stiffly, then her voice softened. 'Now we must clear our minds and free our hearts. Empty yourselves of any thoughts. Release yourselves from all emotions. Focus only on the fire.'

Heads and eyes turned toward the firepit.

'Slowly breathe in and breathe out.' Gina inhaled and exhaled demonstratively. 'Slowly breathe in and breathe out.'

Summer poked her sister's foot underneath the table. Hope had to press her lips together hard to keep a straight face.

'Slowly breathe in and breathe out . . .'

Hope felt the side of Dylan's thigh touch hers, and her pulse quickened.

'Carter Dalton,' Gina said, 'I summon thee.'

TWENTY-FIVE

'**C**arter Dalton, I summon thee.'

The fire crackled.

'Carter Dalton,' Gina repeated a third time, 'I summon thee.'

For a long minute, no one spoke. The shadows of the night deepened around them. A burning log collapsed on itself, sending a spray of crimson sparks into the air. Rosemarie made an anxious mewing sound.

Gina was quick to respond. 'Yes, Rosemarie. I see it, too.'

Everybody looked at the fire closely.

'What do you see?' Miranda asked.

There was a pause. Hope noted how adeptly Gina had taken advantage of the opportunity provided by Rosemarie to suggest that something was beginning to appear amid the flames. And now Gina waited for impressionable Rosemarie to expand on the idea.

'I'm not sure what it is,' Rosemarie answered somewhat timidly, 'but it's down near the bottom of the fire.'

'Near the bottom of the fire,' Gina echoed.

Miranda leaned forward for a better view. 'Where at the bottom?'

Again, Gina waited for Rosemarie to reply first.

'It's on the left side next to the twig that's sticking out.' Rosemarie wavered. 'But maybe I'm mistaken?' She turned to Gina questioningly.

'You should never doubt yourself,' Gina told her. 'Your eyes won't deceive you.'

Hope heard Summer cluck her tongue with annoyance. It was the classic playbook of a fraudulent medium, little altered over the millennia: hint and suggest without providing any substantive details, and then reinforce and reiterate whatever someone else thought they might have seen.

'On the left side . . .' Miranda murmured, leaning further forward. 'Next to the twig . . .' She gave a start. 'There it is!'

A buzz passed through the group, and they all studied the fire.

'Oh, yes!' Rosemarie cried excitedly. 'There it is!'

Paul leaned forward to match the position of his wife. 'Where exactly?'

Miranda pointed. 'That strange spot. Do you see it? It's brighter and more orange than everywhere else, and it's in the shape of a circle.'

Hope looked at the spot Miranda indicated. The flames were indeed slightly brighter and more orange in that area. But it wasn't due to any mystical reason. It was where the log had collapsed earlier.

'It is somewhat circular,' Paul mused.

'It's a face,' Jill declared.

Rosemarie gasped. 'Do you think so?'

'I'm positive,' Jill responded with confidence.

This time instead of turning questioningly to Gina, Rosemarie turned to Hope. 'Do you think that it's a face, Hope?'

Hope hesitated. Although she was supposed to play along with the séance, she didn't want to lie to Rosemarie. The ostensible circle was not a face. She was also wary of supporting any claim made by Jill. But before Hope could decide how best to reply, there was a sudden loud pop from the direction of the firepit.

'He's here,' Jill announced.

Rosemarie gasped again. Miranda gasped with her.

Several more pops followed.

'He's beginning to communicate,' Jill said.

The popping continued. To Hope, the noises were no more mystical than the slightly brighter and more orange part of the fire. They were exploding pockets of tree sap, most likely because Gina – whether deliberately or not – had used too much pine.

Austin nodded at his wife. 'Carter is communicating.'

Rosemarie and Miranda gazed wide-eyed at the Bergs.

'That's jumping to a conclusion, isn't it?' Paul said. 'I mean, how do you know that it's Carter who—'

'Because Carter was the one that we summoned,' Austin cut him off brusquely.

'Of course it's Carter,' Jill corroborated.

There was a rapid succession of snaps and cracks, varying in volume.

Miranda spun in her seat toward Gina. 'Can you understand him? What is Carter saying?'

It was Gina's turn to hesitate. Hope had the impression that the séance wasn't going entirely to plan, and similar to her, Gina was wary of automatically supporting Jill and Austin's claims without knowing where they were leading. During her time on the pebble patio, Hope had observed a decided coolness between the Bergs and their hostess. They didn't converse or make eye contact, and it went beyond mere reserve. There was a palpable tension, as though both sides were on guard, each watching and waiting to see what the other would do.

When no response from Gina was forthcoming, Jill said, 'Carter is trying to send a message.'

'Yes, but what is it?' Miranda asked impatiently.

With a dramatic flourish, Jill placed her hands back on the table, her palms turned up as when the séance had first started. 'Carter, are you here with us?'

Nothing happened.

'Carter,' Jill began again, 'are you—'

She was interrupted by a hollow thud. Rosemarie and both of the Larsons jumped at the sound.

'We hear you, Carter.' Jill raised her hands in the air as though she was communing with the heavens. 'We're listening.'

A pair of thuds came in reply.

Dylan leaned close to Hope's ear. 'Is Austin kicking one of the table legs?'

Although the words were much too quiet for Jill to discern, she must have caught a trace of his voice, because she commanded the entire group sternly, 'Silence!'

Hope answered Dylan with a slight nod.

To impede any further disruptions, Jill went on rapidly, 'Speak to us, Carter. Give us your message from the other side.'

There was one final thud, followed by a low whistle. The whistle stopped almost immediately, making it impossible to detect with certainty what direction it had come from. Hope guessed that it was Austin again.

'We didn't understand you, Carter.' Jill lifted her hands higher. 'Can you repeat yourself, please?'

As requested, the whistle reoccurred, but as before, it lasted only for a moment.

'We're beginning to comprehend,' Jill said. 'Once more, Carter, so that there can be no mistake.'

The whistle was replaced by a brief hum.

Jill dropped her hands to her sides in a shocked gesture. 'It was Gina!'

'It was *Gina!*' Austin affirmed.

Gina shot to her feet. 'No! You two are not going to blame me for this!'

Although it was as fleeting as the whistle and the hum, a smug expression passed across Austin's face. 'Carter's message cannot be denied.'

'There was no message,' Gina retorted angrily. She turned to Nate. 'Did you hear a message?' Before he could respond, she addressed Hope. 'I'm sure that you didn't hear a message.'

Austin gave a biting laugh. 'You think that she's going to support you after you accused her and her sister of murder yesterday?'

Hope felt Dylan straighten in his chair beside her. He was now on full alert, as was she. The séance had moved beyond imaginary faces in the fire and ghostly noises.

'I didn't accuse anyone of anything,' Gina countered. 'I received information from the other side, which I freely admit may have been in error. That's why we're here today, to the learn the truth.'

'And we have learned the truth,' Jill sneered. 'Carter's spirit has told us that you—'

'No,' Summer cut her off, unwilling to continue the charade any longer. 'Hope and I are the ones who know the truth, and it isn't from Carter's spirit. It's from Harriet Lipscomb, fully alive and plenty talkative on this earth.'

Both Jill and Austin flinched at Harriet's name. Gina twisted the pearls on her wrists apprehensively.

'Harriet told us how you' – Summer glared at Gina – 'grew

rich from Carter's tragedy by promising him that you could contact his deceased wife and daughter. And Harriet also told us how you' – the glare switched to the Bergs – 'targeted Carter at his grief support meetings by pretending that you had lost a daughter, too. The three of you should be ashamed of yourselves! And if Carter's spirit really would join us this evening, I have little doubt that he'd be tempted to push you all into the firepit – except he's probably too good of a soul to actually do it. But that doesn't mean you're in the clear. You'll receive your punishment one day in another place. And in the interim, we happily have Detective Nate, who I am certain has a long list of criminal charges in the works against you.'

Summer looked at Nate expectantly, and he didn't disappoint.

'Austin Berg, Jill Berg and Gina Zaffer,' Nate said, 'I am advising you that you will be taken to the police station for a formal interview.'

Jill and Austin exchanged a glance, debating how to respond. Gina was evidently better able to understand the difference between being potentially charged with fraud and being potentially charged with murder, because she didn't vacillate with the Bergs.

'I'll come to the station,' she agreed. 'I'll answer all of your questions. But I am *not* going to take the blame for what happened to Carter. I had nothing whatsoever to do with his death. That's on them.' It was Gina's turn to glare at Jill and Austin.

'*Us?*' Jill cried, aghast.

'How dare you!' Austin hollered at Gina.

'How dare you!' Gina rejoined with equal vehemence.

Austin sprang to his feet, bellowing furiously. In an attempt to keep the situation from escalating out of control, Nate and Dylan rose, too. As Hope also started to stand, there was a sudden gust of wind. It was unexpected, because up to that point, there hadn't been even the slightest breeze. A second gust followed, and with it, the temperature of the air dropped precipitously.

'Did you feel that?' Summer asked her sister quietly through the ongoing shouts and recriminations.

Hope nodded.

There was a third gust. It was the strongest of the three, and the flames in the firepit sparked for an instant with a dazzling brilliance. A moment later, the fire returned to its previous state, except there was now a thin plume of smoke rising from the front that hadn't been there before.

'Do you see that?' Summer said in the same low tone.

Hope nodded again.

The plume of smoke began to dance. It first jumped forward and then darted backwards. It hopped to the left and skipped to the right. Hope and Summer watched it intently, ignoring the surrounding din.

Shivering, Rosemarie approached the sisters. 'Hasn't it gotten terribly cold? It must have dropped twenty degrees in the blink of an eye. How can there be such a chill when it should be scorching hot by the fire . . .' The sentence trailed away with an apparent dawning realization, and her next words were barely audible. 'Doesn't a cold spot usually mean . . .'

'Yes,' Summer answered her.

Rosemarie gulped. She looked at Hope and Summer, and when she saw that they were looking at the plume of smoke, she looked at it, too. 'Is that . . .' she whispered.

'Yes,' Summer answered again.

The plume twisted and curled, drawing gradually closer to them, until it suddenly halted. It flickered in place for a moment, as though deliberating, and then it took a sharp turn to the right.

'Where are you going?' Hope mused.

'I'm not going anywhere,' Dylan said, moving next to her. 'Everybody has calmed down enough that a brawl no longer appears to be imminent. But Nate has called for backup just in case. He and his colleagues are going to have their hands full with those three . . .' It was Dylan's turn to leave a sentence unfinished as he perceived that no one was listening to him. 'What are we staring at?' he asked.

Still whispering, Rosemarie replied, 'The smoke.'

'The smoke?' Dylan frowned. 'When a fire smokes, it's usually because the wood is damp or too fresh.'

'Not the regular smoke,' Rosemarie explained. '*That* smoke.'

As she pointed at the plume, it abruptly switched directions and headed back to the left.

Dylan's frown deepened. 'What the hell is that?'

'Careful of your words,' Summer cautioned him.

'My words? How would—'

Hope didn't let him continue. 'It seems confused,' she said to her sister, 'as though it's searching for something and can't find it.'

Summer nodded in agreement. 'It can't be searching for a person, because we're all right here in front of it. None of us are hidden or—'

Without warning, the plume veered upward. It climbed swiftly and steeply, and then like a raptor hurling itself into an attack, it plummeted down to the ground. It landed soundlessly but with a great gust of wind on the tote bag that Miranda had left lying on the pebbles. An instant later, the plume of smoke was gone, and the air had warmed to its former temperature.

Rosemarie promptly launched into a string of questions, but Hope and Summer didn't respond to any of them. Nor did they pay attention to Dylan as he hastened toward the firepit, no doubt to satisfy his own curiosity regarding the disappearing plume. The sisters' sole focus was on the tote bag.

'Why direct us to the bag?'

'Why care about a cookbook?'

'Unless,' Hope said slowly, beginning to fit the pieces together, 'it isn't actually a cookbook.'

Summer's eyes widened as she followed the direction of her sister's thoughts. 'Gina told us that she wasn't interested in the book. We assumed that she was talking about the cookbook. What if she was talking about our book instead?'

'Then that would mean we were wrong. Gina never had our book.'

'And that would mean Miranda . . .'

They turned to Miranda questioningly. But the moment that they met her belligerent gaze, all of their remaining doubts vanished. Miranda didn't hesitate. She leapt from her chair and raced toward the tote bag. Before Hope and Summer could make any attempt to stop her, Miranda scooped up the bag from the pebbles and threw it into the firepit. There was a rush of flames around it.

Dylan grabbed a poker from beside the firepit and immediately started to dig in the blaze for the bag.

'Oh, don't burn yourself, Dylan!' Rosemarie cried in alarm.

Echoing Rosemarie's concern, Hope was about to tell him that no book was worth the possibility of a severe injury, when Dylan succeeded in pulling the bag out of the fire and dropping it on to the ground. He had been so quick that the fabric hadn't yet fully ignited, and with a combination of the poker and his shoe, he managed to extinguish the burning patches, leaving the bag only mildly charred.

After checking that it was cool enough to touch, Dylan picked up the bag and looked inside. To Hope's surprise, he didn't take anything out. Instead, he walked over to her and handed her the bag.

'I believe,' he said, 'that Volume II belongs to you and your sister.'

Summer didn't wait for Hope to express their gratitude.

'Why?' she yelled at Miranda. 'Why did you have our book?'

Miranda gave her a scornful look, as though the answer should have been obvious. 'So I didn't have to live in that damn brownstone any longer.'

It was the first time that Hope had ever heard Miranda's voice not squeak.

Paul's mouth opened, but not a sound – squeak or otherwise – came out. He was still standing at the table and appeared to be utterly bewildered by what was happening.

Miranda's scornful look moved to him. 'Don't act as though this is news to you, Paul. I've told you for months on end that I couldn't remain in that infernal place, with its leaking cellar and endless repairs and nothing ever working as it should. I wanted to be here on the mountain. I wanted a place like this.' She motioned toward Gina's house.

An indecipherable syllable now emerged from Paul.

'Yes, yes, I know.' The scornful look became a scornful laugh. 'We don't have the money for a place like this. But we would have had the money if I had been able to sell those books.' She turned to Hope. 'Do you have any comprehension what that book you're holding is worth?'

'It can't be sold,' Hope said.

'Of course it can be sold,' Miranda rejoined. 'Everything can be sold. Everything has a price. I told that to Carter. I told him that I had seen the shelves full of old books in your library, and if he took what looked like the oldest and rarest one for me, then I would convince you to hold a séance for him. That's all Carter wanted: a stupid séance! He was too frightened to ask you himself, probably because they' – she inclined her head in the direction of Gina and the Bergs – 'had taken advantage of him previously.'

Summer was livid. 'And you decided to take advantage of him, too!'

Miranda disagreed. 'I didn't take advantage of him. Carter and I struck a deal. The problem came when he gave me the book and said there was another one to match it. I said he had to get it also. He didn't like the idea, but in the end, he took the second book as he had the first. Except then he wouldn't give it to me. He said that his wife wouldn't be happy about the thefts. I said that his wife didn't know and didn't care, because she was dead! Naturally, that made him angry. I got angry, too. And we argued about it by the retention pool.' She gave a little shrug. 'Now Carter is with his wife.'

Paul gaped at her in horror. 'Good God, Miranda! Do you understand what you've done?'

She offered no apology to him or anybody else, and in her eyes, there was not the slightest sign of remorse. 'I understand that I'll never have to go back to that damn brownstone. Maybe in prison, I'll start a séance group. It was a lot of fun pretending this evening, seeing you all make fools of yourself.'

'You may not find séances quite so much fun,' Summer replied, 'after you've had time to realize that this séance is what led to you being in prison.'

A shadow passed across Miranda's face, as though the truth of Summer's words was already beginning to hit her. A moment later, the patio was flooded with police. Nate's backup had arrived, and after issuing a brief set of instructions, Nate let his colleagues take charge of Miranda, Gina and the Bergs. Watching Nate turn his full attention to Summer, Hope smiled to herself. They were already on the mountain, and the weather was clear. It was a good night for stars and fireflies.

'Rosemarie has decided to stay here for a while instead of driving back to the city with us,' Dylan said.

Not having noticed his approach in the waning light of the fire, Hope looked at him in surprise.

'She's worried about Paul,' he continued, 'and doesn't want him to be alone as he comes to grips with what's occurred.'

Hope nodded. 'That's very kind of Rosemarie, as always.'

There was a pause. Dylan took a step closer to her. His eyes mirrored the fading gold of the embers.

'I haven't thanked you yet for saving the book,' Hope said.

'Yes, you do owe me for that.' A smile tugged at the corner of Dylan's mouth. 'And as I recall, you still owe me a kiss from several days ago.'

She laughed. 'You'll have to start keeping a list of my debts.'